A.G. MARSHALL

Second Edition

Published by Avanell Publishing

ISBN-13: 978-1536836493

To Abby
We've told stories together since we were old enough to hold plastic dinosaurs.

I…. Love….You…

Gerta's Farm
Roslynn's Farm
Weeping Mountains
Salt Springs
Ghone River
Salara Museum
William's Farm
Miner's Harbor
Castlemont
Dragon's Cove
Salaria

New Salaria
Castana

The Fairy Snow

From *The History of Salaria*

Long ago, fairies lived in every kingdom and interacted with humans regularly. They often served as godmothers to human children and granted wishes to those who proved themselves worthy. Humans welcomed the fairies into their lives.

The fairies built a great city in the Weeping Mountains, so named because the salt they used for magic ran down the mountains each spring when the snow melted. One spring, so much snow melted that the salt spread throughout the entire peninsula, killing every green thing and making the water undrinkable. The humans fled.

The fairies left the peninsula soon after this disaster. As a parting gift, they covered the land with enchanted snow to heal the salt's damage. Humans returned to the peninsula, formed a new kingdom, and named it Salaria: the Kingdom of Salt.

Minister of History's Revision

Divinia became the first fairy to visit since the fairy snow when she blessed Princess Salara and became her godmother. This act of goodwill is encouraging, but may not mean that the fairies intend to return to Salaria.

Minister of History's Revision

The Fairy Divinia did not come to Princess Salara's tenth birthday party. This is the traditional time for a fairy godmother to give her godchild a first wish.

Prologue

Lady Alma snapped her fingers. The tiny dress on her worktable changed from purple to blue. She frowned and snapped again. The silk turned pink.

"Cliché, but it really does look better that way."

She waved her hands. Red ribbons tied themselves into bows. A needle flew through air, sewing them onto the dress.

"Your technique has improved, darling."

Lady Alma heard the voice before she saw the golden sparkles. Both made her frown.

A tall woman in a green gown appeared. Her skin glowed, illuminated by a light somewhere inside her. She kept her delicate golden wings folded behind her back. Her hair, which glowed even brighter than her skin and wings, hung loose. The green dress and her hair rippled although there was no breeze in the room.

"Divinia," Lady Alma said. "What a surprise."

"And a pleasant one, I'm sure."

Divinia walked around the room, examining the bolts of fabric and spools of thread.

"Is this what you've done with your life, Alma? Become a common seamstress? That is a shame. You always had such potential."

She rested her hand over a carved wooden box on the

table. Alma's eyes narrowed.

"Is that why you've come? After all these years?"

"Well, you're obviously not using it. Do you mind? I know it was a gift, but I really could use it for a project."

Lady Alma shrugged. Divinia smiled and opened the box. A faint glow escaped it. She pulled a silver necklace out, weighed it in her palm, and tucked it into the folds of her skirt.

The door opened.

"Lady Alma, are you ready yet? I-"

The woman stopped and stared at the fairy. Divinia stared back. Lady Alma's lips twitched upwards into a smile.

"Your Majesty, may I introduce the Fairy Divinia? Divinia, this is Queen Ingrid of Salaria."

The Queen smiled.

"Oh, you've actually come! Of course I hoped, but I never thought you'd actually- Oh, Nicholas will be so surprised!"

She clasped the fairy's hands in her own. Divinia shot Alma a questioning look. Alma's smile widened.

"I'm sure you have a lot to discuss. I'll just take this down to the nursery."

"Please do, Alma. The colors are perfect."

Lady Alma curtsied and left the room. Divinia gulped.

"As you, uh, said, Your Majesty. I have come."

The Queen giggled.

"Oh, it is marvelous. They said it wouldn't work, but I had to try."

"And it has paid off?"

The words sounded more like a question than Divinia intended.

"As soon as I realized I was pregnant, I wrote a letter to the fairies. Nicholas said it would never reach them. Said they didn't read letters from Salaria. But I had to try."

Divinia examined the Queen's thin figure.

"And you have had the child?"

"Only a few days ago! You're not so very late. I'm sure I can convince the historians to write that you came on the day of her birth. That sounds much more dramatic. Now, I had some names picked out, but of course as the godmother it is your right to name her."

Queen Ingrid grabbed Divinia's arm and pulled her down the hallway.

"If you have already named her, I don't want to-"

"Nonsense! Nicholas and I hadn't settled on anything. Lucky for us, we haven't christened her yet. A few more minutes, and you would have been too late. Nicholas, this is the Fairy Divinia. She's here to bless our daughter."

The King looked up from his desk. He nodded to the fairy.

"If my records are correct, you are the first fairy to enter Salaria since the fairy snow. To what do we owe this honor?"

Divinia's hand tightened around the charm in her pocket. It would be much easier to tell the truth. Much simpler. The King and Queen would surely understand.

She looked from the King's skeptical face to the Queen's hopeful one and took a deep breath.

"I have, of course, come to bless your daughter."

The Queen jumped up and down and clapped her hands. The King's face relaxed.

"We will need to choose the gift carefully. Perhaps we should delay the christening so we have time to consider it properly."

"Nonsense! Lady Alma will have her dressed by now. I'm sure Divinia can suggest something suitable."

"Perhaps generosity," King Nicholas said.

"No good," Divinia interrupted. "She'll bankrupt the

kingdom before she can walk. Kindness isn't a good one either. You need a strong backbone to rule a kingdom. Difficult if you're too kind."

"But she won't be ruling," Queen Ingrid said. "Of course we'll have a son. I mean-"

She blushed. King Nicholas nodded and turned to the fairy.

"We do intend to have a male heir to take the throne."

"A traditional blessing then. May I suggest beauty? It is always a favorite."

Please let them take beauty. Please.

Ingrid's eyes widened.

"Beauty! Oh, how perfect! Come with me at once. Can you bless her in front of the whole kingdom? Because they're gathered outside waiting for the christening."

Divinia reviewed the spell for creating beauty while the Queen dragged her through the castle. A wailing noise interrupted her thoughts. Every time she had almost worked out the words for the spell, another yell distracted her.

"Why are your torture chambers so near your rooms?" she asked.

"Torture chambers? Oh, the noise. Yes, that's our daughter. She has such healthy lungs. She's been crying like that since she was born."

Unacceptable. Beauty would do her no good with a voice like that. Divinia revised the spell in her head. An enchanted voice would benefit the kingdom more than anything right now. Now she just needed a name. What did one name a human child?

She blinked in the sunlight when the Queen pushed her onto a balcony. The entire kingdom had gathered in the courtyard below to see the newborn princess. Commoners stood huddled on the ground. Lords and ladies watched from windows. A few, the most important, stood in the corners of the balcony. A painter had set up an easel and sketched the scene.

The cradle, complete with crying baby, sat in the middle. Lady Alma stooped over it, straightening the princess's cap. She frowned when she saw Divinia.

"Your Majesty, what is she doing here?"

"Oh, she's going to bless the princess!"

Lady Alma's jaw tightened.

"Your Majesty, I must object. This fairy-"

"Oh, I know it hasn't been done in a while, Alma, but that's what makes it so exciting!"

Lady Alma turned to the King.

"King Nicholas, please reconsider. Divinia-"

Had already started. The crowd's cheers at her introduction drowned out Lady Alma's voice. Divinia picked the baby up awkwardly and snapped her fingers. Golden dust and sparkles filled the courtyard. Peasants and nobles alike blinked at the bright storm of magic centered around the crying baby.

Lady Alma pushed her way through it.

"What are you doing?" she hissed. "Just go home. She doesn't need your blessing."

"Don't be jealous, Alma. Just because you didn't appreciate my work doesn't mean others won't. Now stand back. You don't want any of the beauty to land on you."

Divinia giggled and hugged the child tighter. She spoke the words of the spell, thrust the princess into Lady Alma's arms, and disappeared in a flash of light.

The Fairy Divinia's Spell

Spoken over Princess Salara on the day of her birth
From *The History of Salaria*

Dark as a rook's wing, hair flows like the Ghone.
Night prism eyes reflect colors unknown.

Moonlight complexion, pearly reflection.
By every standard, you are perfection.

Radiant voice like the song of a star.
Reddest of roses, loveliest by far.

I name thee Salara, Salarian princess,
Born to be queen of them all.

Ideals align, beauty be thine.
Names, souls, and destinies all intertwine.

1

I crept through my dark bedroom, pushed the tapestry on the wall aside, and crawled through the opening behind it. Seda, my kitten, ran between my legs and tripped me as he clawed the hem of my night gown. I stood still until he tired of the game. Slivers of moonlight filtered through cracks in the stone. Seda's white fur caught the light as he ran.

As my eyes adjusted I could follow his shape against the dark stones. When we reached the end of the tunnel, even more moonlight flooded through the rotting trap door above us. I climbed the rock wall, and Seda climbed my nightgown until he sat on my shoulder.

Fresh sea air flooded the dank tunnel as I opened the door and climbed onto the tower. Stars twinkled overhead, fading gradually into the predawn light.

Seda walked on the edge of the tower railing, watching birds fly over the ocean. I stood motionless, soaking in the view and solitude. Waves crashed on the shore far below me and drowned out the voices of sailors and merchants getting an early start on the docks.

I joined Seda at the edge and leaned over it. A narrow staircase without a railing wound around the tower. I climbed it once in the middle of the night, clinging to the wall and hoping no one noticed my white nightgown against the dark stone. I expected the stairs to lead somewhere interesting. The castle treasury, perhaps. Or even beyond the castle to a different part of the city. Instead, they led me to the castle's main garden. A disappointing reward for such a dangerous climb, since I visited the garden often. I did not use the stairs again.

Although the staircase stopped at the garden, the tower stretched downwards and blended into the town below. Castlemont, the capital of Salaria, was divided into tiers. Ramps made of large stones and packed dirt connected the flat platforms of earth circling the mountain. Without the tiers, the mountain ground would be too steep for a city. Top levels held large houses inhabited by nobility. The middle tiers, home to artists and servants, held humbler dwellings. Individual houses in Lower Castlemont were indistinguishable from one another. If there were walkways between the shacks, they must be very narrow. The lower part of the city looked like one enormous roof, patched and faded and badly needing repair.

At the bottom, the Ghone River spilled into the sea, and a port just outside Castlemont's protective wall bustled with activity. Sailors loaded crates of salt and checked ropes on massive ships with fluttering white sails. Smaller vessels sailed up the Ghone into the heart of Salaria. They disappeared into the forest, although the sails of larger ships floated above the trees like ghosts. Beyond the forest, open fields and tiny villages stretched to the Weeping Mountains, the source of the Ghone. I could just make out the silhouette of the mountain range in the light of a sun not yet risen.

I rummaged through the crate I kept on the tower. Under the books on magic technique I had sneaked out of the library, I found my gold opera glasses. I turned to the ocean, examining the ships too far away to see without aid. The wind pulled strands of hair from my floor length black braid and whipped my face with them. The usual ships sailed along the coast. Navy vessels, both men and ships clean and polished and identical. I skipped past them. The merchant ships intrigued me. Their stained sails and tattered crews hinted at stories I could only imagine, and they had almost as many canons on their decks as the naval vessels to protect against pirates.

I watched the flags flutter in the breeze. None of the ships in sight flew the flag of New Salaria. Surely the delegation would not be delayed another day? The ocean glowed pink as the sun progressed towards the horizon.

Too near the horizon. I needed to hurry back.

I climbed through the trap door and pulled Seda with me. He yowled as I shut it and carried him back down the tunnel. Golden sunlight slipped through cracks now, but it was still much darker than being outside. Before my eyes adjusted to the dim light, I reached my room and pushed aside the tapestry blocking the tunnel entrance. I took a moment to adjust it so no one would discover my secret. I wouldn't have found the passage without Seda's help, and I had lived in this room my entire life. The secret tunnel continued past my room to Lady Alma's studio and the council chambers, although I never went that way. Too many courtiers wandering around, looking for the latest gossip.

I jumped into bed and tried to smooth my braid. Hopeless. I snapped my fingers, trying to summon magic to help. Nothing happened. My hair remained a tangled mess. If I was lucky, everyone would assume I had been having bad dreams. Rumors would spread throughout the kingdom that nightmares troubled the sleep of Salaria's greatest treasure, but everyone would forget about it in a few days. They would have new gossip after my birthday celebration. I closed my eyes, relaxed my body, and waited.

A breeze rustled through my hair when the door opened, but I did not stir. I kept my eyes closed and my breathing slow and even. Scrapes, scuffles and whispers echoed through my room. They always tried to be quiet, but they seldom were. At least thick carpets muffled the footsteps. I listened for sounds out of the ordinary. My birthday was tomorrow. According to tradition, my fairy godmother should come for a visit. Had the Fairy Divinia come early? Did a fairy's footsteps sound any different?

A string quartet began to play my aria from our latest opera production. I waited. As the violins hit their highest note, I turned my head and opened my eyes.

No fairy. Just the usual crowd. I smiled at them to hide my disappointment.

Divinia would come tomorrow. The Colonial Delegation would have a safe journey.

Everything would be fine.

Lady Alma, my personal designer, opened the curtains with a snap of her fingers. Light streamed down on me. My tangled hair reflected dark colors on the walls. Lady Alma's hair also did a fair bit of reflecting; she wore a pink wig covered in diamonds that towered high above her head. The pink contrasted nicely with her warm Castanian complexion. I once overheard a Duchess complain that Lady Alma had the skin of a sailor as if she spent all her time working in the sun. Lady Alma refused to let her naturally tan skin stop her from making bold fashion choices.

"Night prism eyes reflect colors unknown," Mother said, quoting the spell Divinia spoke over me on the day of my birth.

Because of that spell, I am my nation's greatest treasure. Those words changed my life. They also rhymed. Mother embraced poetry with a passion after the blessing, and I have been surrounded by poets ever since.

I smiled at Mother and nodded to the group of courtiers and artists standing in the back of the room. Sir Quill, Minister of Poetry and unmistakable in his hat that doubled as an inkwell, stepped forward and spoke.

Roses are red, violets are blue
Salara's eyes reflect indescribable hues.

Violets are blue, and roses are red.
Everyone here agrees with what I said.

Violets and roses. Red, purple, and blue.
Colors mean more when reflected by you.

He stepped back into the crowd. Lady Alma came forward, shorter than everyone in the room and as wide as she was tall. Her four chins jiggled as she walked.

Two courtiers pulled back my velvet blankets and satin sheets, and I stepped onto the carpet. Lady Alma raised an eyebrow at my wrinkled nightgown and tangled hair. I ignored her questioning gaze and walked to the center of the room. Light from every window blinded me as I stepped into the sunny spotlight. My hair reflected even more colors onto the wall, a dark rainbow of blue, purple, and green that drowned out the pink light from the wig.

Lady Alma snapped her fingers. Silver sparkles swirled around me until I could see outlines of the crowd, but no details. My nightgown disappeared. A red breakfast gown with a high collar and frilly sleeves replaced it. I gained two inches in height as shoes materialized under my feet.

Jewelry appeared on my wrists, neck, and ears. My hair rippled in a breeze until the tangles from the sea wind became gentle waves hanging down my back.

The sparkles dissolved, and the courtiers gasped and applauded. Sir Quill pulled the feather from his cap, dipped it in the inkwell balanced on top of his head, and wrote. I followed Mother out of the room. Everyone bowed as I passed. Lady Alma walked directly behind me, and the courtiers trailed behind her in order of importance. The string quartet's music faded as we walked down the hall, and a trio of flutes replaced it when we entered the breakfast room.

Father stood in the doorway. Mother took his right arm, and I took his left. Courtiers pulled out chairs for us at the breakfast table. We sat next to each other, facing a wall of windows with a view of the sea.

"I trust you had productive meetings this morning, Nicholas?" Mother said.

Father nodded and took a bite of oatmeal.

"Because you missed waking our daughter. Again. On the eve of her birthday."

The low murmur of a crowd entering the room obscured his mumbled reply. Mother glared at them, and everyone fell silent. They stood behind a velvet ribbon held by guards and watched us eat.

"Is there any news from the Colonial Delegation?" I asked.

Perhaps they were delayed by bad weather and sent a message?

Father shook his head.

"I insist you sanction them if they do not arrive in time for our treasure's birthday celebration," Mother said.

"It isn't their fault they've been delayed by the Dragon!" I said.

"Piracy is hardly suitable breakfast conversation,

Salara," she hissed.

Father ate his oatmeal and read a scroll of parchment.

A courtier escorted the crowd out of the room. A new group replaced them. I pulled a rose out of a vase and twirled it between my fingers. The Dragon was a human pirate, but I had overheard enough conversations to know he was causing far more trouble than most. He sank several official Salarian trade vessels last month, in spite of a naval escort. They called him the Dragon because he set the ships on fire before sending them to the bottom of the ocean. If he attacked the Colonial Delegation, I could only imagine the trouble it would cause.

I couldn't do more than imagine it because I was never allowed into council meetings.

"So your meetings were productive this morning, Father?" I asked. "Did you work on the new treaty?"

"The treaty is finished," Father said.

"Unless the Delegation is late for Salara's birthday celebration. And then you will sanction them," Mother said.

Another crowd entered. Their whispers created a quiet buzz.

"What does sanctioning them mean?"

I leaned forward, trying to look at the parchment in Father's hands.

"We are not sanctioning anyone, Ingrid," Father said.

"Unless they are late," Mother said.

"The Dragon stole another shipment of salt. Castana is threatening to take action against us if a shipment does not reach them by the end of the month. The guest list for a birthday party is the least of our concerns."

I sat up straight, trying to look grown up.

"What action would Castana take?"

"Just raise taxes or something," Mother said.

She dismissed Father with a wave of her hand and turned to me.

"Do you have your lines for the opera memorized?"

"Yes, but what about the sanctions? What about Castana?"

"That really doesn't concern you."

"I'm heir to the throne. I need to-"

"Get ready for your portrait sitting," Mother said.

She stood. I looked at Father. He shrugged and turned back to his oatmeal.

Typical.

2

I followed Mother out of the room. Soldiers pushed the crowd back as I walked past them and turned towards Lady Alma's studio. I flung the door open, not waiting for the footmen standing outside the room to do their job, and stomped into the room. Lady Alma raised an eyebrow at me.

"Breakfast disagree with you?"

"I'm trying to learn things, but they're no help! They wouldn't even explain what a sanction is! And Mother wants Father to put one on the colonies."

"A sanction is a kind of penalty," Lady Alma said. "They would make the colony pay extra taxes on traded goods or some such thing. Your father would never impose a sanction so hastily."

Getting an answer to my question did little to improve my mood, but I made an effort to smile at her.

I stepped onto a pedestal in the center of her studio, an octagonal room with walls covered by mirrors, shelves and drawers. The mirror in the corner behind her sewing table swung out and led to my secret passage. If Lady Alma knew about the tunnel, she never mentioned it. The enchanted ceiling transformed into a mirror, window, or painting of roses depending on what Lady Alma wanted.

So far she had not even sent a calling card.

I stared ahead, struggling to maintain my smile. Was she alright? Could harm come to fairies? Had the Dragon stopped her from traveling? He seemed to take more and more ships every day. Did fairies travel by ship?

Pirates on our shores and bandits within them. Maybe she did not feel safe in Salaria. If she had sent a message by ship, it could easily have been intercepted.

Mother walked to the back of the room and examined the work of the other painters. She stopped to address an apprentice with squinted eyes and frizzy red hair hunched over a medium sized canvas.

"Who is this supposed to be?"

"It is the Princess Salara, Your Highness."

Sir Bristle stopped correcting the color of my dress and approached them.

"Is there a problem? I assure you, Your Highness, Lacquer is one of my best apprentices."

"Indeed? And has he learned how to draw a nose yet?"

"I beg your pardon, Highness?"

"Have you taught him to draw a nose, Sir Bristle? Because this painting, with a nose like that, is not my daughter."

Sir Bristle examined the painting and frowned.

"I don't understand, Your Highness. Until now, all of his work has been exemplary."

"Is this a joke to you, young man?" Mother grabbed the canvas and shook it in Lacquer's face. "Do you think painting the Princess Salara is a joke?"

Lacquer looked from me to the canvas.

"I don't understand the problem, Your Highness."

"Don't understand the problem?"

Sir Bristle bowed low.

"Your Highness, perhaps he lacks the proper experience to do the Princess justice. Lacquer, you will paint eggs for the remainder of this session."

Lacquer opened his mouth to protest, then shut it again. He bowed, collected his brushes, and moved to the back of the room where the youngest apprentices decorated boiled eggs. Mother handed his unfinished painting to a guard.

"See to it that this is destroyed," she said. "I will not have such an inaccurate portrayal of the Princess fall into the wrong hands."

She took a deep breath and turned back to me. I smiled and stared straight ahead, trying my best to look perfect. Mother picked up her brush.

"I prefer blue, Lady Alma. Blue for the Salarian Sea and the Ghone. Blue and white. The sky and the fairy snow. Change her dress to blue."

Lady Alma winked at me and snapped her fingers. My dress shifted back to the original hue. Seda pawed at it and frayed the fabric. Lady Alma waved her hand and wove the threads back together until the fraying disappeared. The painters cleaned their brushes and changed the green paint back to blue with a snap of their fingers.

Mother painted in silence. Sir Bristle examined the work of his apprentices and the guest artists when he was not filling in details for her while she examined the scene.

I always had plenty of time to think during portrait sessions, which is the polite way to say they were dreadfully boring. I stared at the wall and let my mind drift. What would I do when I met Divinia? It would be against every tradition if she did not come to celebrate my coming of age. Fairies didn't bless people often these days, but against all odds she had blessed me. What would I say? Thanks for the beauty and great voice?

And what would I wish for?

Right now, a more comfortable chair. Salaria's most

3

The rehearsal dissolved into chaos. Mother rushed away to get ready. Sir Lefting tapped his baton and insisted the rest of the cast stay to rehearse the revisions. Lady Alma pulled me down the hall to her studio, still in my saltshaker costume.

I stood on the pedestal, catching my breath. Lady Alma looked more winded than I was, but she snapped and waved her hands like mad. The diamonds, salt crystal necklace, and silver hat flew off. My hair hung loose down my back. A servant entered the room.

"The King has already received the ambassador in the throne room! The Queen says to send Princess Salara to the Salara Gallery immediately."

"She is still in her costume!"

"Immediately!"

I followed the servant out the door. Lady Alma ran behind me, flinging rubies onto the dress. The charm for holding diamonds kept them floating just above the fabric. I caught my reflection in a window and frowned. The gems made me look more polished, but the white dress was such an odd shape.

The servant bowed and left me alone in the gallery. I paced the floor, wondering how I should look when the ambassador entered. Sitting or standing? It was always dramatic to rise from a seated position and give guests a gradual full effect, as well as an excuse to offer their hand. But the light from the windows reflected unknown colors from my hair onto the walls. Everyone enjoyed that. If I stood in the center of the room, I could be in full sunlight and dazzle them as they entered.

The highest curtains, far out of reach, were closed. More light would make this scene more dramatic. I waved my hand and snapped my fingers, trying to open them. They did not move. I gave up and turned to the rows of picture frames lining the room.

The portraits in the Salara Gallery were arranged chronologically so visitors could witness the story of my beauty from birth to present. Mother and Sir Bristle had painted all of them. Sir Bristle, in spite of years of training apprentices, had not found anyone who could capture my beauty to Mother's satisfaction.

The first picture showed the scene of my blessing. The Fairy Divinia held me, and a cloud of gold sparkles surrounded us and illuminated the crowd below. I had seen so many depictions of this moment I felt as if I had been there in another body, seeing my blessing through many viewpoints at once.

I examined Divinia. She did indeed wear a green dress. Her skin glowed from within as if she were a lantern. She cast a warm light over everyone in the scene. She was taller than Mother. Much taller than Lady Alma.

The next painting showed a crowd of peasants. Sir Bristle painted it the day of my blessing. The commoners' faces were rapturous as my cries, now uttered with an enchanted voice, rang through the courtyard. Nobility watched from balconies and windows while peasants crowded into the courtyard below. One peasant had lifted his dark haired son onto his shoulders to give him a better view. I stepped back to get a better look and tripped on something. I lifted up my skirt to see.

My foot rested on an invisible platform. I pulled the silver bracelets off my wrists and fell back to the floor. I put both on my right arm and stepped backwards.

Nothing happened.

Good, I could leave them there until I had a chance to return them to Lady Alma.

"They were lucky to be there."

His voice startled me. I turned and met the green eyes of a stranger. His skin was tanned darker than any fashionable member of our court, and his blond hair curled around his head in a wind-blown manner. He wore dark clothing a few months out of fashion.

"I am Sir Gilbert, ambassador from New Salaria."

"Welcome to Castlemont."

"I feel at home already."

I smiled at him. A real smile. In spite of my calculations, he had caught me in an unguarded moment. He did not tower over me, but I had to tilt my head upward to meet his eyes. He was younger than I had expected. Far younger than any of the other ambassadors that had visited us.

About my age, actually.

Sir Gilbert gestured to the painting.

"Those peasants were lucky to be there. At the scene of your blessing."

"I expect as many came to see the fairy as came to see me."

"I very much doubt that."

He offered me his arm. I rested my hand on it, and we proceeded down the gallery. He skipped a few paintings that showed my progress from dazzling newborn to dazzling toddler and stopped at one that showed me playing with three blond ladies in waiting.

"Your dress is quite interesting," he said.

"It is actually my costume for the opera tomorrow."

"You still fit into that?"

"Oh, you meant the painting."

He turned and examined me. I looked at the canvas. My dress in the painting was the shape of a castle. Literally. I had been unable to move my arms because of the towers sticking up from the square skirt. I couldn't remember why Lady Alma had designed such a horrid thing.

"What are you in the opera? A triangle?"

"A snowflake."

"After a battle?"

I looked down and laughed. The ruby jewelry did look like drops of blood against the white fabric.

"I wear diamonds in the opera. We are telling the story of the fairy snow. Highly symbolic."

"I had noticed a certain amount of symbolism in these portraits."

"Are you a painter, Sir Gilbert?"

"No. I spend most of my time as a sailor. Pirate attacks on the colonies provide plenty of opportunity for glory. But since this is a delegation of peace, I intend to join the poets in my free time. Shall I recite something for you?"

"No, please. Don't trouble yourself."

"Perhaps later then."

"That really won't be necessary."

He laughed.

"Then you have my word as a poet. And poets value words most highly."

We progressed to a painting of my sixth birthday.

"Ah, the day you received Seda. How charming. We have a copy of this painting at the colonial palace."

I nodded, and we examined the painting. Seda had

been added as an afterthought; the portrait had been finished before I received him as a gift. He sat next to me, sleeping peacefully. Wishful thinking on Mother's part. The kitten never stayed that still.

"Ah, forgive my rudeness. I also have brought you a gift."

He pulled something out of his coat and handed it to me with a flourish.

I took it and gasped.

I held a red rose, but made of gems. The petals and leaves were transparent and no thicker than those of an ordinary bloom. They had veins and the texture of a flower, but were unmistakably rubies and emeralds.

"Smell it."

I lifted it to my nose and inhaled. It smelled like a real rose.

"It is magnificent."

"I found it on a pirate ship after a battle."

"With the Dragon?"

"You know about the Dragon?"

"Everyone knows about the Dragon."

And no one would tell me about him. I watched Sir Gilbert's face, waiting for him to decide that piracy was an unsuitable topic of conversation for a princess. Instead, he met my eyes.

"He burns ships and sailors alike. I have been lucky never to see him."

"But he robs ships in colonial waters."

"And somehow avoids our Navy. I would have chased him down if I had known you were interested in such things."

"But you said he is dangerous."

"He is just a man. I fear disappointing you more than any pirate."

He stared into my eyes. I stared back, vaguely aware

that he had clasped my hands in his. The green of his eyes mixed with swirls of hazel and something darker. Possibly the colors from my hair.

"Is that a Rosas Rojas?" Lady Alma asked. She pulled our hands apart, took the ruby rose, and sniffed it.

"It came from a pirate," I said.

"It came from Castana. I haven't seen one in so many years. Watch this."

She pinched the stem. The rose glowed. She pressed it against my shoulder, and it stuck to my gown.

"At parties in Castana, noblemen give these to the lady of their choice. Rosas Rojas, the reddest rose, the most beautiful. The lady with the most at the end of the evening wins."

"What does she win?" Sir Gilbert asked.

He smiled at me. His teeth looked very white against his tanned skin. He and Lady Alma had similar complexions, although his features did not look Castanian.

"Oh, generally marriage to her choice of the men in the room. I won once."

Sir Gilbert and I stared at her. Lady Alma's bright pink dress, covered in frills, flounces, ribbons, gems, and other embellishments I don't know what to call, enhanced the cube-like shape of her body. Her towering pink wig turned her head into the base of a column of hair.

"No need to look so surprised. Beauty is in the eye of the beholder."

"And who were your beholders?" Sir Gilbert asked.

"That's enough of your sass, young man. Aren't you a bit young to represent New Salaria?"

"Everyone else was afraid to sail so far."

"Yet you made it with a skeleton crew."

Sir Gilbert flinched.

"A what?" I asked.

"It is a nautical term. It means I have one sailor per job. No extras."

"Yes, that's exactly what it means," Lady Alma said.

She stared at Sir Gilbert until we both fidgeted.

"So the Rosas Rojas was stolen from Castana?"

Lady Alma pulled the rose off my shoulder and handed it back to me.

"It takes the souls of a hundred rose bushes to make one of these. Very precious."

"Rose bushes have souls?" Sir Gilbert asked.

"Most things have souls."

She stared at Sir Gilbert while she said it. He met her gaze this time and smiled.

"Sir Gilbert is a warrior and poet," I said.

"Oh, I'm sure he's much more than that," Lady Alma said. "Lunch will be served shortly, and you must change, Princess. Please come with me."

Back in her studio, Lady Alma snapped me into a deep yellow dress without saying a word. The dress had waves of dark orange and bits of light that moved like reflections in water. She braided my hair, then twisted the braids into a familiar shape.

"Not the butterfly chignon again," I groaned.

"This is one of your most popular styles. And we have never done it with braids before, so this is new."

My hair stuck out on either side of my head like a butterfly's wings. Lady Alma secured it with a hair ornament carved from salt. Once the charm absorbed all the salt's magic, my hair would cascade down my back.

"You shouldn't be so rude to an ambassador," I said.

"He didn't seem to mind. That was a nice gift he brought you. Rosas Rojas don't often find their way out of Castana. A pirate must have stolen one from a lady traveling."

"Like the Shadow stole the gems for my gown?"

"You were safe in the palace when that happened. The poor lady would have been carrying this with her."

She shuddered. The motion made her body and the gems in her pink wig jiggle.

"I trust you can find your own way to the dining hall?" she said. "I have to meet with Madame Delilah. She's making me a new wig to match your snowflake costume."

I clipped the Rosas Rojas onto my shoulder while I walked. It didn't match the dress, but I didn't care.

Sir Gilbert sat next to me at lunch: a place of honor.

"I am sorry Lady Alma was rude to you," I whispered.

"You owe me no apology, Princess."

"But you are our guest and represent our colony! You deserve every courtesy, and I will make sure she apologizes to you."

"Please, do not trouble yourself. I am sure it brought back painful memories for her to see something from her homeland. Do you know why she left her home country? Why she lives in exile?"

"She is not in exile."

"She works day and night serving your mother's whims- Forgive me, Princess. I should not be so blunt."

"No, please. It is refreshing."

"I have prepared a surprise tomorrow for your birthday," Sir Gilbert said. "An excursion of sorts."

"Make sure you check with my mother. She'll have the day planned down to the minute."

He raised my hand to his lips. The salt charm chose that moment to dissolve. The silver grew dark, as if tarnished, and my hair cascaded down my back.

"I already have. She couldn't resist the symbolism."

The afternoon passed in a blur of opera rehearsals and dress fittings. Mother fretted about everything, and Father kept Sir Gilbert and the rest of the delegation busy discussing treaties.

activated a charm built into the dress, and the skirt billowed like ocean waves.

"Is the ship really necessary?" I asked.

"You would prefer the rose?"

"They're already going to compare my hair to the Ghone. Putting a ship there just makes it obvious."

She smirked.

"Would you rather dress up as a snowflake again? Your mother wanted to save the costume for the opera, but I suppose she would make an exception."

She pulled the round silver hat out of a drawer.

"No need," I said. "Who doesn't love a good Ghone metaphor?"

Lady Alma nodded.

"You'd better go. They'll be ready for you."

The dining hall was empty when we entered it. I took my place on an elevated throne, ignoring the smells of the feast I wouldn't get to eat. Lady Alma arranged my skirt so the waves would billow around my chair. I sat tall, but far enough back in the seat that I could lean against the back. I knew all too well how tiring it was to sit properly all night.

Lady Alma stepped off the platform and signaled to a pair of footmen. They swung the doors open, and dinner guests filed into the ballroom. Most of them wore red. Trying to stay on trend no doubt. But the red breakfast gown had been this morning. Those who had fast enough seamstresses wore yellow, to match the gown I had worn at lunch.

Only one noblewoman wore blue, and her dress was too light to match mine. I smiled at all of them as they walked past me. Those who lived in the palace smiled back. First time guests whispered and pointed.

After everyone found their seats, Mother and Father entered and sat at the head table. Servants in the corners of the room worked a spell to dim the candles in the chandeliers.

The candles by me brightened. A tilted row of mirrors behind me reflected the colors of my hair onto the ceiling. Every time I moved, the lights flickered through the room. I shook my head and watched the colors dance. Guests gasped in delight.

Seda, who had a bad habit of stealing food from people's plates, remained in my room for the evening.

A set of doors at the other end of the room swung open. The Minister of Poetry, Sir Quill, entered. His apprentice Sir Inkling followed so close behind him he stepped on his foot. A dozen other poets, still in training at the Royal Academy of Poetry, trailed behind them. Sir Gilbert stood in the middle. He winked at me. A smile spread across my face.

The poets gasped when they saw it. In unison, they pulled their feather quills from their inkwell hats and began to write.

4

Sir Gilbert did not wear the traditional garb of a poet. In fact, he did not even carry a quill. He simply looked at me, taking in every detail. I watched him. The rest of the room faded away.

Servants brought out plates of food, and the guests ate. Normally musicians played at dinner parties, but the poets demanded absolute silence. People tried not to clink their silverware. I had already eaten, but smelling the feast made me hungry again. And the food kept coming. I had heard rumors they had a special surprise for the end of the meal. Maybe someone would think to bring me a plate of it.

The poets gathered in a semicircle around my stage. Sir Quill stood in the center. As the head poet, he had the right to the best view. Apprentices and students fell into place behind him based on their order of importance.

Sir Inkling, the chief apprentice, walked past Sir Quill. He stepped up onto the raised platform and examined my face. He drew so close I could smell his breath.

"Remarkable," he said.

I looked down at Sir Quill. Surely he did not want his apprentice getting the best view. But Sir Quill smiled at his protégé and continued to write.

Sir Inkling walked around, examining me from every angle. His footsteps echoed through the silent ballroom.

I stared straight ahead, gripping the armrests of my chair. I didn't dare meet Sir Gilbert's eyes and bit my lip to keep from speaking.

Sir Inkling raised a hand and stroked my hair. Then my forehead. He reached for my eyes. I closed them automatically and felt him stroke my eyelashes.

An ode to my hair, perhaps?

My eyes were watering by the time he stopped. I resisted the urge to brush away a tear. It rolled down my cheek and dripped off my chin.

I lowered my eyes. Sir Gilbert caught my gaze and raised an eyebrow. I shook my head slightly.

Sir Inkling's breath smelled terrible. He leaned even closer, staring at my eyes. I stared into his nostrils. I could count the hairs.

The nostrils flared, blowing a puff of air into my face, and Sir Inkling stepped back.

Sir Gilbert's hand rested on his shoulder.

"Excuse me," he said, "but you are blocking my view."

Sir Inkling frowned.

"Student poets must take whatever view they can get. I am a knighted apprentice."

"And apprentices should stand behind their masters."

They stared at each other appraisingly.

Lady Alma hopped onto the platform, sensing a quarrel.

"This is unacceptable, gentlemen," she said. "You have not written a word yet, either of you. Please step back so Princess Salara can inspire you with her enchanted voice."

Sir Inkling stalked away. Sir Gilbert walked behind him.

Lady Alma rearranged my hair and stepped back.

without delay!"

Musicians played the royal fanfare. Everyone stopped talking and turned to stare at me. I descended the steps from my stage slowly, making every movement as graceful as possible. Mother and Father took my arms and led me across the room. Courtiers bowed and applauded as I left. I nodded to them, waited for the door to close, and collapsed against the wall in the hallway.

The door opened, and I jumped. Sir Gilbert slipped through the door and closed it behind him.

"Something for you, Princess."

He handed me a plate with a tiny silver ship on it.

"You brought me one!"

I examined it and found a perfect replica of the Navy ships I watched from my tower. I popped it into my mouth. It dissolved into sugar flavored with strawberries.

"Thank you, Sir Gilbert."

"I hope you do not mind if I escort you to your room, Princess?"

"Not at all."

He offered me his arm, and I slipped my hand over it.

"I apologize if I was out of line this evening, but Sir Inkling seemed to be making you uncomfortable. We do not have poetry sessions in the colonies."

"As far as I'm concerned, you were the only one in line. Did you not prepare a poem?"

He laughed.

"I did, but seeing you in person made me realize how inadequate it was. Besides, I think I used my turn on the stage getting Sir Inkling off it."

Too soon, we reached my room.

"Thank you again," I said.

Sir Gilbert pressed my hand to his lips and turned to go.

"I would rather stay in your charming company," he

said. "But I am here to represent the interests of New Salaria. I'd best make sure no one is plotting against us."

"Gossiping against you, most likely."

Seda attacked my skirt when I entered the room. I trailed the fabric from one of my sleeves along the floor so he could play with it.

Lady Alma entered.

"Princess Salara!" she said. "He is ruining your gown!"

"I won't wear it again. Why does it matter?"

"And you have been instructed numerous times to wait for an escort before leaving parties!"

"I had an escort. Sir Gilbert walked with me."

Lady Alma bristled.

"Why don't you like him?"

"He is a stranger to the court."

"He is the ambassador from our colonies. If he is not to be trusted, perhaps we should rethink this treaty."

"That is not your concern."

"It is my concern! As heir to the throne, it is very much my concern!"

Lady Alma snapped her fingers. The gown, jewels, and ship disappeared. My nightgown replaced them. The same one I had worn last night. The sleeves and hem were frayed from Seda's playing with them in the tunnel that morning.

"Shouldn't I have a new nightgown? Has the Shadow so depleted your fabric supply that you can't even make such a simple garment?"

"Goodnight, Princess Salara."

She slammed the door on her way out.

I lay on my bed and picked at my frayed sleeves. Music from the ball drifted up to my room. Would it really spoil the opera if I danced? I came of age tomorrow. I would officially be named heir to the throne. But I was still sent to bed early like a child.

I remembered Sir Inkling touching my eyelashes and rubbed away angry tears. Seda curled up on my chest, and I stroked his fur as I fell asleep.

5

A dark shape hovered over me. The Shadow. He reached his inky hands forward and covered my face. I couldn't breathe. I tried to push him away, but my arms were tied down. I gasped one last time, desperate for air.

And inhaled cat hair. I coughed and opened my eyes. Seda sat on my face, flicking his tail. I untangled my arms from the blankets and pushed him off the bed. Ignoring his protesting yowls, I stared at the stars through my window.

My birthday. Would Divinia come?

At least Sir Gilbert had prepared a surprise for me.

I smiled and shut my eyes.

A single violin woke me. I waited for the rest of the quartet to join him, but they didn't. When I opened my eyes, only Mother, Lady Alma, and Sir Inkling greeted me. No courtiers. A single musician. Lady Alma held my opera costume from the third revision when I had been a shepherdess in disguise, a pink and beige confection covered with bows. In keeping with typical peasant immodesty, the skirt was short enough to show my ankles.

Mother held long boots.

"I name thee Salara, Salarian princess. Born to be

queen of them all," she said.

I waited for Sir Inkling to speak, but he just dipped his quill into his inkwell hat and took notes.

Mother put down the boots and pulled back my blanket herself.

"Where is everyone else?" I whispered.

"I thought an intimate celebration of your birthday would be best. Of course your father couldn't make it."

I walked to the center of the room. Lady Alma snapped me into the boots and shepherdess costume.

"No painters?" I said. "No birthday morning poem?"

"You're not disappointed are you? We have something very special planned. Full of symbolism."

Sir Gilbert's surprise.

"This dress isn't a breakfast gown."

Lady Alma rolled her eyes. She wore a green wig covered in bows shaped like miniature trees.

"We're not having breakfast in the usual place today," Mother said.

I followed her down the hallway. We walked past the empty breakfast room and kept going until we reached our largest courtyard. The scene of my fairy blessing. Courtiers and musicians surrounded us. They sang as I walked through the crowd.

Sir Gilbert stood by a roofless carriage, dressed as a shepherd. He took my hand and helped up, then jumped and sat beside me. Everyone else climbed into identical carriages. I watched Father help Mother into one.

"What in the world is going on?" I whispered to Sir Gilbert.

"Symbolism."

The trumpets played a fanfare. Ten soldiers on horseback rode through the courtyard and down the road to the sea. Our driver snapped his reins. I grabbed Sir Gilbert's arm for balance as the horse lurched forward.

My parents and a line of carriages full of courtiers followed us.

The music should have faded as we left the courtyard. Instead it grew louder. Singers on horseback rode on either side of us, performing music from Mother's operas. We followed the guards down the road. When we reached the gate, two soldiers waved their hands and opened it with an enchantment. We descended a steep ramp and entered the second tier of the city. Sir Gilbert glanced around with interest.

"Lesser nobles and artists live here," I said. "There is a rather nice park though. You can see it from my garden. Is that where we're going?"

He shook his head.

The guards at the front opened another gate. The wood shimmered as their charm pulled it open. This ramp was bumpier. I gazed at the third tier of the city. The houses were smaller. Upper level servants and wealthy merchants, mostly. I turned to Sir Gilbert.

"Is this enough guards? I usually have more."

"You're not usually with me."

The sea grew nearer and nearer. After a few more gates, we reached the port. It was empty. Perhaps everyone was taking a holiday for my birthday. We passed the harbor and drove into the forest. I heard the Ghone rushing toward the sea, but the trees blocked my view.

"Would you like some breakfast?"

Sir Gilbert reached below the seat and pulled out a basket. The seat across from us folded up into a table. He placed pastries, fruit, and cheese onto a plate.

"This is symbolic?"

"Very."

We both laughed. I caught a glimpse of a ship's mast through a gap in the leaves. They must be sailing upriver.

"A bandit hides in these woods," I said. "Worse than

any pirate, so they say."

"What makes him so bad?"

"No one has ever seen him. He steals our treasures like a ghost. Could you fight someone like that? An invisible bandit?"

"Of course. Let him try to attack us!"

We gazed into the woods, searching for bandits. The trees grew in a scattered manner, not at all like the orderly groves in our palace garden. Leaves fluttered in the wind, and I almost believed the Shadow was hiding in the dark spaces waiting to attack us.

"Tell me about your most exciting battle."

"Only if you tell me about yours."

"I've never been in a battle."

"Surely you've taken a swing at a poet at some point over the years."

I laughed.

"I was attacked once," I said, remembering.

"Someone dared to attack you?"

Sir Gilbert turned to face me, his chin resting on his hands like a child and his eyes wide. I ignored him.

"It was two days after I turned six. I was playing with Seda with a group of my companions."

"Your blond companions?"

"Yes, they were all as blond as you. Mother insists on that. Symbolism, I'm sure."

He ran a hand through his curled, golden hair. It looked striking against his sun tanned skin. The opposite of my pale skin and dark hair.

"I was playing with Seda when one of my handmaidens ran towards me. She screamed that she hated me and tried to hit me. I let go of Seda and hit her back. Guards picked her up and dragged her away. Seda ran after them, hissing and scratching, trying to protect me. A courtier brought him back to me a few minutes later."

"What was her name?"

I shrugged

"I don't even remember my handmaiden's names now. They come and go, depending on whose father tells my father what he wants to hear."

"Did you ever see her again?"

"I doubt it, but I can't be sure. As I said, they come and go. No one ever attacked me again. Now tell me about a pirate battle."

"I'm not sure it can compare."

"That's the point."

The trees cleared, and we drove through a collection of rundown houses and shops circled around a fountain and courtyard. Our carriages rattle through empty streets. The peasants must still be asleep. Most of the houses had no windows. How could anyone stand to live in such a small, dark place?

"I was at sea," Sir Gilbert said when we entered the forest again.

"Were you sailing with your skeleton crew again?"

We both laughed.

"Yes, I had my skeleton crew for that voyage. You don't find many sailors willing to chase pirates. We hadn't been sailing together long and were traveling light. Just trying to get a feel for the ship. No cannons, no cargo. The boy in the crow's nest didn't notice the pirate ship until we were sailing side by side. I gave my first mate the wheel and rushed to the side of the deck just as the pirate captain gave the order to board. Pirates swung across on ropes and pulled out their swords. I stabbed the pirate nearest me and tossed him overboard. This really isn't appropriate breakfast conversation, Princess."

I swallowed a bite of pastry.

"I told you my story. What happened next?"

"I knew the pirates would keep attacking us as long as their captain ordered, so I grabbed a nearby rope and swung over to the pirate ship. The coward had stayed behind while his men attacked. He pulled out his sword, and we fought across the empty ship while my men fought his. I managed to fling his sword into the sea. I grabbed his arm, twisted it behind his back, and held my sword to his throat."

We left the forest and traveled across gently sloping striped hills.

"The different colors are different crops," Sir Gilbert said. "Farmers plant crops like that in the colonies."

"Did he call off his men?" I asked, leaning toward him.

"Yes, they returned to the pirate ship. I couldn't let them go, but my men were in no shape to bring prisoners back. So I took one of their own canons, pointed it downward, and shot a hole through the pirate ship. As it sunk, I swung back across and ordered my crew to sail for home."

"And the ship sank? What about the pirates?"

"As I said, it is hardly proper breakfast conversation."

The carriages stopped on top of one of the striped hills. Sir Gilbert jumped out and offered me his hand.

"What now, defeater of pirates?" I asked.

We walked into the forest side by side. Music floated down from the trees. I glanced up. Members of our orchestra sat in the branches. In the shifting light of the forest, a bandit could easily have been among them.

"His name is the Shadow," I said.

Sir Gilbert's arm stiffened. "Who?"

"The bandit. He stole a shipment of gems from the museum a few days ago. I had to wear lace instead."

I glanced back, hoping I looked casual. A line of couples, led by my parents, followed us.

“Does he steal from you often?”

I tightened my grip on his arm. Just a little.

“Often enough. There are even songs about him.”

I sang softly, so only he could hear.

The Shadow comes when the sun goes down.
The Shadow comes to steal.
Your silk, your crown.
Your jewels, your gown.
The Shadow comes to steal.

I took his smile as encouragement and sang the second verse.

The Shadow slips through the moonless night.
The Shadow climbs the tiers.
Though guards are keen.
He goes unseen.
The Shadow climbs the tiers.

Sir Gilbert stared at me as if in a trance. I looked away unsure what to say. Finally, he shook his head, and his expression cleared.

“It sounds as if he has caused quite a bit of trouble for you.”

“Once he stole an entire shipment of silks that had just been unloaded in the harbor. No one knows how. There were crates and crates of them. Lady Alma had to take apart dresses from the museum to make a new one for me to wear when I met a Duke from Castana. I’ve never been so embarrassed in my life. Everyone whispered about it. She started keeping extra supplies in her studio after that. And she’s been gathering even more since the gem theft."

I mistook the glint of a flute for a dagger and jumped. Sir Gilbert pulled me closer until he saw the musician and relaxed.

"I've never told anyone about that," I said. "I'm sure I'm supposed to be impressing you with the wealth of the mainland."

"I won't tell anyone. And I'm sure you looked lovely."

"Lady Alma changed the color of the fabric. It didn't looked recycled."

We followed a path that was hardly a path at all. It zigzagged through the trees, littered with rocks and roots.

"The gardener should clear the path more often," I said after tripping on a root.

Sir Gilbert laughed for some reason. We both jumped as a violist sitting in a tree began to play.

"I am sorry. I thought it would be fun to have the musicians hide in the woods and serenade us."

"Who said I'm not having fun?"

But I couldn't help singing the third verse of the song in my head.

Beware, beware, oh Princess fair.
The Shadow's always near.
Cares naught for charm.
He means you harm.
The Shadow's always near.

We reached a stream with no bridge across it. Sir Gilbert caught my hand as I jumped and helped me over. We walked along the bank.

"This is a charming surprise, Sir Gilbert. I've never been to the woods. I rarely leave the castle."

"Don't be disappointed, but this isn't the surprise. We're almost there."

The stream disappeared into a hole in a hill. We walked up, and I gasped when I saw the other side. A rolling valley covered in snow stretched before me. Horses hitched to sleighs stood to the side.

"How is this possible?" I asked, looking back to the forest. It was as green as ever. I stepped into the valley and felt the snow crunch beneath my shoe.

"Welcome to the fairy snow."

Sir Gilbert helped me into a sleigh, and we sat for a moment watching everyone react to the valley.

"What magic have you used?" I asked.

"Only the magic of Salaria."

He snapped the reins, and our sleigh glided across the winter valley behind a white horse. Sir Gilbert handled the horse masterfully, avoiding the other sleighs and taking us around the valley. The sparkling snow was almost blinding.

Sir Gilbert handed me the reins.

"Oh, I couldn't!"

"No one is watching."

I glanced around. Everyone was staring at the snow. I took the reins and almost ran into my parents as they drove over to give me a parasol. Sir Gilbert grabbed the reins before they noticed I was driving, but he handed them back to me when they left. I snapped them, and the horse bolted forward. I struggled to regain control.

"Stay calm and know where you're going," Sir Gilbert said.

I managed to make a loop around the valley before handing him the reins. Then I opened the parasol and waited for my heartbeat to slow.

"Beautifully done. I would expect no less from the heir to Salaria's throne."

"I wasn't supposed to be, you know. Everyone thought my parents would have a son."

"Well, thank goodness they didn't."

Long before I was ready to go, a trumpet sounded. Everyone guided their sleighs back to the top of the hill.

"You have an opera to perform tonight," Sir Gilbert said before I could protest.

A silver fountain sat in the stream now, shooting crystal drops of water into the air. Sir Gilbert got a cup from a servant and filled it for me.

"A lovely touch," I said.

"And necessary. This stream flows straight from the salt mines, so it is undrinkable."

"How so?"

Sir Gilbert filled his cup from the stream and handed it to me. I took a sip and gagged at the salt.

"Our greatest treasure," I said after a few gulps of the filtered water to get the taste out of my mouth.

"Yes, to Salaria's greatest treasure," Sir Gilbert said. He kept his eyes on me as he took a drink.

6

I found it hard to concentrate when we arrived back in the palace. The day flew past in a series of portrait sittings and opera rehearsals. I ate supper backstage while Mother made a few last minute revisions.

I wanted to be back in the woods, walking with Sir Gilbert. Daydreams of summer snow filled my head while Lady Alma snapped me into the snowflake costume. She piled my hair up until it fit under the silver hat. She had changed into a white wig with spikes. It was meant to look like a snowflake, but the overall effect was more like a spider web. Another classic Madame Delilah creation. My silver hat was ridiculous, but it looked better than that.

"The bracelets!" she said, looking through her drawers and chests.

I was still wearing them. How could I have forgotten to give them back? I slid one onto my left arm.

"You already put them on me," I said.

She checked my wrists and shrugged.

"I am going crazy trying to finish everything. You may wait in your dressing room."

Now that I was in costume, I had to stay backstage. I glanced at the audience from behind the curtains.

Everyone came early to make sure they got their seat. Guards paced the aisles, escorting uninvited guests back to the garden. A place in the opera audience was the highest honor. Even listening from the garden was a sign of status.

Mother, Father and Sir Gilbert sat in the center box, high above the crowd of courtiers and dignitaries. Sir Bristle stood behind them sketching the scene so it could be painted later. An empty chair sat next to my mother.

Divinia.

As a fairy, she might materialize at any moment. There was still time for her to arrive.

Sir Lefting ran around checking everything. Lady Alma stood with the dancers and singers lined up in front of her.

"Act one," she said.

The dancers tapped silver charms etched with curved engravings on their dressing tables, and simple red dresses wrapped around their bodies in a swirl of silver sparkles. The short dresses left their arms and ankles exposed. Brown ballet slippers appeared on the dancers' feet. The singers wore boots. Lady Alma walked down the line, examining everyone.

"Act two."

Two taps, and everyone stood in green dresses with wide skirts, gold trim and fairy wings. Mother would be devastated if Divinia didn't see this tribute to her.

"Act three."

Three taps. Pale blue dresses with silver trim.

I had only one costume. And about three hours of opera to go before I needed it.

The orchestra tuned and began the overture. Dancers tapped back into the red dresses and took their places. The lead singers moved past them with perfect posture and stood on the stage. They wore white with gold trim.

The curtain opened, and a soprano and tenor sang about Salaria and love. Dancers moved across the stage, twirling as they went. The chorus sang behind them.

Lady Alma tapped me on the shoulder and led me to my dressing room.

"Divinia is late," I said.

"Don't hold your breath."

She polished the silver hat. It reminded me of a knight's helmet, but far rounder. I really did look like a salt shaker.

"You're so sure she won't come. How do you know about fairies?"

She opened the chest and diamonds floated to the surface of my gown.

"There are still fairies in Castana."

"So you've met them?"

"Once. They live in the mountains. It is not an easy journey to reach them."

"Why did you leave Castana, Lady Alma?"

She stopped polishing the silver hat and looked at me. I met her gaze.

"Why ask this now?"

"It was your home."

"It wasn't that great."

"But you were given a Rosas Rojas. You had your choice of the men."

She winked at me.

"They weren't that great either. I'm here because I want to be, Salara."

I should have scolded her for not calling me Princess, but instead I examined my white swan feather boots.

"Stay quiet, now," Lady Alma said. "You've been talking to Sir Gilbert all day. Best give your voice some rest."

She left to check on the other costumes.

I tried to imagine Lady Alma as a young, beautiful girl, but the image wouldn't stick. Castanian visitors always treated her with respect. She was a Lady there, a noblewoman.

And one day, she left.

I had never been to another country. It was too dangerous with so many pirates on the seas. This morning, with Sir Gilbert, was the longest amount of time I had spent outside the castle. But people from many places came to see me. And they all lived somewhere.

In Castana, for example. What was that like? Or a tiny village in a houses with no windows? Or in New Salaria, the island colonies to the south?

I sat on the chair in my dressing room. Fortunately, the diamonds spread out so I didn't have to sit on them. Someone had left an opera program on my desk. I flipped through it.

The First Snowflake

Book, music, and choreography by Queen Ingrid
Directed by Sir Lefting, supervised by Queen Ingrid
Costumes by Lady Alma, supervised by Queen Ingrid
In honor of the coming of age of Princess Salara
Blessed by the Fairy Divinia and raised by Queen Ingrid

The Legend of the Fairy Snow

Long ago, fairies lived in the Weeping Mountains. The salt they used for their magic ran down the mountains as the snow melted. The salt poisoned the land, killing every green thing and ruining the water. When the fairies left the mountains, they created an enchanted snow to heal the land. The people gave the land a new name. Salaria: the Kingdom of Salt.

Plot Summary by Queen Ingrid

I left my dressing room to watch the opera from backstage. The audience knew the story of the fairy snow, so Sir Quill had taken a lot of poetic license with the lyrics. Mostly the queen fairy sang about how beautiful the land had been before her salt poisoned it and how difficult it was to leave her beloved home. The ballerinas danced around her, agreeing without saying a word. I looked up into the royal box. Still no sign of Divinia. There was plenty of time for me to sneak up and say hello to Sir Gilbert, but Mother would be furious if I left the backstage area.

I stepped back from the curtain and stumbled onto the invisible platform. I pulled the bracelets off to reset them and fell back to the floor.

The opera continued.

I turned back to my room and stumbled into a stage hand. Her ring dug into my arm. It flashed silver in the low light as she hurried away without a word.

I watched her go and noticed the other stage hands. Black clad figures moved in the dark backstage with ease. They ran around, climbing ropes, pulling curtains, and running the show from the darkness.

I stepped into my dressing room and blinked. It was far too bright. I waited for my eyes to adjust, but they didn't. I snapped my fingers to dim the lamps.

Nothing happened.

It really was annoying, not being able to work magic. These enchanted lamps obeyed magical commands, but the hand gestures never worked for me, no matter how much I read and practiced.

I turned a knob on the side to dim the lamps to a reasonable brightness and sat. The stage hand's ring had left a red mark on my arm. I rubbed the sore spot and hummed along with the music to warm up my voice. The audience applauded as the first song ended.

I picked up my mask and traced the lines of the lace. Mother had planned a masquerade for the after party when the plot of the opera had featured me as a shepherdess in disguise. The silver lace was coated with salt. It hardly covered any of my face. But that didn't matter. No one else would be wearing a salt shaker dress. I would hardly be in disguise.

I leaned my head back and fell asleep. The noise of the door opening woke me some time later.

Lady Alma entered my room and turned up the lamps. I blinked in the sudden brightness.

"What in the world happened to your arm?"

"I bumped into someone."

She pulled something from her sleeve and rubbed it on my arm. The mark disappeared.

"A bracelet on each wrist!" she said.

I moved the bracelet and followed her to the stage. The entire chorus of green clad fairies sang a spell to create snow. Dancers in blue swirled around them as the enchantment grew stronger. The lights dimmed, and I walked onstage. The musicians stopped playing. My footsteps echoed through the hall. The entire audience held its breath.

The lights came back on, and I found myself surrounded by white. I couldn't see my parents and Sir Gilbert. I couldn't tell if Divinia had come. I couldn't even see the dancers I knew were standing next to me. Had the stage lights always been that bright?

The orchestra played, and I danced. I knew the moves well enough that I didn't need to see to perform them. I heard shuffling as everyone leaned forward and gasps as I rose above the stage. The dancers should be offstage now. I couldn't see the stage floor in the brightness, but I felt every eye on me.

My diamond rays spread out across the stage, and my

skirt expanded to a full circle. I stood in the middle, at the top of the stage, took a few deep breaths, and sang. Enchantment swept over the crowd. Music echoed through the theater. There were no clinking dinner forks. No scratching quills. I had everyone's full attention. My voice rang through the opera house.

I began my final note and took a step forward to descend. The invisible platform collapsed. My feet landed on another platform a few inches below. I waved my arms until I caught my balance and glanced backstage. Lady Alma stood somewhere in the darkness. What should I do?

Keep singing, for one thing. I caught my breath, sang my final note again, and took baby steps down the invisible staircase. Halfway down, I stepped into nothing. My song became a scream as I fell towards the stage. The diamonds wrapped around me and pulled me back to an upright position. They slowed my descent but did not stop it. My right ankle hit the stage. Something cracked, and I collapsed to the floor.

Diamonds scattered across the stage and into the orchestra pit. Someone closed the curtain as the audience burst into applause. Lady Alma ran out to me.

"They will riot if we don't open the curtain," she whispered. "Can you stand?"

I tried and bit back a scream when I put weight on my ankle. Lady Alma wrapped my arm around her shoulder and propped me up. The curtain opened, and the audience stood and cheered for me.

Mother ran onto the stage and bowed until the curtains closed.

"Really, Alma, trying to steal the spotlight," she said.

Then the curtains opened again, and she resumed her bowing.

The audience wanted more. An encore. Another song.

Another dance.

We had prepared several, of course, but my whole leg throbbed. Pain shot through my ankle when I put weight on it. I leaned against Lady Alma and waved. Finally the curtains closed and didn't open again. Mother slipped between them to the front of the stage to continue bowing and invite the audience to the masquerade in the gardens.

"Bring a chair!" Lady Alma said.

Singers and stage hands brought chairs from backstage. I eased into one and propped my foot up on another. Lady Alma snapped my boots off, and I groaned. My ankle had swollen to three times the normal size and turned purple.

"I'll fetch a doctor," the lead soprano said.

"No need," said Lady Alma.

She pulled a flat silver disk from somewhere in her dress and sprinkled it with salt from a crystal vial. She fastened it around my neck, and silver swirls of magic cascaded over my leg. The pain stopped, the skin's color returned to normal, and the swelling lessened.

Mother slipped back through the curtain. Behind it, applause gave way to general commotion as everyone scrambled to find their way to the garden for the party.

"How dare you rewrite the scene without my permission? Improvising in this carefully planned masterpiece? Do you know how many times I revised?"

"I fell."

"The fairy snow crashing to earth like a rock! And changing the notes of your song! I have never been so insulted."

Lady Alma sighed.

"Our sincerest apologies, Queen Ingrid, but the audience loved it nonetheless. Go on to the party, we'll join you shortly."

"And find a way to ruin it, no doubt. Come help me change, Alma. I can't stand this green dress another moment. The whole chorus looked dreadful in those green gowns."

"Just because Divinia did not come-"

"Don't speak her name! I declare from this day forth the name Divinia and the color green are banished from Salaria!"

Lady Alma looked at me.

"I'll be fine," I said.

"Stay here and leave the charm on until I come back."

Mother had already gone. Lady Alma hurried after her.

I glanced around the empty stage. Everyone had rushed away to the garden to prepare for the masquerade. I put weight on my ankle. The pain had disappeared. I took a few steps, testing it, and picked up my boots.

I was supposed to go out and address the crowd now, but how could I after ruining the opera? Why didn't I stay in the air when I realized the charm was failing? They could have brought me down with a ladder after the curtains closed.

I felt so stupid.

I wandered around the empty theater and found myself in the chorus dressing room. Props and costumes draped over chairs and tables. I found a spare charm on a table and tapped it.

A red dress wrapped around me. The skirt fell just past my knees. One of the ballerina costumes! A pair of brown leather ballet slippers appeared on my feet, and my white boots vanished. I stared at my ankle. No trace of the injury remained. I glanced in a mirror and jumped at my reflection. The charm had given me a long blond wig. I looked just like a member of the chorus! My bracelets glittered as I twirled around, imitating the dance moves from the first act.

I wandered back to my dressing room. No sign of Lady Alma. I tied the silver lace mask around my head and looked in the mirror. I hardly recognized myself. The charm had sent my white saltshaker dress and boots to the wardrobe in the corner. The hat sat upside down, filled with the diamonds.

I slipped the silver bracelets onto my right arm and stared in the mirror

Sometime tonight, I would address Salaria as heir to the throne.

But did it have to be right now?

I slipped out the back door and into the garden.

I hardly dared to breathe as I entered the bustle of the party, expecting each person to stop and shout, "I've found her!"

But no one did. One by one, people passed by me. I stood still, savoring the experience. The ballerinas and chorus members still wore their costumes. I blended into the sea of blond hair and red silk.

"May I have this dance?"

I turned and froze. Sir Inkling smiled at me and held out his hand. I shook my head. He had written so many odes to my enchanted voice, he would recognize me if I answered out loud.

"If you can dance on the stage, you can dance in the garden," he said. He grabbed my arm and pulled me towards the dance floor at the center of the party.

I resisted as quietly as possible, pushing him away. If I made a scene or spoke a word, I would be discovered. The poet ignored me and pulled me behind him. My ankle buckled, and I grimaced in pain until the charm provided relief. Sir Inkling caught me as I fell and pulled me close.

"Tipsy?" he asked, smiling.

I found myself staring up his nose again. I closed my

eyes and turned my head. The mask hid my face, but not very well.

Sir Inkling pulled me closer and closer to the dance floor. Were they always lit so brightly? Ladies' gems sparkled as their partners twirled them. Courtiers stood on raised platforms watching. Mask or not, someone would recognize me by the way I moved.

"I do not wish to dance," I whispered, trying to disguise my voice.

What scandal would there be if Princess Salara was caught attending her own party disguised as a ballerina? On the evening she came of age and was pronounced heir? Plus I had already ruined the opera. My face burned red. No wonder they didn't take me seriously.

I tried to push his hand off my waist, but Sir Inkling was stronger than he looked. Lights from the shimmering marble dance floor blinded me. We stood on the edge. I leaned back and pushed against his chest as he pulled me forward.

"I believe your partner has had enough dancing for one night," a voice behind me said.

Sir Inkling stopped. We both turned. A dark haired courtier about my own age smiled at us. His black mask covered most of his face and matched his gloves and clothes.

"It is an honor to dance with a poet," Sir Inkling said.

"And an honor to take refreshments with a nobleman. Let the lady choose which honor will be hers."

I glanced at the refreshment table. Crowded, but not as well lit as the dance floor. I shook my arm out of Sir Inkling's grip and accepted the courtier's hand. I smiled at him, hoping that was thanks enough to be polite. He did not look familiar, but my voice could still give me away.

Sir Inkling bowed and stalked off in search of another partner.

7

I examined the interrupter. Behind his mask, dark eyes reflected the bright lights of the dance floor. He took my hand and led me to the refreshment table. I accepted the glass of punch he offered and sipped it in silence. He did the same. The silence should have been awkward, but somehow it felt comfortable.

Sir Gilbert approached the table. I wanted to speak to him, but what would he think of me in this state? I turned to my companion. He also had noticed Sir Gilbert and stared at him.

"He is from the Colonial Delegation," I whispered, trying to make my voice sound raspy. "His skin is tanned from sailing."

"I know who he is."

But he did not know me, thank goodness.

"Thank you for earlier. I did not wish to cause a scene."

"Poets are idiots."

I nearly spit punch out my nose. I swallowed and regained my composure.

"You dare to criticize the Queen's favorites so freely?"

"Why not? You agree with me."

I laughed.

"What is your name? I must have seen you somewhere in the palace before," I asked.

"Excuse me."

He grabbed a handful of boiled eggs with my portrait on them from the table, tucked them into his sleeve, and disappeared into the crowd.

Behind me, Sir Gilbert moved nearer. I ducked my head and examined an egg. It featured a close up portrait of me surrounded by gems, flowers, and salt crystals. My nose was crooked.

I reached to put the egg back, and my hand brushed against someone's skin.

I raised my head to apologize and found myself face to face with Sir Gilbert.

We stared at each other. He searched my face as if trying to remember why he should know me.

I didn't dare talk to him surrounded by so many people. I grabbed a glass of the nearest drink and limped away. He did not follow. I made it to the edge of the garden and stood alone in the moonlight. An ocean breeze stole the warmth from my body.

The edges of the garden were empty and dimly lit. I walked into the darkness and stared over the wall at the moon's reflection on the sea.

This night seemed to be the fulfillment of a wish I had never found the courage to make. For one night, I was free.

I stared back at the light. The dazzling crowd swirled around the dance floor. I should join them. I should be the center. But I couldn't quite do it yet. I wandered back through the grove of evenly spaced trees, watching everything. Servants ran behind the scenes like stage hands, bringing food and drinks and taking empty plates. Everyone whispered when Mother arrived dressed in a gown of white lace trimmed in blue. In certain light, the blue looked green. She must have had Lady Alma change the color. Sir Gilbert spoke with her for a moment then walked to the theater. Was he looking for me?

I walked towards the theater and passed the dark clothed courtier. I hesitated. He had saved me from Sir Inkling. I should at least learn his name. I could grant him a favor as thanks. Perhaps a place at the next portrait sitting. It wouldn't take long. I could find Sir Gilbert afterward.

I turned and followed the courtier. He slipped behind a bush in the corner of the garden. I followed and descended the dark staircase I found on the other side. Flickering light grew stronger the lower I went. Where was he going?

A smoky haze enveloped me as I reached the bottom of the stairs. My eyes watered, blurring my vision. Servants rushed past me carrying overflowing trays of food. A huge fire filled a corner of the room. The light from it glinted off knives wielded by muscular servants carving meat. Red faced lads threw logs into the fire. Chefs used large bronze charms to adjust the heat to suit what they were cooking. I had read about charms like this, but never seen them. I stood for a moment watching their technique. It was a simple motion. I mimicked it, trying to dim the fire in a lantern.

The fire flickered as bright as ever.

The dark clothed courtier was not in the room.

I had no idea where the door at the end of the kitchen might lead, but I followed it anyway and found myself in an art studio. Painters copied famous portraits of me onto cakes and boiled eggs. I recognized Lacquer, the red haired painter from my latest portrait session. Were unskilled painters banished to the kitchen, then? Other artists sculpted bits of sugar into replicas of my shoes, clothes and even hairstyles. I grimaced at the butterfly chignon. Servants examined each finished work and put them in baskets.

I ran to the doorway across the room, keeping my head down. It would be foolish to linger in a room filled with my portraits.

Still no courtier.

The rooms grew calmer and calmer the farther I went. Some were empty. Some held piles of food. A few servants gave me strange looks, but most were too busy to care that a dancer had lost her way in the kitchens.

The heat from fires and the weight of the wig made me sweat. I passed a door with a cool breeze blowing through it and hurried inside.

Or should I say outside? I entered a small garden filled with rows of ugly plants without flowers or even ornamental leaves. Were unskilled gardeners banished to the kitchens as well? At least the plants smelled nice. A short wall separated the outer edge of the garden from the seaside wall. I stood for a moment, grateful for the cool air. A small fountain bubbled in the center. I sat on it and scooped up water with my hands. My ankle tingled as I took weight off it, but the pain did not return. Moonlight sparkled in the fountain.

How would I explain my presence here if a servant came? I found a corner of the garden hidden by a plant with giant bushy leaves and sat underneath it. I just needed a few more moments to catch my breath before I returned. Surely they had missed me by now. If I could find Lady Alma, she would help me make an excuse for my absence.

I heard a rustling in the leaves and turned my head. A pair of dark, shining eyes stared at me from under the bush.

I gasped, and a gloved hand shot out from behind the leaves and covered my mouth.

"Don't scream," someone whispered. The hand released me.

I sat still for a moment catching my breath. The eyes belonged to a face in a black mask. His dark clothes blended with the plants, making it difficult to see him. Only the whites of his eyes and thin rim of pale skin surrounding them were visible as they reflected the moonlight. Even his eyelashes disappeared in the darkness.

Someone else entered the garden. The stranger stood and offered me his gloved hand. I took it, and he pulled me to my feet. A young man in a red tunic, gold cape, and green mask stared at us. The sea breeze ruffled his brown hair. Moonlight shone on his white teeth when he smiled.

"Sneaking beautiful women away from the party is my job, Will."

The dark clothed courtier pulled his hand away from mine.

"You're late, William."

"Apparently not late enough. I can come back later if you need more time."

"Your names are Will and William?" I asked in the raspiest voice I could manage.

"Second cousins," William said. "Our parents weren't very creative. As the clear superior, I kept the full name."

He kissed my hand and swished his gold cape.

"But we'll be going now," Will said, pulling William across the garden.

They jumped over the low wall and climbed down. By the time I made it to the edge, they had disappeared.

I stood looking over the wall for a moment before following voices to another part of the castle. I was nervous I wouldn't be able to find the main garden, but I was too afraid to ask anyone for help. How long would they wait before sending soldiers after me?

It would be the scandal of the century. On the night I was supposed to be proving my responsibility. I had to get back.

I found the kitchens and wandered through room after room full of food in various stages of preparation. Finally, I entered the room where they were painting eggs. Heat from the main kitchen's fires streamed through the door. The masquerade was just beyond that.

My stomach rumbled. If I had to face the whole kingdom as heir after ruining my birthday opera, I shouldn't do it on an empty stomach. I grabbed a Salara egg from a basket and cracked it against the table.

"Stop!"

I looked up. Everyone in the kitchen stared back at me. Their knives glinted in the firelight.

"Stop, thief!"

I ran for the nearest door. Someone beside me did the same. Lacquer grabbed my skirt and pulled me back. Someone else grabbed my hand and pulled me forward. Lacquer lost his grip, and I ran down the corridors, clinging to the hand that had saved me. Servants chased us waving knives, paintbrushes, and anything else they could find.

I lost track of where we were, but the person in front of me kept running. People shouted behind us. We darted in and out of rooms before dashing into an open courtyard. No, a stable judging from the smell of it. William stood there, holding a horse harnessed to a cart full of hay. He had changed from courtier clothes to peasant clothes.

"What now?" he said.

"No time," the person in front of me said. I turned and realized I was holding Will's hand.

He picked me up and set me on the cart.

"Crawl in."

"What?"

"Do it now!"

He jumped up and crawled into the hay. I followed him. It was itchy. Beyond itchy. At least the mask kept it off most of my face. William rearranged the hay behind us, covering our feet. I heard him walk back to the horse. A crowd of people ran into the courtyard.

"You, there! Did anyone come this way?"

Silence. William must have shrugged or shook his head.

The crowd moved on. I realized I was holding my breath and exhaled. Will's hand bumped into my nose. I put my hand up to push him away, and he handed me a handkerchief. I took it and put it over my mouth. Breathing became easier, but my heart did not slow down. My hand, still holding the cracked egg, trembled.

8

The wagon rattled as we left the stable. Horse hooves clicked against cobblestones, and I bounced against hay until I reached the bottom. I held as still as possible, watching the road pass through a gap between the boards.

We slowed, and the wagon tilted as we descended a ramp. I slid forward, gasped, and inhaled a piece of hay. William whistled a tune to cover up my coughing.

The wagon reached the end of the ramp, and I bumped against the wood with such force I was certain to be bruised. Me, bruised. What would Lady Alma say?

"Easy, there. Quiet, girl," William said, clucking to the horse.

I gripped the gaps between wood to prepare for the next gate.

"Quite a load there, William," a voice said. The guard at the gate?

"I thought they'd need extra hay with all the guests here, but no such luck," William said. "There's more honor than crops at our farm this year."

"And what an honor! I'd give my sword arm for that."

"Wouldn't we all?" William said. "Although I guess I'd be giving my plow arm."

The soldier laughed. The gate creaked open. Light

from the opening charm shone through the cracks in the boards. Splinters dug into my hands as I clung to the wood, but I didn't slide forward.

We passed through two more gates without a problem. I smelled the sea mixed with the hay. It occurred to me we were leaving Castlemont about the time the cobblestones gave way to a dirt path.

I was out of the palace! On my own! We traveled long enough for my heart to stop pounding before the wagon stopped. The hay rustled as Will climbed out. I tried to do the same, but my skirt had become one with the haystack. I found Will's leg and pulled myself up. He reached down and grabbed my shoulder.

"Nice to see you again," William said. The moon reflected off his teeth like a marble dance floor.

I felt to make sure my wig was still on and breathed deeply, enjoying the scent of hay now that it wasn't smothering me. Behind me, Castlemont glowed brighter than the moon and stars.

"Thank you," I said to Will.

He nodded. His eyes reflected the moonlight. For a moment he looked like a ghost. His dark hair fell over his eyes, giving the impression that the top of his head was missing as it blended in with the trees surrounding us.

"Again, Will, sneaking away with beautiful maidens is my job."

William winked at me. Will sputtered.

"I didn't- I mean, I'm not sure how this happened."

"He saved me. From servants with knives," I said.

"Ah, the old servants with knives routine," William said. "Well, you two have fun!"

He jumped off the wagon seat.

"Where are you going?"

"I've got my own blond beauty to see."

He disappeared into the woods.

Will and I stood in the hay. He still wore his mask. So did I. Neither of us seemed inclined to take them off.

I had encountered awkward situations before. Diplomats who forgot the little Salarian they knew when they saw my beauty and babbled on and on in their native languages. Walking in Lady Alma's more outrageous gowns. Sir Inkling stroking my eyelashes.

This was the worst.

He would recognize me at any moment. He had seen me in the opera and eaten eggs with my portrait on them. I breathed the night air, taking in the scents from the ocean and forest.

"I should go back," I said.

The party lights flickered above us. Music and laughter echoed through the forest when the wind blew our way. I should be addressing that crowd, and instead I was in a wagon with a stranger, covered in hay.

I had managed to sneak away on my own, but what now? The guards would never look for me here.

"You can't go back now."

"What else can I do?"

I jumped off the wagon and gasped as my ankle popped and gave out. The eggshell dug into my palm as I caught myself. I stared as drops of blood formed against my pale skin.

Will helped me up and lifted me to the front of the wagon so I could sit. He jumped up and sat beside me. My ankle tingled as the charm relieved the pain.

"I'm going to Salt Spring Village. You can ride with me and hide there. The soldiers will be looking for you. Stealing this is a crime against the Princess."

He held up the crushed egg and tossed it on the ground. I remembered I was still hungry and sighed.

"I was supposed to do something tonight."

"It will have to wait."

I glanced up at the palace lights. Were they panicking yet? Had they closed the gates and canceled the party? Mother would probably faint. Lady Alma would rant in Castanian. Father would get even quieter and gather his advisers around him.

Sir Gilbert-

To him, it would be just another adventure.

For me, it could be my first.

I was free! I was actually outside the palace. Away from everything I had ever known.

"Alright. Let's go to Salt Spring, then."

I shivered.

Will pulled off his dark cloak and wrapped it around me. He swished the reins, and the wagon moved through the forest.

"Here."

He reached into his sleeve and handed me a Salara egg. I tapped it against the wagon seat and peeled it. The artist had not quite gotten my eyes right.

"I thought stealing these was a crime against the Princess?"

"You weren't the only one who ran when they yelled 'thief.'"

I chewed the egg as we traveled in silence. Was this the same road I had traveled with Sir Gilbert? I couldn't tell in the dark. I pulled hay out of my wig in between bites of egg. Neither of us removed our masks.

Will handed me another egg when I finished the first. I ate a third and refused a fourth.

"Why did you steal so many?"

"Just a hobby."

"Stealing Salara eggs is your hobby?"

He laughed. "Life gets boring sometimes."

I should definitely not take off my mask. Apparently it covered more of my face than I thought. It had fooled even Sir Inkling. Maybe I could actually do this!

"What about you? You danced with the Princess in the opera. There was plenty of food at the masquerade. Why steal an egg?"

Right, he thought I was a ballerina.

"I was hungry."

"There's safer food to take."

"I'll remember that next time."

The stars flickered through the tree leaves.

"I missed it," I said, needing to hear the words out loud. "She's coming of age tonight. They'll announce her as the official heir."

"She'll make a terrible queen."

"What?"

People treated me as if I was incompetent, but no one had ever voiced the thought out loud. At least not in my presence.

"A good ruler should know the people. Know their struggles. The King does a decent job. But Salaria can hardly support Salara as a Princess. Her rule will be a disaster."

"Princess Salara is a national treasure!"

"She costs the nation plenty of treasure!"

I stared at him.

"You have some nerve!"

"You don't know anything about it."

"Apparently not. Your opinions seem quite contradictory. You steal eggs with her portrait then complain about her. Who are you, anyway? How did you get into the palace?"

"You should be glad I did. You'd be in a dungeon right now if not for me."

Wrong. I would be in a garden dancing with Sir Gilbert.

We drove in silence. The sky turned from black to

blue, and the moon faded. We turned a corner and entered a village. I recognized it. In the early morning light, I saw the same fountain and town square surrounded by tiny houses and shops with no windows. I had passed them just yesterday. It all seemed like a long time ago.

Will parked the cart in front of a trough and tied the horse's bridle to a post. He helped me out of the seat.

"Keep the cloak."

He disappeared into the crowd of peasants, slipping off his mask once his back was turned to me. He had straight hair almost as black as mine.

I would have to remove my mask. There was no way around it. If I kept quiet, maybe no one would recognize me. I untied the strings and crumpled the mask into a ball. I straightened the blond wig and wrapped the cloak around me, covering as much of my dress as I could. The cloak had a hood. I pulled it over my head and walked to the fountain.

First things first. I was thirsty.

9

No one noticed me in the bustle of the town square as I walked towards the fountain. Several peasants wore cloaks similar to mine. I blended in! When I reached the fountain, my rippling reflection showed a face covered with dust. Bits of hay stuck out of the blond wig. I wiped at a speck, afraid it might be a freckle. It smeared on my face.

I stood, waiting for someone to offer me a glass. No one did. Right, I was in disguise. I cupped my hand and scooped up a mouthful of water. The peasants drawing water with buckets ignored me. I drank a few more mouthfuls and sat on the side of the fountain. My ankle ached. Still not completely healed, then.

My stomach made an odd growling noise. A few boiled eggs were not enough not replace dinner and breakfast. My skin tingled, and I felt light-headed as the excitement and lack of food caught up with me. I kicked my feet against the fountain. Where did peasants get food, anyway? No servants with silver trays bustled around, but everyone here would need breakfast. A movement in front of me drew my attention away from the courtyard.

I turned and found myself face to face with a blond

peasant wearing a decent imitation of Lady Alma's butterfly chignon. She had secured the elaborate style with green ribbons instead of a salt charm, and her hair stuck out on either side of her head. She stared at the fountain wall beneath me.

"Have you lost something?" I asked, trying to sound casual.

"Shoes," she whispered.

I glanced down. She wore plain brown boots, dusty from the dirt paths around the village.

"You have shoes," I said.

She kept staring. I followed her gaze and realized she was staring at my feet. I examined the ballet slippers, puzzled. They were dusty from the hay and dirt and much plainer than my usual footwear. I glanced around the town square.

All the peasants wore ankle length boots. Their skirts varied from knee length to almost floor length. Was that why they wore short skirts? To show off their boots?

So I didn't have the right shoes to be a fashionable peasant. She didn't have to be rude about it.

I stood, ignoring a stab of pain in my ankle. The peasant lowered her head, following my feet.

"Salara preserve us," the girl muttered.

I stepped backward. She followed.

If I ran now, I would have a head start. I might be able to make it to the woods and hide. Was my ankle healed enough to walk back to Castlemont?

Before I could move, the peasant grabbed my hand and pulled me towards the edge of the courtyard. We ducked between two buildings, and she pushed me through a door. I blinked in the sudden darkness.

A male version of the peasant who had kidnapped me stood at a high table cutting something with large scissors. Twins, perhaps? He stared at us, looking as surprised as I felt. An oil lamp on the table cast light upwards onto his face, making him look like a phantom from a ghost story. A pot hung over red coals in a fireplace in the corner. The whole room smelled of leather.

"Elsie?" he said.

"Her shoes, Edsel! Look at her shoes!"

Were all commoners this rude?

The two identical peasants knelt to the ground and examined my feet. I could have kicked them in the face and run, but sketches on the walls caught my eye. Detailed drawings of every outfit I had worn for the past two months covered every flat surface in the room. My birthday portrait gown. My past two opera costumes, including the shepherdess gown I had worn to the picnic. My red breakfast gown. Replicas of my footwear rested on shelves around the room. I shuddered.

Edsel tore himself away from my feet and offered me a chair. As soon as I sat, Elsie pulled off my slippers and tossed them to Edsel.

"You shouldn't wear such things out in the dirt," she scolded, offering me a glass of water.

"You shouldn't wear them out at all!" Edsel said. He pulled a paintbrush from his table and flicked dust off the leather.

"Dangerous," Elsie agreed.

My face grew redder and redder. The coals produced surprising amount of heat in the tiny room. I pulled off my cloak.

Edsel dropped the paintbrush. Elsie gasped.

"Salara preserve us," they said together.

They stared at me. I stared at them.

"Who are you?" Elsie said.

I wanted to ask them the same question.

"That dress is from Princess Salara's birthday opera,"

Edsel said.

I shifted my weight to my feet, ready to run for the door if they attacked. How far could I make it barefoot? Of all the stupid things to do! Why had I removed my cloak?

"So you were in the opera, then!" Elsie squealed. "Did you see Princess Salara's dance? Oh, you must have! Tell me all about it!"

"It was marvelous," I said without enthusiasm.

At least two people did not know I had ruined my own birthday opera.

Elsie clapped her hands together.

"Oh, I knew it would be. Queen Ingrid writes the best operas! And to cast Princess Salara as the fairy snow! Her skin glistens like enchanted snow. That's what all the poets say!"

"What was her costume like?" Edsel asked. "We haven't heard yet. They revised the opera so many times. This is the latest design we have, but she wore this to a picnic instead."

He gestured to the drawing of the shepherdess costume.

If I kept them distracted, maybe I could escape before they recognized me.

"She wore white silk. And Lady Alma enchanted diamonds to float around her like a snowflake."

They both clasped their hands to their chests.

"Do you think you could draw it for us?" Elsie asked. "I have some white muslin. I could make a replica to wear to-"

A beam of sunlight blinded us as someone opened the door. Elsie recovered first.

"William! I was just planning what to wear for, well, never mind that."

She giggled and threw her arms around him.

William returned her embrace with three pats on the back and stared at me.

"Oh, my manners!" Elsie said. "William this is- Um, well, I don't know actually."

"Sa- Sara," I said, instantly regretting using a name so close to my own. "And William and I-"

"Are pleased to meet each other," William said. He took my hand and kissed it, frowning at me.

"What? Oh. It is charming to meet you, William."

"Out with it, William. All the latest news! Did Divinia come to the opera?"

Elsie served William a bowl of oatmeal from the pot hanging over the coals. Edsel brought me one and watched me eat it. I picked my way around burnt lumps. Disgusting, but I was too hungry to care. Much.

"The majestic Fairy Divinia did not make an appearance. Naturally, everyone was devastated."

"Princess Salara will be so disappointed," Edsel said to me. "She has been longing to have her blessing confirmed by her fairy godmother. And of course she has wishes lined up."

"I managed to catch a glimpse of the opera," William said. "Salara wore white silk-"

"With a diamond snowflake around her!" Elsie said. "Sara told us all about it. She was in the opera. Her costume is just like the sketch of the ballerinas you brought me. They didn't revise those outfits at all!"

"Anything else Sara told you?"

"Did they sign the treaty?" Edsel asked.

"Yes, Princess Salara took a fancy to the head of the delegation. A dashing young sea captain."

"He must be dashing if he can outrun the Dragon," Elsie said.

"Is Roslynn here?" William asked. "I thought she might be working today."

Elsie crossed her arms.

"She went home."

"Business has been slow," Edsel said. "And her parents need help on the farm."

"Any idea when she'll be back?"

Elsie tossed her head, making her butterfly chignon flap.

"Oh, we won't need her anymore now that Sara has come."

William and I both choked on our oatmeal.

"You will stay, won't you?" Edsel said. "You could tell us all about the latest fashions."

"And palace gossip!" Elsie said.

"That's my job!" William protested.

"Don't be jealous, William," Elsie said. "Of course we'll still need you."

"Jealous?"

"Yes, don't be jealous, William," Will said.

I jumped. When had Will entered the room? He stood in the corner farthest from the fireplace watching us. I stared at him. He had removed his mask, but his dark hair covered most of his face. I still couldn't tell what he looked like beyond a narrow chin and infuriating smirk. He now wore the baggy shirt and trousers of a peasant, but in a darker color than William and Edsel's outfits.

"Oh, please stay, Sara," Elsie said. "It will be such fun! We're about the same size. You can borrow my clothes until we make you new ones. My shoes might even fit you!"

"I doubt that."

"You would be very helpful," Edsel said. "You could model our clothes at parties. Everyone would want them if you wore them."

He stared at me. His expression reminded me of the poets. I stared back for a moment, then nodded.

"Then it's settled," Will said.

I glared at him, but kept silent.

The door burst open, filling the room with sunlight. Will lifted his arm to shield his eyes.

"Elsie! Edsel! Just wait until you see what I've got!"

The girl stopped. She dropped her basket and put her hands on her hips.

"I see you've started the party early. Who on earth is that?"

"Estrella, this is Sara," Elsie said.

Estrella crossed her arms and glared at me. She had blond hair pulled back in a braid that reached her knees. Her green dress brought out her blue eyes. At least, I thought they were blue. It was difficult to tell in the dim light.

"Why is she here?"

She directed the question to Will, but Edsel answered.

"Sara is from the palace."

"I can see that," Estrella said. "The palace is in a quiet uproar today. Guards everywhere. Lots of whispering and running. Everyone is trying to act normal, but the royals didn't have their public breakfast today. I had to borrow a boat to get out."

"I knew it," Edsel said. "They're devastated the Fairy Divinia did not come."

"How do you know?" I asked.

"Princess Salara has been looking forward to meeting the Fairy Divinia for-"

I waved my hand at him.

"Not that. The things about the palace."

Estrella ignored me and turned to Will.

"Something is up. Something big. The New Salarians even cut their visit short. They're leaving this afternoon."

"Sir Gilbert is leaving?" I exclaimed, my voice louder than I intended.

Everyone turned and stared at me.

"I mean, the delegation just got here, and they barely made it past the Dragon."

"As I said, something is up. I don't suppose you know what it is?"

Will shook his head.

"Nothing seemed unusual last night."

I laughed and covered my mouth to make it seem like a cough. Nothing seemed unusual last night?

"Enough gossip," William said. "What did you get, Estrella?"

"See for yourself. I think you'll like it."

Elsie and Edsel transferred the basket to a table and pulled out yards and yards of red fabric. The silk matched my ballerina dress perfectly.

"Lucky I grabbed the red," Estrella said. "We can copy that gown exactly now."

"Three at least," Edsel said, his eyes darting between me and silk in his hands. "And if Sara wears one to a party, they'll sell for double the price!"

"No time to waste!" Elsie said. "I'll help you change!"

She grabbed my hand and pulled me up a flight of stairs.

"What is going on?" I asked as she unbuttoned my dress. I turned my necklace backwards to hide the healing charm under my wig.

"I'm sure my clothes will fit you. Not as nice as your dress, but you definitely can't wear this out. What if someone recognized it?"

I could hardly be in more trouble than I was now. I stood in my chemise while Elsie rummaged through a wardrobe. Downstairs were the most devoted Salara fans I had ever met. Sir Gilbert was leaving. And I was trapped barefoot in a peasant village. I twirled my fingers around a lock of blond hair. What would happen if I removed my wig, revealed my true identity, and demanded passage back to the palace? If we left now, I might arrive in time to say goodbye to Sir Gilbert.

Or convince him to stay.

That would almost make life in the palace bearable.

Almost.

"You should hide your jewelry," Elsie said, gesturing to the bracelets. "Someone might try to steal it. I'll give you an apron. Very useful for storing things. Estrella enchants the pockets so things won't fall out, and it will keep your dress clean."

She shoved an itchy brown dress over my head. I struggled until I found the sleeves and pulled it past my shoulders. I had never put on a dress without magic. Elsie found a pair of socks and peasant boots like the ones she wore and helped me lace them. To my surprise, they fit. She helped me with the buttons on the front of the dress and tied the apron around my waist. I slipped the bracelets into a pocket on the side.

"I told you we were the same size! You can trust a cobbler to know these things."

She rushed downstairs with the ballet dress. I stayed upstairs, looking for a mirror. There wasn't one, but surely I looked less like a princess than I ever had. I went downstairs with my head held high.

Will and William had gone. Estrella and Edsel stood over the ballerina costume. A ball of light floated near the ceiling, a miniature indoor sun. It lit the worktable far better than the fireplace and candles. I squinted at it, trying to see how it worked. My magic books never mentioned a spell like this. The others focused on the gown and didn't notice my fascination.

"This will be a bit tricky," Estrella said, her blue eyes narrowed. "I may not be able to duplicate it exactly."

"If you can get anywhere close it will be a huge

success," Edsel said. He smiled at me.

Estrella nodded and waved her hands in the air. Without a hint of sparkle, the bolt of red silk floated into the air and split into pieces. Elsie also waved her hands. As they worked together, the pieces shuffled around and arranged themselves into the same shape as the ballet costume. Estrella snapped her fingers, and a needle with red thread zipped around the pieces and sewed them together. Elsie hemmed the skirt. They lowered the completed dress to the table. Estrella collapsed into a chair and poured herself a glass of water.

Edsel examined the dress.

"Oh, well done!"

"You'll have to do the shoes on your own," Estrella said, panting. "I can't handle any more today. Watch out for that swan feather lining. Alma's construction is always tricky."

"Of course!" Edsel said. "If we can copy these, oh!"

He cradled the ballet slipper as if it were a kitten, stroking the brown leather.

Elsie tugged at my sleeve.

"Let's go."

"Where?"

"Don't you want to see what you look like in your new clothes? And we need swan feathers for the shoes."

We left the shop. Edsel tried to follow us, but Estrella pulled him back and handed him the other shoe.

10

Elsie and I walked to the outskirts of town and entered a small pink gypsy wagon with green and gold trim. There was no sign of the horse that pulled it. A wooden plaque painted with colorful pictures of wigs, ribbons, and feathers hung on the front.

"Madame Delilah's wig shop," a voice crackled. "Are you buying or selling?"

Madame Delilah? Had Lady Alma's crazy wigs really come from this tiny wagon? I glanced around. I didn't see anyone in the dinghy interior. Just shelves full of boxes, bottles, and hair in the tiny portable shop.

"Buying, Madame Delilah. We need swan feathers and a glimpse in your mirror."

"Ah, Elsie, how nice to see you. I have some new trim you might like."

A wrinkled face emerged from a pile of blankets on a chair. Her clothes, draped randomly over her body, blended with her shop. She smiled at Elsie, then stared at me.

"Ah, I would recognize one of my creations anywhere. I am always happy to buy them back if you need extra coins."

"You made this wig?"

"You're wearing a wig?" Elsie asked.

"I make wigs for Lady Alma and every noble mother who wants her dark haired child to have a chance at being Salara's companion. They used to try dying their hair blond, but wigs are easier."

"Salara's companions wear wigs?"

Why had I admitted to wearing a wig?

"So they can be blond like me!" Elsie said.

I had always assumed it was natural.

"And what does your real hair look like?"

Before I could protest, Madame Delilah waved her hand. A lock of my real hair appeared from under the wig.

Elsie gasped. The old woman smiled.

"Almost dark enough to pass the rook test."

"The what?" I asked, stepping into the door to get further away from her. The sunlight hit my hair and reflected a dark prism of colors into the wagon. I jumped back into the shade.

"They say Princess Salara's hair is dark as a rook's wing. I have a rook feather here for comparison. Ten gold coins for hair that passes the test."

"You'll pay me because my hair is dark?"

"No, dear. I buy hair. To make my wigs."

"I'm not interested in selling my hair."

Elsie pulled me forward.

"Of course you're not. But wouldn't it be fun to know if your hair is as dark as Princess Salara's?"

I already knew the answer to that question and shook my head.

"No need to be shy, dear."

The feather might as well have been a dagger. I pressed against the wall, grimacing. Madame Delilah advanced. Her wrinkled smile collapsed when she held the feather up to my hair. She squinted at the feather, and then at me.

"Well?" Elsie said. "Does she pass?"

"Not quite."

Was she blind? It was identical. Madame Delilah examined me and the feather.

"You are sure you will not sell? The wig or your hair? You didn't pass the test, but I'll still give you a fair price."

I shook my head and backed away to put as much distance between me and the rook feather as possible.

"Well, if you ever change your mind, blow on this feather and I will find you."

She handed me the feather and waved her hand. The strand of dark hair disappeared back into my blond wig. I ran outside while Elsie ordered the swan feathers.

In the sunlight, the rook feather reflected the same spectrum of purples, blues, and greens that my hair did. I stared at it until Elsie came out. Madame Delilah followed her. She pulled a curtain back from the wagon's side, revealing a full length mirror. Elsie pushed me in front of it.

I stared at myself. This was not the face Salaria's poets spent hours describing. I was still beautiful, but I did not look like myself in the rough brown dress and disheveled blond wig. My face was smudged with dust and creased with worry.

"See, the dress looks great!" Elsie said.

She pushed me away from the mirror and adjusted her green hair ribbons so her hair stuck out more on either side of her head.

"Those are getting a bit frayed, dear," Madame Delilah said from the wagon door. "I've got some pink ribbons that would suit you very well."

"Oh, I couldn't replace these. Are you staying in town long?"

Madame Delilah shook her head.

"I'm on a gathering mission, but no one around here seems interested in selling."

Elsie straightened with pride.

"Salt Spring is prosperous, Madame Delilah. No one here needs to sell their hair."

"I can see that. You girls have a nice day."

Elsie waved at her as she closed the curtain. I tucked the feather into my apron pocket and exhaled.

As soon as we returned, Edsel handed me giant scissors and a piece of brown leather. Estrella sat at the table sketching. She did not acknowledge our entry.

"Cut this to fit the pattern," Edsel said. He pushed a handful of paper across the table.

"I can't do magic," I said.

I pushed the pattern back to him.

"Who said anything about magic?"

"You're not going to replicate these by hand?"

I stared at the shoes. No one in the palace made things without magic.

Edsel handed me the patterns and clasped my hands for a moment.

"It takes a lot of fairy salt to power this kind of spell. We would have to sell our shoes for double the price if we put them together with magic."

"But it will take days!"

"Weeks!" Elsie said. "But it will go faster if you help. Edsel will show you how to follow the pattern."

Edsel unfolded his pattern, placed it on the leather, and cut around it until he had a piece shaped like the parchment. I slipped my hands into the scissors and snipped the air. Had it really come to this? Salaria's greatest treasure earning her keep in a cobbler's shop?

"It will take years if you go that slowly," Estrella said.

She pulled the scissors from my hands and cut the pieces herself.

"You used magic a moment ago," I said. "Why are you doing this by hand?"

Estrella rolled her eyes.

"You've lived in Castlemont your whole life, haven't you? There are salt charms in every room, waiting to power your spells. Magic is precious out here. Fairy salt is expensive."

"It doesn't matter to me," I said. "I've never been able to work charms."

They stared at me.

"Perhaps with proper training," Elsie said.

"I can teach you," Edsel said. "I'll show you every charm I know."

"You should change your name," Estrella said.

"What?"

"If you're going to stay, you should change your name. You'll put Elsie and Edsel in danger if someone finds out they're harboring a refugee from the palace."

"You should be Leslie!" Elsie said. "Elsie and Leslie! We can be sisters!"

"Edsel, Elsie, and Leslie, cobblers and more. It does have a ring to it!" Edsel said. "I, um, don't have to be your brother though."

He smiled at me. His cheeks flushed pink.

"You could take off your wig!" Elsie said.

Estrella nodded. "That might be wise."

I clutched the wig as if she might rip it off by force. The colors shining from my real hair would give me away faster than anything.

"Fine, keep the wig, Leslie," Estrella said.

"Rook."

"I beg your pardon?"

"I'll be Rook."

I wasn't sure why I chose it. Leslie just didn't feel right.

"You did almost pass the rook test!" Elsie said.

"That's not a real name," Estrella said. "You're supposed to be blending in!"

"I like it," Edsel said. He put his hand on my shoulder and glared at Estrella. "Rook is welcome to stay here as long as she likes."

Estrella sputtered.

"You're all going to hang, and you don't even care! I've dealt with nobility. I know how they think! They won't let a companion run free when something big is going on!"

"You used to know how they think," Elsie said. "You haven't lived in the palace in years. Rook lived there yesterday. She'll have lots of valuable things to tell us I'm sure."

"You're all impossible!"

Estrella threw her hands in the air and muttered to herself in Castanian as she rushed out of the room. The gesture reminded me so much of Lady Alma a wave of homesickness sweep over me. The star on the ceiling disappeared when Estrella left, plunging us into darkness.

"I've never seen her so mad," Elsie said.

She lit some candles with the coals in the stove. The room brightened a little.

"You can tell us about the latest fashions, can't you?" Edsel asked. "We're in trouble if you can't. Estrella is our best source of information."

"William tries, but the poor boy has no sense for fashion," Elsie said. "Last week he told me short sleeves were in."

"But everyone wore long sleeves last week!"

"I know! The layering confused him. He thought the full sleeves were some kind of cape. We looked like fools, trying to sell short sleeved dresses with capes."

"So you make clothes and shoes?"

"Edsel specializes in shoes. I make dresses when we

can get the fabric."

I nodded.

"Even Lady Alma has had trouble finding fabric with the Shadow and Dragon on the loose."

Elsie and Edsel stared at the floor. I bit my lip. I had said too much. They would figure it out now! Why would a simple ballerina have such a close connection to Lady Alma?

"Our fabrics aren't fine enough to tempt the Shadow," Edsel said after an awkward pause.

"But this silk is identical to the fabric in the ballet costume."

"We get lucky sometimes. But not often enough to make us a target."

Edsel didn't meet my eyes as he spoke. Elsie fiddled with her hair.

"Well, you shouldn't be ashamed. No one can measure up to Lady Alma."

They brightened.

"Of course not! But I do so adore her designs," Elsie said. "She is my inspiration every day!"

"Do you mind helping us?" Edsel asked. "I can teach you what to do. You'll be a natural. And it isn't hard work. It won't ruin your hands."

I nodded. If I was going to stay here, apparently I would have to work.

Edsel showed me how to cut strips of leather into even lengths. He and Elsie cut pieces of patterns and stacked them by shape.

"Is the colonial ambassador as handsome as they say?" Elsie said.

"I've heard the delegation from New Salaria is shockingly tan," Edsel said. "We work inside, so our complexions are almost as fashionable as yours, Rook."

"The ambassador is very nice," I said.

My first strip of leather was crooked. Elsie trimmed it, and I tried again.

"Does Princess Salara like him as much as everyone says?"

I ducked my head to hide my blush.

"How much do they say she likes him?"

"Oh, I heard she didn't take her eyes off him at all their first dinner! And he arranged a sledding party for her! And she held his hand the whole time they walked through the forest."

News traveled fast, apparently.

"Could you sketch what she wore for the Castanian Duke's visit last month?" Edsel asked. "I haven't been able to get any information about it."

My face burned crimson.

"Lady Alma created the design from, well, from a dress she had already worn."

They both gasped.

"A repeat?" Elsie asked.

"It was short notice. The Shadow stole fabric meant for the dress before it reached the palace, and the Dragon stole a shipment from New Salaria the same week."

"But still, to repeat a gown," Edsel said. "Is the Shadow really causing that much trouble for Lady Alma and Princess Salara?"

They set down their tools and stared at the drawings on the wall. The expression on their faces was identical. I wouldn't have been able to tell them apart except for Elsie's butterfly shaped hair.

"It was one time," I said. "Lady Alma has started storing extra fabric in her studio so it won't happen again. The Shadow stole a shipment of jewels from the museum a few days ago, but she had enough extra lace on hand to improvise an embellishment for the gown."

Even if they were as embarrassed by the repeat as I

was, I couldn't admit the palace was having any trouble.

"The sleigh ride was such a romantic gesture on Sir Gilbert's part," Elsie said, "but it is inconvenient when men don't give notice of their plans. William never tells me when he's coming to visit. I have to look nice all the time in case he shows up."

"What about Will?"

She laughed.

"He's never made a romantic gesture in his life."

"But is he here often?"

She and Edsel glanced at each other.

"Hardly at all," Elsie said.

"Good."

"He is rude," Edsel said. "Not very considerate."

"I had noticed."

We laughed and continued to cut leather and talk about palace life. By the time the sun set, I had a pile of thirty-six leather strips. My fingers ached. Elsie had to help me unbutton my dress and unlace the boots. I pulled the socks off by myself. It was a triumph, somehow.

I stared into darkness from my place on the floor. The thin mattress underneath me did little to soften the wood planks. Elsie lay on a similar mattress across the room. Edsel slept downstairs in the cobbler shop.

"Elsie, do you ever go to Castlemont?"

She sighed.

"Sometimes, but I've only been to the third tier. William goes to the palace kitchen every week during the summer to sell vegetables. That's in the first tier."

"Could I go with him sometime?"

I heard her roll over.

"Why do you want to go with William?"

"I'm just homesick. I'd like to see the palace again."

"Oh. Good. Will goes with him sometimes."

I said nothing. Once I got to the kitchen, could I find

my way back to my room? And how would I explain my absence?

"I'd love to see it," Elsie said. "Even the kitchen. But William says it is too dangerous."

"Why would it be dangerous?"

I had been chased by angry servants with knives my first time in the kitchen. But if Elsie didn't wander off, she would be fine.

She didn't answer. Her steady breathing turned into a raspy snore. She had fallen asleep. I rolled over and tried to do the same. The noise and lumpy mattress kept me awake.

William went to the palace every week, and he had just come back. I would stay here for a week and return to the palace the same way I came. Maybe Elsie could come along. I could have my adventure and return before anyone got too worried.

What was this mattress filled with? Certainly not enchanted swan feathers like my palace bed. And I missed the weight of Seda on my feet. Where would he sleep while I was gone? I stared at the ceiling for hours before drifting to sleep, feeling every bump in the mattress and floor. Elsie's snores continued in a rhythmic pattern. At least Madame Delilah's wig was comfortable.

11

I awoke to a hand over my mouth and gasped for breath. Where was I?

"Quiet," someone whispered.

"Will?"

His hand muffled my voice. I squinted into the darkness, trying to see his face. Why didn't peasants have windows? Elsie's breathing continued in a steady rhythm across the room. The details of yesterday's activities came back one by one until I remembered why I was laying on a lumpy mattress in a cobbler's shop.

"Don't scream," Will said.

I nodded, and he removed his hand from my mouth.

"What are you doing here?" I whispered, pulling the blankets up to my chin.

"You need to come with me."

"You're insane."

If I screamed, would it wake Elsie? I had never tried to wake someone. She probably wouldn't be much good in a fight. Maybe I could get Edsel's attention. He could grab the scissors for a weapon.

Unless Will had already silenced him.

"Soldiers are on their way."

I stiffened.

"It is the middle of the night."

"No, it is almost dawn. They're looking for someone. It has to be us."

Us. Not likely.

They were looking for me.

"I am not running away with you."

"Do you want to die? You're wanted for crimes against the Princess."

I grimaced. I wouldn't die, but I would be disgraced. Princess Salara working with peasant cobblers? Oh, the soldiers would try to hush it up once they realized who I was, but word would get out.

I leaned forward, trying to make out Will's face.

"Where are we going?"

"A farm. William will meet us there."

Perfect! William had access to the kitchens. He could take me back.

"Ok."

"Get dressed. I'll wait for you downstairs. Don't wake Elsie."

Apparently, not much would wake Elsie. She kept snoring while I fumbled around the room looking for my clothes. I couldn't dress myself in the light, and it was harder in the dark. I got stuck with both arms above my head before pulling the dress onto my body.

Backwards.

And this was a different dress. I had grabbed one of Elsie's. Too late now. I managed to turn it around and buttoned the front. Somehow, I got it wrong. There was a gap at the bottom, and the top didn't line up. I tucked the extra fabric at the top into the collar and tied my apron around my waist. It covered the gap where there were extra buttons.

I had done it! I had dressed myself. If only there was a mirror so I could make sure I got it right. I pulled the boots over my feet. How had Elsie laced them? I should have paid closer attention. I wrapped the laces around the ankles of the boots to keep them closed. They still flopped when I walked.

I clunked down the stairs. My loose boots made a lot of noise. Neither Elsie nor Edsel stirred. Had Will cast a spell on them? He stood by the doorway, holding the door open so a thin stream of moonlight illuminated the shop. I made it outside without tripping over Edsel, the workbench, or the various tools on the floor.

Will closed the door. I stared at him. Nothing covered his face, but the moonlight was not bright enough for me to make out his features. He was paler than me, but no one would ever call his skin pearly.

I laughed to myself. That was a silly thing to call a peasant boy's skin. What would Sir Quill say of his long hair, swept out of his face and tucked behind his ear?

Hair like a dirty bird's wing, pale skin unlike pearls.
Eyes reflective like the mirror of a girl.

Maybe the castle poets worked harder than I gave them credit for. I examined Will and tried again.

Side-swept bird's wing hair over lusterless face
Hides reflective eyes that seem out of place.

What else rhymed with face? Lace, race, trace-

"Is something funny, Sara?"

I jumped. He didn't look offended, just confused. I had been staring at him and laughing. No way could I tell him I had been writing a poem.

"I'm called Rook now."

He raised an eyebrow.

"Estrella thought it would help me hide."

"And she suggested the name Rook?"

"Elsie and Edsel wanted to call me Leslie."

"That's better than Rook."

"I like Rook."

"This isn't a game. I don't know what you meant by stealing that egg, but the guards will try you for crimes against the Princess if you're caught."

"How could stealing an egg harm the Princess?"

He grabbed my arm and pulled me towards him. I felt rough patches of skin crisscrossing his hands. No wonder he wore gloves in the palace. I stared into his eyes. Dark eyebrows lowered. His lips clamped together, merging into a single scar across his face.

"If they catch you, they will kill you. Do you understand?"

I nodded. I wanted to laugh again, but his face looked so serious I swallowed the sound. The guards would not kill me for crimes against myself.

Will examined me for a moment, then let go of my arm. I tugged at my collar and followed him through the village. My shoes smacked with every step, but I refused to ask this rude peasant for help. The fountain sparkled in the moonlight. I walked towards it.

"What are you doing?"

"I'm thirsty."

"We don't have time for this."

I cupped my hands, took a drink, and gagged as the salty water hit my tongue. What had happened to the well? Will ignored me and walked in the shadows of the ramshackle houses until we left the town. I had to jog to catch up with him. The briny taste stayed in my mouth as we walked through hayfields and gardens.

By the time we reached the forest, the moon had

almost set, and the sun had almost risen. I studied Will's face in the morning light and considered continuing my poem. His skin did not look so strange in the daylight, and his features were pleasant. Too thin for the poets to rave about, but they would like his defined jaw and prominent cheekbones.

Will noticed me looking at him and swept his hair over his eyes.

Birds sang. Soon, the murmur of a brook joined them. Will meandered through the woods. He found a stream and walked beside it. My boots bumped, and my feet ached, but I inhaled the fresh forest air with enjoyment.

"Are you hungry?"

Will stopped so suddenly I ran into him.

"Yes."

I was always hungry lately. Peasants ate such small meals. Will sat on a flat rock on the bank of the stream. I joined him and kicked off my boots. Raw spots and blisters covered my feet.

Socks. I should have worn socks. I moved to the edge of the stream.

"Don't!" Will said just as I put my feet in the water.

It burned. I pulled my feet out at once. My eyes filled with tears as I used my apron to dry my feet. The fabric further irritated my wounds.

"This creek is salt water," Will said. "It flows straight from the mines into the Ghone."

I glared at him and blinked back tears.

He produced a Salara egg from his pack and handed it to me. Was this all he ate? I turned it over in my hand. The egg had a border of Seda chasing butterflies around it.

Poor Seda. I missed him. Surely someone in the palace would think to feed him.

"Behold, our Princess," Will said.

I examined the picture on his egg and laughed. My nose was far too large. I squinted at the portrait on my egg and showed it to him. The painter had given me eyes the size of an owl's.

At least Will wouldn't recognize me from these portraits.

He smashed his egg against the rock, portrait side down. I winced as he peeled away bits of the shell and tossed them into the stream.

I tapped the top of my egg and peeled away the shell, doing my best to keep the owl-eyed portrait intact. I set it on the ground next to me.

Will pulled more eggs from his bag.

"How many of these do you have?"

He shrugged.

I took another egg.

Will smashed his next egg so hard that half the white stuck to the stone. He tossed the entire egg into the river.

"Why steal so many eggs if you don't like her?"

He didn't answer.

I thought back to my days as Princess. I had never done anything to anger peasants. I had even performed for them a few times in the large courtyard. Thousands gathered to hear me sing.

"You've never met her," I said.

"I know her."

His voice contained an edge. Something dangerous. If he knew who I was, would he smash my real head against a rock?

Surely not.

And how did he know me?

"Tell me."

He shook his head and smashed another egg.

The sun rose above the horizon. It cast slanting shade through the trees, and beams of light darted across the forest floor like the reflection from a fairy's skin.

Will pulled off his boots and handed me his socks. I wrinkled my nose.

"You won't have skin left on your feet if you don't wear them."

"Worry about your own feet."

"We have to keep going."

The thought of putting anything against my feet made me want to cry. At least my ankle did not hurt. Lady Alma's healing charm had done its work well. But shouldn't it heal my feet?

I pulled the charm off and examined it. The metal had lost its shine and darkened. The curved engravings had faded. There was no trace of the salt crystals.

Empty, then. All the power from the fairy salt had been used. I tucked it into my apron pocket and took the socks. The thick wool looked mostly clean, and they didn't smell. I pulled them over my feet. It hurt. A lot. It hurt more when I put the boots over them, but once I tightened the laces everything was too snug to rub against my skin. That was something.

Will tied the laces of his boots together and slung them over his shoulder. He offered me his hand, and I stood, testing my feet. My soles were raw. It hurt less if walked on the insides of my feet.

Will kicked my pile of eggshell portraits into the creek and walked down the path. Mud stuck to his bare feet. I limped forward. Keeping up with him would be impossible. Without a drink, the egg taste lingered, reminding me how thirsty I was. I watched the stream as I walked. If only I had the purifying charm we had used at the picnic.

Once out of the forest, we walked through sloping striped fields. Hills. So many hills. My feet pressed against the boots at all angles as we crossed them. Drops of sweat formed on my brow as the sun climbed high and grew hot.

Will did not slow down. He walked barefoot, ignoring the rocks and roots that tripped me. I twisted my ankle in a hole and fell behind even further. It held weight, but the soreness returned. Will disappeared from my view more than once, and I took short breaks to search for him when I reached the tops of hills.

Just when I thought I had lost him for good, I saw him standing at the top of a large hill. He stood motionless, staring forward. Finally, he was waiting for me. I tripped up the hill, struggling to breathe. He did not acknowledge me when I joined him. I gasped as I realized why.

In front of us stood a desolate valley. Cracks and bits of withered plants covered the earth. I turned. On one side of the hill, green grass and flowers waved in a breeze, leading to the woods.

On the other, no living thing. Not even animals. Not a sound except the wind. The parched ground stretched over hills to the horizon, silent.

12

Will's hands shook at his sides, clenched into tight fists. I stepped towards him, and my ankle gave out. I fell and would have rolled down the hill if he had not caught me. My hand stung. A drop of blood formed on my palm, a ruby against a pearl.

Will offered me his hand.

"I can't."

Now that I was down, I couldn't imagine getting back up. My feet throbbed, and my palm stung. The fall had reinjured my ankle, and now I had no healing charm. A ball of pain formed just above my heel and stayed there.

"We're almost there."

He said it through gritted teeth.

"Then go ahead. I can't walk anymore."

I pulled off my boots to make it clear I had no intention of taking another step. The socks stuck to my feet when I removed them. Quite a bit of wool stayed behind in the blisters.

"The soldiers will find us."

"Great! I won't have to walk anymore."

I meant it. At this point, I didn't care about a scandal. They would take me back to the palace. Lady Alma would heal me. Everything would be better.

Will retrieved his socks and slipped on his boots. I watched, picking bits of wool off my skin and cringing every time.

As soon as he was out of sight, I would start screaming. The soldiers would find me eventually.

Will wrapped an arm around my waist and another under my legs. Before I could protest, he lifted me up and carried me into the parched valley. His feet crunched against the ground as if he were walking on brittle bones.

"Put me down," I managed to say. We were halfway down the hill by then.

He shook his head.

"I want them to find me. I want this to end."

"You think this is bad? You have no idea."

His face was too close to mine. Hair stuck to his forehead, damp with sweat. His eyes looked straight ahead. I diverted my gaze and watched the passing rows of the petrified plants. Will stepped between them.

A breeze cooled my feet. I should have struggled. Made him release me. But that would mean walking again. I felt Will's sweat through his tunic. He didn't smell very nice. I probably didn't either. A drip of his sweat landed on my face. I wiped it with my sleeve.

The dead valley stretched on for an eternity.

"Thank you," I said after a while.

He nodded. Possibly smiled a little. He was breathing too hard to speak.

Was I really that heavy? Sir Inkling once said I was delicate as a butterfly wing. Sir Quill said I was a snowflake come to life. But neither of them had ever carried me across hills and valleys.

Finally, at the top of a hill, Will's crunching boots met living grass. In front of us, surrounded by green grass and gardens, stood a tiny house and barn. Peeling red paint revealed weathered wood, and chickens pecked around the front yard. A group of children ran and laughed. A boy caught a chicken and chased a girl with blond hair so short I thought she was a boy until I noticed her dress. The whole group laughed and waved to us as we approached.

Will walked to the house and kicked the front door three times. A woman with a single streak of gray in her hair opened it.

"Will! I'd expect William to bring home a half-dressed girl in the middle of the night. Don't tell me you've picked up his bad habits."

Some of my buttons had come undone, revealing my chemise. My face flushed.

"It's morning," Will said.

"Even worse."

She smiled at me and opened the door wider to let us inside.

"Is she going to stay here?" a boy asked as we entered.

He looked younger than me, but he sat up straight, trying to look taller.

"Finish your breakfast and go help Samuel in the field."

"He won't need much help," the boy said. He stood and held out a chair. Will set me down in it.

"My name's Thomas," he said. "If you stay, you can have my bunk. I don't mind sleeping outside if it means you'll be comfortable."

"Um, thanks," I said.

"Anything for you, angel."

He winked at me.

"Thomas! Get outside this instant!"

The woman shooed him out the door.

"I am sorry about that. He has been spending a lot of time with William lately. My name is Gerta."

"Rook's feet are hurt," Will said. "Do you have

anything? We may need to leave soon."

I wouldn't do it. I couldn't do it. I couldn't walk any more today.

"Oh, I've treated my fair share of injuries," Gerta said. "I'll see what I can do. What are you on the run from?"

"Soldiers came to the village."

"Oh."

Her smiled faded. She poured the contents of a green bottle on my feet. I waited for the instant relief of a magic spell, but felt only a slight tingle. The translucent silver liquid smelled like a garden after rain. I fumbled with my dress and managed to refasten the buttons while Gerta bandaged the blisters.

"You can stay as long as you need to, of course. I'm a bit short on supplies though. Even feeding the children-"

"We'll get you some as soon as we can," Will said.

"I know you will."

"Has William come back yet?"

Gerta shook her head.

"He should be back soon, but it is hard to say. He's gone to visit Roslynn."

"The girl that helps Elsie and Edsel?" I asked.

"She lives on the farm next door," Will said.

"Will is at her farm as often as he is here," Gerta said. "Roslynn does come here to help sometimes, though."

"It looks like you need it," I said.

Gerta raised an eyebrow.

"I mean you have a lot of children!"

She laughed.

"They're orphans from all around Salaria. They do pretty well. The older ones especially."

Across the room, Will rummaged through a dresser and pulled out a clean pair of socks.

"Stealing my clothes again?" William asked.

He stood in the doorway, arms crossed.

"Just socks," Will said. "You can keep these."

He threw his dirty socks at William's face. William dodged and punched him on the shoulder.

"How's Roslynn?" Gerta asked.

"Not home. But her parents invited you to stay with them."

"That's kind, but they barely have enough food for their own family."

"I know. What are you doing here?" He pointed at Will.

"Rook and I came to visit."

He nodded in my direction. William jumped.

"I thought you were with Elsie."

"I was kidnapped."

"Rescued," Will said.

"Again? Rook, you should take better care of yourself."

"William, can I come with you next time you go to the palace?" I asked.

"I won't be going anytime soon."

"Elsie said you sell crops there every week. I can disguise myself. I need to get back."

"You can't, Rook," Will said. "We're running from soldiers."

"I could hide in the hay again."

"No."

"William has no reason to go back," Gerta said. Her voice shook. William put his hand on her shoulder.

"I just need you to get me in! I'll be fine! You'll be going to sell crops anyway! Why is this a problem?"

"We need to check for soldiers," Will said.

He picked me up.

"Put me down! You have no right!"

I struggled, but he carried me to the barn and set me on the back of the wagon. Thomas waved at me. He and a group of orphans were putting blankets on bunk beds that lined the barn wall.

"No soldiers in sight," I said, staring at Will.

"You were upsetting Gerta."

"It is a simple request! I won't be any trouble. I just need a ride to the castle."

"Will you listen? That black patch of land we walked through was Gerta's farm. William isn't going back because there's nothing left to sell."

"Maybe he should water his crops instead of flirting!"

Will brushed his hair aside and stared at me with dark eyes.

"This is not a joke, Rook!"

"Don't yell at me! None of this is my fault!"

The children looked at us. Will waved his hand, and they left the barn. Thomas came back.

"Something for the lady," he said.

He handed me a cup of water. I drank it in a single gulp.

"Thank you."

"Hey, is this guy bothering you?"

He gestured to Will.

"Get out of here, Thomas," Will said.

"Because if he is-"

Thomas rolled up his sleeves and flexed his skinny arms.

"I'm fine, Thomas. Thank you for the water."

"Hey, there's more where that came from. I've got a whole well of the stuff."

He winked at me and left.

"So all these beds are used by orphans?"

I gestured to the beds that filled the barn. Will nodded.

"With this much help, why did the farm dry up?"

"Royal servants coated the fields with salt. So Princess Salara could go sledding."

13

I gaped at him.

"The picnic happened on that field?"

"And the salt soaked into the ground. Estrella is coming later, but even if she can heal the land this year's crops are ruined."

"But, but-"

Will shook his head.

"They mowed the crops to make a flat surface for sleighing. Even if we can remove the salt, there's nothing left."

I stared at the dusty barn floor. It wasn't my fault. Not really.

"Salt powers charms, right?" I said. "Can't they sell the salt?"

"Only fairy salt from the mountains works for charms. Regular salt that has been trampled by horses is useless."

"Oh, right."

I had read about different types of salt, but had assumed the author was exaggerating. All the salt in the palace powered charms.

Will held out his arms, offering to take me back to the house. I shook my head, and he left me alone.

Salt.

The snow was made of salt.

I twisted my apron in my hands.

How did a farm work, exactly? They grew food, and now they had none. I glanced around at the beds in the barn.

There were a lot.

If I could get back to the palace, I could send them plenty of whatever they needed.

I just needed a way to get back.

Something fell out of my apron pocket. I watched it flutter to the ground.

A rook feather.

So much for Estrella's enchantment. It couldn't even keep a feather in the pocket. I jumped off the cart and groaned as my feet hit the floor. A blister burst, covering my foot in sticky liquid. My ankle ached. Gerta's potion had done some good, but I was far from being able to walk anywhere. Walking to the palace was not an option.

I brushed the dust off the feather and twirled it around, watching the dark prism of colors it reflected. Maybe I could arrange a trade.

I inhaled and blew on it.

Dust swirled around it. The feather melted into the air and floated around me in inky droplets. More and more droplets circled around me until the barn faded to black. When the darkness cleared, I stood in Delilah's wig shop.

"Welcome back, Sara," Delilah said. She did not look up from the blond wig she was styling. The wagon's doors and windows were closed, and her wrinkles looked deeper than ever in the flickering candlelight.

"I'm called Rook now."

"Ah, yes, the girl who almost passed the rook test. I can give you five gold coins for your wig."

"Is that enough for passage to the palace?"

She stopped working. The hair she held quivered as

her hand trembled.

"I should think you'd want to avoid Castlemont."

"I'll trade you the wig for passage to the palace. You could give me another feather to send me there."

"I'm not a courier service, dear. But let's figure out what's really going on, hmm? Someone's in trouble, and you'd like to help. Admirable, but whatever valuables you had at the palace are long gone."

"I'll give you these, then. I'm sure they're valuable. They were in the opera."

I pulled the bracelets out of my apron.

"I specialize in hair accessories, dear. Those would be no use to me."

I returned the bracelets to their place in the apron and offered her the healing charm. She shook her head. I started to tie it around my neck, then shoved it into the apron pocket as well.

"I just want to go home."

Madame Delilah gestured to the chair with the smallest pile of fabric on it. I collapsed in it and propped my feet up on an overturned mannequin.

"Have a snack, dear, and let's talk business."

She handed me a plate of cheese and crackers and a cup of water. I ate while she talked.

"The wig is valuable, even used. I'll give you five for it. That will help your friends. But a little more, and you could set Gerta and the orphans up for the rest of the winter."

"How do you know about Gerta?"

"Her girls sell me their hair when things get rough. This hair is from one of hers. I'm making it for Lady Alma."

She held up a blond wig shaped like a Castanian star. Eight points jutted out from the head.

"I just need to get to the palace."

"She's a good woman, Gerta. Been taking care of orphans since she was one herself. And with you being a former member of the court, you must feel some responsibility for her plight."

The party had been Sir Gilbert's idea, and of course he wouldn't have planned it if he had known the consequences. But he was gone now.

"The wig is all I have. You used a charm to transport me here. Can't you just send me to the palace?"

"No, I can't. And you have much more than this wig, dear."

"I don't even have shoes!"

I gestured to my bare feet. Delilah snapped her fingers, and my wig appeared in her hand. My own dark hair tumbled down around my shoulders.

Oh.

"Normally there's not much demand for dark hair, but I had a request yesterday. I need more hair to fill the order."

"Dye some."

"I've tried that. Bit of a disaster. Getting the hair to look natural is harder than you would think. Five for the wig and seven for your hair. That's more than fair. Enough to help Gerta and pay someone to take you back to Castlemont if you're crazy enough to try."

"Out of the question."

"Nine for your hair then. The short hair will be a nice disguise for you."

"Would you trade my hair for transport to the palace?"

"I already told you, no. But I can give you a little something extra."

She waved her hands in the air, and a small bottle appeared.

"A healing potion for your feet. Takes away the pain and repairs the skin instantly. It will even do the bone in your ankle some good."

The crystal vial flickered in the candlelight. The throbbing in my feet grew worse.

"And one more bit of magic jewelry since you seem fond of that sort of thing. This one is rare. The last I have."

She pulled a blue charm shaped like a tear drop out of her apron. It hung on a silver chain.

"This makes your hair grow faster. It will be past your waist again in no time."

"How long is no time?"

"Ten seconds once the charm is activated. I hate to give away my last one, but this wig is for one of my best clients."

My ankle ached. Moisture from the popped blister oozed through my bandages.

"Fine. I'll do it."

Delilah's face disappeared into a pile of wrinkles as she smiled. She handed me the bottle. I uncorked it and rubbed the contents on my feet. The pain stopped the moment I applied it, and the throbbing in my ankle lessened. I unwound the bandages and poured more on. My skin showed no trace of the blisters.

"Have a seat."

Madame Delilah pulled a wooden stool to the center of the room. I sat, and she brushed my hair. I stared ahead, trying not to imagine what Mother and Lady Alma would say if they knew. They never had to. My hair would grow back before I saw them again.

The scissors reflected candlelight onto the walls. The first snip made me jump. Delilah laid a lock of hair on a table. It seemed alive. A part of me removed.

The pile grew. I grabbed the sides of the stool to keep from falling over. My head spun, my scalp tingled.

It was so odd to see my hair detached from my head.

It rippled like the Ghone on a starry night, absorbing the light around it. Purple, green, and blue rays filled the tiny wagon.

My head grew lighter and lighter. I felt dizzy.

Delilah circled around me. The scissors flashed in my eyes. Finally she put them down and handed me the hair growth charm and a pouch of coins. She gathered my hair off the table and put it in a box.

"Be careful standing up. You're literally light headed."

She snapped her fingers, and the room blurred. I heard her laughing as everything went dark. The last thing I saw was the scissors, sharp and silver and lit with flames.

I reappeared on the barn floor under the wagon. Thomas stood in front of me.

"Thank goodness you're back!" he said. "I saw you get swallowed up by ink and thought you'd been kidnapped."

I crawled out from under the wagon. His jaw dropped.

"That's, um, quite the makeover, angel," he said.

I winked at him and ran to the house. My feet did not hurt at all.

Will and William stared at me when I entered. They stood on either side of Gerta, holding her hands. Gerta blinked away tears and rubbed her eyes. Estrella stood in the corner of the room slicing bread. She crossed her arms, and the knife glinted. She had dark circles under her eyes, and bits of hair stuck out from her braid.

I handed Gerta the bag of coins. As she took it, I realized I hadn't kept any to pay for transportation to the palace. Too late now. Gerta weighed the bag in her hand and raised an eyebrow. William's eyes grew wide as she pulled gold coins out of the bag. They clinked together. Will remained stoic.

"Where did you get that?" Estrella asked. She pointed the knife at my chest.

"What?"

She snatched the charm out of my hand and examined it.

"It makes hair grow faster."

She laughed.

"What is so funny?"

"Who gave it to you?"

"Madame Delilah, as part of the trade for my hair. It will make my hair grow, won't it?"

"Yes, but not much faster. And it won't grow at all while you're wearing the charm. When you take it off, the growing will happen all at once. Your hair will be longer than it would have been otherwise, but not by much. You'd better put it on."

I groaned and combed through what was left of my hair. My arms flew through the few inches, used to combing feet of raven tresses. I fastened the chain around my neck and fought back tears.

"You're lucky Delilah didn't make this charm herself," Estrella said. "She's a decent wig maker, but a terrible magician. When it was decided that all Salara's companions should be blond, many courtiers hired her to dye their hair with magic. It never went well. My mom made these hair charms for a friend of mine after a Madame Delilah dye job went horribly wrong."

"So the hair could grow back?"

"So it wouldn't grow under his wig. The hair was permanently damaged."

I swallowed. Estrella examined my head.

"She did this with normal scissors. You'll be fine."

"And dark hair suits you better," Gerta said.

She brought me a piece of polished metal. Some sort of farm equipment, I think. I stared at myself in it and gagged.

Beauty had never looked worse. Hair stuck out all over my head in uneven clumps. It didn't even reflect colors onto the wall anymore. There must not be enough left! Tears rolled down my face. I couldn't go home looking like this. I pulled off the charm and counted to ten.

Nothing happened.

"Perhaps it is out of magic?" I said.

Estrella shook her head.

"This charm draws energy from the person wearing it. My mother's trick. I'd recognize it anywhere."

Gerta retrieved a pair of scissors from her desk.

"Let me even it out for you. I have lots of experience from cutting William's hair. He is very particular."

"I can't help it if I need to look my best," William said. He combed his hair with his fingers. Will and Estrella rolled their eyes.

"She cuts mine too," Thomas said. He ran his fingers through his hair, imitating William.

I laughed through my tears. Gerta cut bits and pieces of what was left of my hair. When she showed me my reflection again, I looked much better. She had coaxed the front piece of hair into lying across my forehead like a bird's wing. You noticed my face more with all the hair gone. My eyes looked larger than ever and twice as luminous. And my skin seemed pearlier with dark hair to contrast.

I glanced around the room and noticed a faint purple spot on the wall. It moved when I turned my head. So my hair did still reflect colors. At least they were faint. No one noticed.

"Would you like me to look at your feet?" Estrella asked. "I don't have much magic left, but I can ease the pain."

I shook my head.

"Were you trying to heal the field?"

"Yes, and the village well went salty. The water purification spell backfires sometimes. I fixed the well, but the field won't grow anything for ten years at least. I didn't know it was possible for the ground to hold so much salt."

"Let me finish lunch, dear," Gerta said. Her eyes sparkled as she handed each of us a slice of bread and a Salara egg.

"Are there any eggs left in the palace?" I asked Will.

He smiled at me and shrugged.

"Thomas, can you and Samuel take this to Castlemont and buy supplies?" Gerta said. "You're my best traders."

"It's because I'm so charming," Thomas said. "But I was really hoping to stay here and help."

He watched for my reaction as he said it.

"You can take the horse," Gerta said. "You'll need him to help you carry everything back."

"Alright!"

Thomas ran out the door, then turned to me.

"Don't go anywhere, angel," he said. "I'll be back soon with supplies."

"And smelling like a fish," William said. "The market stinks. Estrella still smells fishy when she sweats."

"You're fishy," Estrella muttered with her mouth full of Salara egg. She swallowed and turned to Will.

"The soldiers set up camp in the village. They'll be there at least another day."

"They'll be searching the surrounding areas then."

She nodded. Will turned to me.

"I hope your feet really are feeling better, Rook. We need to take another walk."

14

I spent the rest of the day helping William and Estrella around the farm. Will stayed in the house with Gerta.

The wind chilled my bare neck and rustled my hair like grass. When no one was looking, I took off the hair growth charm and counted to ten.

Nothing happened.

I would have a few choice words for Madame Delilah when I found her. Better yet, I would send Lady Alma and the poets after her. They would be ready to fight when they saw me with short hair. The thought of Sir Quill and Sir Inkling chasing Madame Delilah around cheered me up.

The moment the sun began to set, Will packed food and supplies into his bag. A fistful of stars twinkled above us as we walked into the early evening light. My feet did not hurt at all. At least one of Delilah's charms worked.

"Where are we going?" I asked.

"The soldiers will search the surrounding area for us first thing in the morning. We need to hide before then."

"How do you know that?"

"They've done it before. Our royal troops are nothing if not predictable."

We did not cross the salt field. Instead, we walked

towards the mountains, following paths between rows of crops.

"Was losing one field really that bad?" I asked. "Gerta has plenty of crops here."

"These aren't Gerta's. We're crossing through Roslynn's farm now."

"Ah, the elusive Roslynn."

Will raised an eyebrow.

"Elusive?"

"William has been looking for her since we arrived. She seems very mysterious."

He laughed.

"She's a farmer's daughter. The most exciting thing she does is come to town to help Elsie and Edsel at their shop. And she won't even be doing that now that they have you."

"Oh."

It was silly to feel disappointed, but I did.

The fields stopped at the edge of cliff. Far below us, sluggish water carved a deep, muddy scar through the land. It smelled like rotten fish. Across the river, trees grew in clumps. In the dark, they looked like groups of courtiers gathering to gossip. The moon was up now, and the dirty water reflected slivers of light.

"Welcome to the Ghone," Will said.

I took another look. There was no way this could be the Ghone. The poets had compared my hair to Salaria's mightiest river a thousand times, and the curving water I saw shining from my tower could not be this muddy.

"We'll find a safe place to cross," Will said, mistaking my silence for nerves.

"We have to cross?"

"Our hiding place is on the other side."

We walked along the bank. Had any of the court poets ever seen the Ghone? Actually seen it? Or did they secretly think my hair was disgusting? Soon there were trees on our side of the river. They stretched across the water on both sides, blocking the moonlight. I stumbled over roots and rocks, but Will continued as if it were daylight.

A twig snapped in the forest. Will and I stopped. I heard voices.

"Soldiers?" I whispered.

"Impossible."

The voices grew nearer.

"When we find her-" a man's voice said.

I stiffened. Will looked up into the trees.

"Can we climb them?" I whispered. "They won't look for us in the trees."

"We are not climbing the trees."

He pulled out a knife, sliced through something, and handed it to me. I grabbed it. Some sort of rope?

"We'll swing across," he said, just as the men appeared.

Will jumped, and the vine carried him across the river. He hopped off, landing on the other side. The men yelled and ran towards me. There were three of them. I recognized the crests on their armor: Salaria's royal guard.

I lost my footing and fell forward. My hands tightened around the vine as I swung over the water. Will reached his hands out to catch me, but I didn't have enough momentum to make it all the way across. I came within feet of the bank before swinging back towards the soldiers.

This was good, right? Soldiers could take me back to the palace. Soldiers would obey their Princess. I twisted on the vine to see them and gulped. They had pulled out their swords and pointed them towards me.

I swung over the bank, nearer and nearer to the gleaming guards and blades. They looked ready to slice first and ask questions later. I aimed for the nearest head and kicked.

Years of ballet training served me well. My foot connected with the soldier's helmet, and I swung back across the river. The force of the blow made me spin. I saw Will at the river bank, holding a stick over the edge. I reached for it, but spun away before I could grab it. The soldiers grew closer and closer as I whirled out of control, dangling from the vine by one hand. Desperate, I swung my body around and tried to get my other hand around the vine.

I lost my grip and tumbled into the river.

From the bank, the Ghone looked lazy. From my new vantage point, it seemed ferocious. The current pulled me towards the sea with a force too strong to fight. My head bobbed under as waves pushed me and my skirt soaked up water like a sponge. The soldiers stood on the bank, too heavy in their armor to dive after me.

Will had disappeared.

My boots filled with water. Every kick took a tremendous amount of effort. I looked for something to grab, but saw only streaks of moonlight against the inky surface. I inhaled water and spit it out.

Salt.

Behind me, something large splashed. Light danced in the ripples. What sort of fish lived in the Ghone? I kicked harder, not wanting to find out.

Something touched me. I inhaled to scream and gagged on salt water.

"Relax," Will said.

He swam closer. I could make out the outline of his head bobbing in the waves. His arm wrapped around me.

"Stay still, or we'll both drown."

I coughed and tried to obey. His bare foot brushed against my leg as he kicked for both of us. I focused on breathing, trying to regain my calm.

We hit solid ground, and Will pulled me onto the bank. We lay on our backs gasping for air. I coughed up salt water.

"Thanks," I said.

I felt him nod.

"They'll try to follow us," he said. "Can you walk?"

I pushed myself up to a sitting position, shaking.

Above us, the bank turned into a sheer cliff. The ledge we sat on was barely wide enough for two. We were trapped.

"I can't climb that," I said, gesturing to the smooth rock above us.

"Can you crawl?"

"There's nowhere to go."

I shivered as a breeze blew past me. I turned to Will, but he had disappeared.

"In here."

He stuck his head out of a hole in the cliff. I gathered my sopping skirts in one hand and crawled towards him. The hole was a tunnel. I followed the sound of Will's knees shuffling against the rocks. It was completely dark.

"To the right," Will said.

His voice echoed. I felt the wall and found an opening. I entered and collided with Will.

"Sorry."

"Close your eyes."

"What?"

"Just do it."

I closed them and heard a snap. The darkness behind my eyelids lessened. I opened my eyes and blinked. The cave walls glowed. Not much, but enough to show we were in a small room with sloped walls. Will leaned against one side. I crawled over and took the other.

My skin itched from the salt water, and my clothes

clung to me. Hair plastered Will's face. He wiped it to the side. I did the same with mine.

"Where are we?"

"A mining tunnel. Not quite the hiding place I had in mind, but it will do the job."

"You know magic?"

"All miners learn the basics. Mines are the easiest place to work magic since you're surrounded by fairy salt."

I sat for a moment, just breathing.

"I kicked a guard in the face."

It seemed funny for some reason. I giggled. To my surprise, Will joined me.

"He'll never live that down," he said.

"Sir foot-to-face."

We smiled at each other.

"They shouldn't be out after dark," Will said. "They never search after dark. Too dangerous."

"Yeah, they might get kicked in the face by a girl swinging on vines."

He smirked.

"I'm serious. Did you steal anything when you left the palace? Besides the egg?"

"You're one to talk. You took way more than I did."

"I'm just wondering what they're looking for. It must be something big. Something important."

"Just the costume and the wig I was wearing. Oh, and these bracelets."

I showed him the thin silver bands. My face flushed as I thought about the opera.

We sat in silence. It was comfortable in the mine, warm and still and dry except for us.

"So you're a miner?"

Will opened his palms, showing me hands lined with white scars and calluses. I clenched my own smooth hands into fists and hid them in my wet skirt.

"I worked with my father. The salt scars can't be healed."

"So you wear gloves."

"In polite company."

We lapsed into silence again. I leaned my head against the wall and closed my eyes.

"How long are we staying here?" I asked.

"A day at least, but most of our food got lost in the river. We'll have to sneak out to get supplies if we stay too long."

"So I have time for a nap?"

He chuckled.

"I mean it."

I leaned forward and looked at him.

"You've saved me twice now. Thank you. I will repay you somehow."

"No need. Just don't go back to the palace and get yourself killed. You saw how those guards were ready to cut you down for no reason. You're not a noble anymore."

I ran my fingers through my short hair. It was dry already. The salt made it stiff, and it stuck up in spikes.

"I suppose not."

"Will you stay with Elsie and Edsel?"

"For a while."

"And after that?"

"I don't know."

Will nodded.

"You won't be able to join Elsie and Edsel until the guards leave. I can't go to town either. It makes sense for us to stay together."

"I suppose."

I watched him, waiting. Where was he going with this?

"I have things to do, Rook."

"Running out of Salara eggs?"

"Important things, and I think you can help. If I can trust you."

"Will, I'm no good at farm work. I know how to dance and paint and sing. I can speak all the courtly languages and spot a Lady Alma design from a mile away. I'm not sure I'll be much help."

"Oh, you'll be perfect. How are you feeling towards Princess Salara now that her guards tried to kill you?"

"She didn't order them to do that."

"Not that you know."

I knew.

"Let me try a different question. You committed one crime against the Princess. How would you feel about a few more?"

"I stole an egg."

"Would you do it again? Maybe take something larger?"

I narrowed my eyes.

"What are you trying to ask?"

"I'm trying to see how loyal you are to the Princess. Some people think everything she touches is sacred. Are you willing to cross some lines?"

I shrugged. He had no idea how many lines I had already crossed.

"This is important, Rook."

"I don't mind taking more of Salara's things if that is what you are asking. What's next? Her oatmeal? Her hair ribbons?"

"Rook, please."

"I said I don't mind."

Especially if we had to go to the palace to get those things. Not right away though. I was still hoping the hair growth charm would do some good.

"So you want to help?"

"Sure, Will. I'll help you overthrow Salara through

petty theft."

I smiled. Will did not. He reached out his hand, and I shook it. The calluses etched across his skin pressed into my palm.

"There's one more thing you should know."

He leaned his head back, a bit too casual.

"My name is Shadow."

15

Shadow?

The Shadow?

I stared at him in the blueish cave light, searching for a sign of the notorious bandit of song and legend. I saw nothing new. Just a pale boy about my age with dark hair and scars on his hands. His eyes looked black in the strange lighting, and they were focused on me.

I swallowed.

"That doesn't change things, does it, Rook?"

Of course it changed things. It changed everything. But I shook my head.

"So we both have false names."

The Shadow laughed.

"Will is my false name. I use it around strangers, and they usually remember William since our names are so similar."

"So your parents named you Shadow?"

An emotion too brief to register flickered across his face.

"Yes." He said it slowly. Deliberately. "My parents called me Shadow."

"They sing songs about you in the palace. You're infamous."

"I know."

Questions swirled around my head, but wouldn't form into words.

"Get some rest, Rook," he said. "We're stuck here for a while."

He leaned back and closed his eyes. His breathing became soft and even. I stared at him, wide awake.

The Shadow.

I was trapped underground with the Shadow.

As the shock wore off, I felt sleepy. The strange events of the past few days had taken their toll. I glanced at the sleeping bandit. Would he cut my throat in my sleep? I leaned against the wall and closed my eyes. Focus. I had to find a way out of this.

Just.

Focus.

I woke up with a stiff neck and numb legs. Shadow sat against the opposite wall, watching me. It seemed darker than before. His eyes shone like metal.

"The fairy salt in this cave is almost drained," he said. "We need to move, or we'll be trapped in the dark."

"I might be able to swim if I take my boots off."

Shadow shook his head.

"I'm not really up for another swim."

I followed him into the tunnels. The cold light illuminated the path around us. We crawled away from the Ghone. I think. I had no sense of direction underground. After a few minutes of crawling, I realized how hungry I was. My clothes were stiff, and my skirt dragged along the tunnel edge. The tunnel expanded as we went until there was enough room for us to walk side by side.

"So you know your way around down here?" I asked.

"All salt mines lead to the mountains."

"We're going to walk all the way to the Weeping

Mountains underground?"

"We could crawl instead."

He handed me an apple from his pack and took one for himself. I brushed bits of salt off the skin, but it still tasted odd.

"The last from Gerta's cellar," he said. "But she can afford more thanks to you. That was a good thing you did, Rook."

At least Salaria's most notorious bandit approved of my actions.

"How long have we been down here?"

"If we're lucky, we'll find a way out by sunset."

"And then what?"

"If the guards are gone, I'll take you back to Elsie and Edsel's. Otherwise, we stay hidden."

A noise echoed through the tunnel in front of us. Shadow and I froze.

"They wouldn't search for us in here," he whispered.

"Maybe it's a miner?"

"These tunnels are abandoned. If there's not enough salt left to power the lights, there's definitely not enough left to mine."

"An animal?"

We listened. The footsteps stopped.

"They heard us," Shadow said.

"We could hide in one of the side tunnels."

"You can hear breathing here if you listen close enough. We'd better face it head on. Stay behind me."

Shadow pulled a dagger from his pack and walked ahead. He kept his arm out as if to prevent me from dashing ahead to face the threat by myself. Nothing could have been further from my mind. What sort of creatures lived in abandoned salt mines? And was the bandit of legend also a fighter? In the stories, he relied on stealth alone.

A light glowed in the distance. It had a warmer tint than the salt mine walls. Shadow relaxed.

"Identify yourself!"

"Oh, thank goodness!" The voice echoed through the tunnels.

Shadow put his knife away.

"Who is it?" I asked.

The warm light hurried towards us, and Estrella came into view. She wrapped her arms around Shadow.

"Some soldiers were bragging in town. They said they'd killed two bandits, a male and female, and dumped their bodies in the river! You weren't at the hideout, so I thought- I thought-"

She looked up at him, tears sparkling in her eyes. Shadow smiled and put a hand on her shoulder.

"They tried, and we did end up in the Ghone. After Rook kicked one of them in the face."

Estrella pulled back from Shadow and glared at me.

"Typical amateur, trying to be the hero. Do you have any idea what you've done? They'll be looking for us now."

"Not if they're saying we're dead," I replied.

"Will," Estrella said, "can't you see this is bad? They'll be on high alert now. They're forcing peasants to house them, and one of the captains is staying in Elsie and Edsel's shop. They just managed to hide all the Salara drawings and supplies. You should have given them some warning."

"You can call me Shadow," Shadow said. "I told Rook."

"You did what?"

Estrella's face grew pale.

"Shadow, you just met her. And she's from the palace. You can't trust her."

"She's one of us now. And if she's on the run with us

it will be easier if she knows."

Estrella glared at me.

"She'll have a chance to earn her keep soon, then. I got word that Captain will be docking in a few days. And he's buying."

Shadow nodded.

"Do we have an event?"

"Tonight. Elsie and Edsel are on their way. The northern hideout."

Estrella led us down the tunnel. Shadow snapped his fingers, and the cool blue light faded from the walls. Estrella waved her hand, and the warm light above her head shattered into countless stars that followed us through the tunnel.

Estrella glared at Shadow occasionally and at me often. If Shadow noticed, he pretended not to. He stared at the walls, the stars, and the dark passage ahead, lost in his thoughts.

I had plenty of thoughts of my own to keep me busy. My skin itched, and I rubbed my arms trying to remove the salt residue. My dress crackled.

Estrella and Shadow stopped. I stepped on Estrella's foot, and she elbowed me. Shadow stepped back, pulling me with him, and Estrella waved her hands in the air. A blinding patch of light opened above her, and ladder rungs slid out from the wall. Estrella climbed the ladder without a backwards glance.

"I'll be back tonight," Shadow said.

He disappeared into the tunnel. I climbed the ladder and found myself in a valley. Flowers waved in the breeze, and birds sang. Water rippled somewhere nearby. The fresh air smelled wonderful. I turned around and saw the Weeping Mountains looming over me. They looked enormous this close. We had walked much further than I thought. Had I spent days in the tunnel?

"Will- um, Shadow said he'll meet us tonight."

Estrella rolled her eyes and snapped her fingers. A patch of grass slid over the hole, leaving no trace of entrance. She walked towards the mountains at a brisk pace, and I jogged to catch her.

"Where are we going?"

"The hideout."

"And Elsie and Edsel will meet us there?"

"Yes."

"Do they know Will is the Shadow?"

"Yes."

"What are we doing tonight?"

"Stop asking questions."

"But I-"

She did not slow down and refused to look at me.

"Shadow is a fool to trust you, but I know who you really are."

I swallowed.

"You do?"

"I was a companion to the Princess once. I am not fooled so easily."

"You were?"

I glanced around the meadow. A forest of pine trees surrounded the Weeping Mountains, but we were in the middle of a field of flowers. I had nowhere to run. Nowhere to hide.

"I know the games of court. I know the politics. You think if you come back with interesting stories, your precious Princess will make you her favorite. If you catch the dreaded Shadow, so much the better. You might even earn a title."

I tried to muffle my sigh of relief.

"I didn't know who I would meet. You think I planned this?"

"We don't need your help. I know the court. I know

the fashions. We haven't had any problems so far."

"How long has it been since you lived there? The fashions change every day."

"Then you're not up to date either."

It was true. I let that sink in. I had no idea what was happening in court. No idea what Lady Alma had designed for the day.

And I didn't care.

I smiled to myself as we walked. I didn't care! It didn't matter what Lady Alma had designed that day. I was wearing the same dress I had worn yesterday, and I would wear it again tomorrow. And no one would scold me for doing it.

We reached the edge of the valley and stopped in a cluster of trees. The beginnings of the forest that climbed the base of the mountains.

Estrella stood between two trees and stomped her foot three times. The grass rolled back, revealing a rough wooden staircase descending into the dirt. I hurried to follow her before the hole closed.

The underground room was well lit. Sunbeams filtered through the dirt above us. Tree roots draped with fabric, sketches, and ribbons formed the ceiling. Doors covered the packed dirt walls, and the wooden floor had been smoothed and polished. I spun around, taking in the circular room. Elsie and Edsel ran through the door nearest the staircase.

"You made it!" Elsie said.

She and Edsel froze when they saw me. Edsel stared at my hair. Elsie's face burst into a huge grin.

"Rook! So you know all about it then! I hated keeping this a secret from you! Pull your wig out. You'll need it tonight!"

"It is good to see you, Rook," Edsel said. "I wanted to chase after you when I realized you had been kidnapped, but the soldiers delayed us. The troop commander chose our shop to stay in."

"Nice to see you all again," Estrella said. "Is my outfit ready?"

Elsie pointed to a door, and Estrella stomped away.

"You look good with dark hair," Edsel said. "If it were longer, it would flow like the Ghone."

"Almost like the Princess!" Elsie said. "Except her face is rounder than yours."

"You think so?" I asked.

She and Edsel nodded.

"What is this place?"

"Our secret workshop," Elsie said. "We have much more space here."

"Elsie, those mountains are the Salarian border. It takes three days to reach them on horseback. If you have a good horse. How did you get here so fast?"

"You travel faster in the salt tunnels," Elsie said. "The salt affects your steps somehow."

"Fairy magic lingers in the salt," Edsel said. "The closer you are to the mountains, the stronger it gets."

"Estrella could tell you more about how it works," Elsie said.

I had no intention of asking her.

"So I didn't walk three days underground? I've never been this close to the mountains before."

They laughed.

"You walked a few hours if you came from Gerta's farm," Elsie said. "Was William there?"

I nodded.

"And Roslynn?"

I shook my head. Elsie smiled and grabbed my hand.

"I need to get you dressed! Your wig is enchanted, right? I didn't bring any wig supplies."

"I don't have it."

Elsie and Edsel stared at me, horrified.

"What do you mean?" Elsie whispered.

"I sold it to Madame Delilah."

"Oh, Rook!" Elsie said.

"We have money," Edsel said. "Whatever you needed, we could have gotten it for you. I have plenty of things I could have sold."

"But you have a growth charm!" Elsie said, gesturing to my necklace. "I've heard about those from Estrella. You've had that wig for a while, I'm sure. Just take off the charm, and I'll style your natural hair."

I took off the charm. My hair did not grow.

Edsel frowned. Elsie blinked away tears.

"Please, don't sell anything else," Edsel said. "If you need anything, just ask us. Rook-"

He grabbed my hand and squeezed it, looking like he might cry at any minute.

"Of course she'll ask," Elsie said. "When the guards are gone, she'll share everything we have!"

"Will they leave?" I asked. "I kicked one in the face, and Will, I mean Shadow, thought that might make them stay longer."

"You did what?" Edsel asked.

"They're leaving tomorrow," Elsie said. "We got that straight from their commander. You can move in with us for good after we finish this job."

Job? I smiled at them. Elsie and Edsel beamed back. If they were working with the Shadow, their job might be more complicated than it seemed. What exactly had I agreed to do?

"You're sure you don't want to be called Leslie?" Elsie said.

"I like Rook," Edsel said.

He bowed and left the room.

"Where did he go?" I asked.

"He hasn't finished Shadow's outfit yet. You know, it really is a shame. I designed your dress to go with blond hair."

"What are you talking about?"

"I made you a costume. Just in case Shadow decided to trust you."

"A costume for what?"

"The masquerade. Didn't he tell you?"

I shook my head.

"Typical. It's tonight, and you're helping. Your outfit is already finished."

"I need special clothes to steal things?"

"I'll have to cover your short hair. You don't want to stand out too much."

I followed Elsie through one of the doors. We entered a dressing room. A blue silk dress on a mannequin glittered in the sunlight. The wide hoop skirts filled half the room. The dress was trimmed with lace that I recognized.

I had worn it a few months ago.

Elsie noticed me staring.

"I tried to disguise it," she said. "Is it too obvious that I copied Lady Alma's design?"

"It is pretty obvious you copied her lace."

Elsie blushed.

"Most people won't recognize this as the exact same lace. They'll think I imitated it. We'll sell all this to the pirates, but I like to make things with it first."

"The same lace? So you stole this from the palace?"

Elsie nodded and watched me. I took a deep breath. If I was going to be a bandit, I couldn't let this shock me.

I walked around the dress. It really was lovely.

"You should trim this with some sapphires."

"That would be perfect! If only I had some!"

I stared at her, uncertain what to say. I knew they had

sapphires. They had stolen Lady Alma's shipment from the museum. But it seemed they weren't ready to trust me with everything just yet.

"I was counting on your blond hair," Elsie said. "Obviously I have to modify it now. If I cut off the train, I can make a hood out of it. Don't worry. It will be elegant. And since you have bangs, no one will know your hair is short."

"What exactly are we doing tonight?"

Elsie snapped her fingers, and the train ripped off the dress. She waved her hand to hem the raw edge. It was not as clean as Lady Alma's magic, but the result looked acceptable.

"We're close enough to the mines that I can use their power," she said. "Not the best, but at least I can get this done fast."

Elsie continued to wave her hands, shaping the fabric into a hood.

"There's a masquerade at the Salara Museum tonight. You, Shadow, and Estrella will sneak in disguised as guests. William usually makes deliveries to the kitchen and asks servants what people want to buy, but without any produce to sell that cover doesn't work. He's gone to Castlemont to arrange a meeting with the pirates."

"What do you and Edsel do?"

She pinned the fabric to the mannequin's shoulders and enchanted a needle to sew the hood.

"We'll be outside selling clothes and accessories to guests. Where else could we find so much nobility in one place?"

Equipped with magic, Elsie worked quickly. The hood looked as if it had been part of the dress from the beginning. While she put the finishing touches on, I washed my skin and hair in the underground bath next door. The water was crystal clear without a trace of salt.

After I dried, Elsie helped me into the gown.

Even with magic to help, it was difficult to slip myself into the bodice while wearing the enormous hoop skirt, and even harder to fit through the door into the main room. When we made it through, Elsie handed me a familiar, if crumpled, silver lace mask.

"You left this at our shop," she said.

I tied it around my head and examined my reflection in a pool of water. The hood gave me an air of mystery. It felt strange to be dressed up after being a peasant. The fabric was smooth against my skin.

Estrella entered the room, dressed in a red gown with a skirt even wider than mine. She wore a red mask that matched her dress. Bits of magic light sparkled like jewels in her blond hair, now piled above her head in a mass of curls. As the sunlight filtering through the ceiling faded, she created more lights. They danced and flickered around the room like fireflies.

Edsel entered the room and offered me his hand. I took it, and he twirled me around. My skirt bumped into Estrella, and she sniffed. Edsel danced well, although he used last month's waltz style. I smiled at him when we finished, and he kissed my hand.

"Your dress has pockets," Estrella said, rolling her eyes. "Enchanted baskets are built into the hoops. There's a slit under your flounces so you can access them."

She pulled up the flounces by her hips and pushed her hands into her skirt. I did the same. There were indeed baskets under there.

Clever.

Elsie pushed my peasant clothes into the pockets.

"So you can change when you're done," she said.

I reached into the skirt, rummaged through my apron, and pulled out the opera bracelets.

"Perfect!" Elsie said. "Jewelry will definitely help you

blend in! Put one on each arm. Princess Salara wore a bracelet on each arm in the opera."

Well, I could certainly imitate Princess Salara's look. At least the stage magic charm had worn off. I slid the bracelets on my wrists, and Elsie clasped her hands in approval.

"You won't actually steal anything tonight," Estrella said. "You'll stay with Shadow and pocket the things he takes. And you'll distract anyone who gets too interested in him."

"How do I distract people?"

"Tell them stories," Shadow said.

I had not noticed him come in. There were no corners in the round room, but somehow he had found the darkest spot. He wore a black suit, cape, and mask. His hair swept over his face.

"Are you trying to stand out as a thief?" I asked.

"There are lots of shadows to hide in, even at parties. You were at the opera, and it should still be a topic of conversation. Get people talking about it, and they'll forget they ever saw me."

"I thought you wanted me to blend in?"

"It is all about the timing," Estrella said. "Shadow, she has no idea what she's doing. It would be better to leave her here."

"Don't you dare!" Elsie said. "I put a lot of work into that hood!"

"No one will take her seriously in that. Who ever heard of a hood on a formal gown?"

"Rook will be fine," Shadow said. "Just follow our lead."

I nodded.

16

Shadow opened the door nearest him and stepped into a salt tunnel. Estrella snapped her fingers, and our skirts folded in on themselves so we fit in the narrow space. Elsie and Edsel grabbed full baskets covered with cloth, and we walked into the darkness.

The stars in Estrella's hair lit our way. The path sloped uphill. It would have been easier in my peasant clothes. The wide skirt and baskets weighed me down. We walked until we reached a dead end. Shadow motioned for us to stop. Elsie and Edsel exited first, climbing a ladder. Estrella followed them a few moments later.

"Will I really be okay?" I asked Shadow. "I have no idea what I'm doing."

"Just act like you're back at court."

He helped me onto the ladder, and I climbed out. The tunnel opened behind a patch of bushes on a hill overlooking the museum. Stars shone above me, but they were no match for the spectacle below. The Salara Museum sparkled with thousands of candles and magical charms of all shapes and sizes. A steady stream of nobles in colorful hooded capes and masks entered.

This was foolishness! So a few peasants didn't recognize me. That didn't mean I could fool nobility!

Especially now that my hair was dark again.

Below, Estrella entered the museum. She walked through the line with her head held high. No one questioned her.

Shadow snapped the tunnel shut and offered me his arm. I took it, and we walked down the hill. He wore dark gray leather gloves. No one said anything as we approached, although a few people stared at me. I told myself it was the hood. It really was an odd fashion choice. We climbed the stairs and entered the museum. I turned to Shadow, searching his face for reassurance. His eyes remained confident behind his mask. How many times had he done this?

I shivered, looked around, and gasped. The noblewomen had not been wearing capes. They had hoods on their gowns! Elsie's design showed my face, but the nobles wore hoods that draped nearly to their chins. Estrella's starlit blond hair looked out of place in the sea of colorful fabrics. She glared at me and snapped her fingers. The stars in her hair disappeared.

Nostalgia swept over me as I turned my attention from the guests to the exhibits. Nostalgia and a bit of nausea. Mannequins painted to look like me and wearing my latest gowns stood in scenes around the edge of the room. "Dinner with the Castanian Duke" Salara was having tea with "Last Week's Garden Party" Salara. Two mannequins wearing my breakfast gowns played cards. At the far end of the room, mannequins in my five most recent birthday gowns played croquet on a fake lawn.

People in masks and hoods wandered around the room, talking in whispers and studying the gowns. Music echoed from somewhere further in.

Shadow pulled me forward. I shook myself out of the daze and followed him.

It was like traveling to the past. I walked by outfits I

remembered and outfits I didn't. In the room dedicated to my hair, sketches and dark wigs on mannequin heads recalled the ghosts of styles past. Was this where the hair I sold Delilah would end up? As an immortalized butterfly chignon?

"Wait in there," Shadow whispered. He nodded towards a door and disappeared into the crowd.

I entered the room and looked around.

Poetry.

Books and pages covered tables throughout the room. Quotes from famous Salara poems were painted on the wall. Bold script on the ceiling stated, "Words prevail where images fail."

"The Princess is notoriously difficult to paint," a young man next to me said. He wore the inkwell hat of a poet, but I didn't recognize him from court. I ducked my head and made my voice as raspy as I could.

"How do you capture perfection?" I asked.

"How indeed? The Queen is the only one who does it well at all in the visual arts. That is why I stick to poetry. Do you write?"

"No."

"This is my poem here, in this book."

He flipped open a large book titled "Salara around the World: Poems Praising the Princess Salara in Styles of Every Nation." He pointed at a page headed "Castanian Styles" and read aloud:

Roses are red, but she on the throne
is lovelier than the star-lit Ghone.

"A Rosas Rojas," I said, tracing the illustration on the page.

"You're a poetry fan! No one around here understands the reference. I actually had to explain to the illustrator what a Rosas Rojas is. It is the perfect symbol for Salara, but everyone here is obsessed with salt. So overdone. I think they included this one in the anthology because it compares her to the Ghone. My early work was better, but you have to know your audience, am I right?"

I nodded and edged towards the door. Shadow would be able to find me in the next room. The poet followed me.

"I'm published under the name Plume. It would be Sir Plume, but Sir Quill chose that idiot Inkling to be his apprentice instead of me. We were in the same class, you know, me and Inkling. He stayed in Salaria to schmooze, and I studied a year in Castana to better my art. I should have known better than to leave him alone at court. Who knows what he told them about me? I came back months ago and still haven't had an audience with Princess Salara! I can't even get a place in the breakfast tour! If I could just see her in person, I would write a poem that would force them to notice me! Of course, she isn't seeing anyone right now."

"No one?"

I stopped moving towards the door.

"She hasn't done a poetry or portrait sitting since the opera. I heard she's resting. Probably devastated that Divinia didn't show. She ate breakfast with her parents yesterday morning, and she had a hood on her breakfast gown! Lady Alma is quite the genius."

"She appeared in public wearing a hood?"

"I know! Edgier than Lady Alma's usual designs, but it really caught on. Well, I don't have to tell you that. You're clearly in the know. Who designed your dress?"

"Um, Elsie. Of Elsie and Edsel's Cobbler Shop in Salt Spring."

"Never heard of her. She must be pretty exclusive."

"This is the only one she made."

He nodded.

"What else have they said about the Princess? Was the opera a success?"

"Oh, everyone loved it! I heard the masquerade was cut short though. Again, everyone was expecting Divinia. I'm lodging in the same house as Sir Bristle's brush cleaner, and he told me they haven't made a new painting in days! Even the Queen isn't painting."

"And Sir Gilbert is gone?"

"Yes, back to the colonies. I stayed in the colonies for a while on my way back from Castana. The art scene is terrible. No one appreciates poetry. I read a cycle of Salara poems at a pub there. Way over their heads. You'll appreciate it though!"

He struck a pose and recited:

Roses are red, violets are purple
with your lovely figure you don't need a girdle.

Roses are red, peonies are pink-

"Please excuse us," Shadow said.

When had he come back? I slipped my hand over his arm.

"Hey, the lady and I are having a conversation!" Plume said.

Shadow did not answer. Plume stared into his dark eyes, and his face paled a little. We left, and he didn't protest.

"Any problems?" Shadow asked.

"Just a poet reciting his work for me."

"Was he any good?"

We both laughed.

Shadow handed me a book of portraits. I slipped it into my pocket. We walked through the museum until we reached the back. Shadow tapped three times on a wall, and a panel slid open. I squeezed my skirts through just before Estrella slammed it shut. I looked around. Piles of mannequin body parts filled the room.

"Back here," Estrella said.

I tried not to look at the stacks of arms, legs, and heads as we followed Estrella. She led us to a room filled with bolts of fabric.

"Extras for repairs," Shadow said.

Estrella put a bolt of bright pink brocade on a table and unwound it. She cut off a piece and folded it.

"Put this in your skirt," she said.

I pulled up my hip flounce and slipped the silk into my hoop skirt pocket. Shadow and Estrella continued to hand me fabric until my skirts were so heavy I struggled to stand.

"They're full," I said as I stuffed a piece of green velvet into my skirt. "Time to load Estrella up."

Estrella tossed her head. Her golden hair gleamed even in the dim light.

"I had my pockets full before you made it to the poetry hall. I'll leave first."

Music drifted through the secret door as she slipped out. Shadow and I waited by a pile of legs.

My legs. They were perfect replicas of my legs.

"Have you ever seen the Princess?" I asked. "In person?"

"Once."

"Do you think she's worth all this?"

He shrugged and opened the door in the wall. My skirts were so full of stolen fabric, I barely fit through.

Instead of walking through the poetry room, we turned left and entered a room full of portraits. I examined them with interest. Only my mother's paintings were displayed in the palace. These had unfamiliar artist signatures in the corners.

Each painting was beautiful in a slightly different way. The basics of my face were there: pale skin, dark hair and eyes, and delicate features. But one had bigger eyes. Another's lips were thinner than they should have been. Some faces were heart shaped, others were oval, one looked quite round. I stroked Seda in one of the pictures. While the artist had painted my hair lighter than it actually was, he had captured my kitten perfectly.

Shadow considered the portraits. They might have been cousins or siblings, but they did not look like the person my mother painted or the face I saw in the mirror. I started to ask his opinion of them, but the expression in his eyes stopped me.

We continued through the gallery. Music, laughter, and light filtered through a door to my left. I stopped and saw a ballroom filled with dancing couples.

And tables of food.

Shadow pulled on my arm.

"We need to go."

"I haven't eaten since the tunnel, and that apple hardly counts as a proper meal. Just let me grab something."

"We don't have time."

I ignored him and entered the ballroom. Shadow didn't follow. Candles and magic gleamed on mirrors and polished gold on the walls. I ignored the dancers and stuffed a savory pastry in my mouth. I grabbed a napkin and poured a plate of tarts onto it.

"Hungry?"

I turned, my mouth still filled with half a pastry. Plume stood beside me, smiling.

"You disappeared before I could ask you to dance," he said. "I've been looking everywhere. Where did you go?"

"The museum is vast," I shrugged and swallowed the remaining bit of pastry.

"The food will be here all night," he said. "Come dance with me."

"I really need to go."

His hand clamped around my arm. I resisted, but my heavy skirts hindered my movements. Plume pulled me onto the dance floor just as the musicians began a waltz. The napkin full of tarts in my hand made the movements difficult. I fought the urge to stuff it in my skirt pockets and glanced around the room, searching for a way to escape.

"The chandeliers are made of her old tiaras," Plume said. "And the music is from her latest opera. They only play music from Salara productions here, of course."

As I danced with him, I glanced at the tiara chandeliers. Most I had worn only once. They caught the candlelight and sparkled with dazzling brilliance.

"Finally, someone who knows the new style of waltz," Plume said. "I danced with a girl earlier who was absolutely clueless."

I wasn't dancing particularly well with my skirts stuffed solid, but at least I knew the steps. Plume stumbled and gripped my shoulder to keep from falling.

"Someone from the palace must have taught you. Do you think they could help me get an audience with Princess Salara or Sir Quill?"

I shook my head. Where had Shadow gone? I stepped back and tripped. Plume held me steady. I glanced down. Our feet hovered just above the floor on an invisible platform.

Why were the bracelets working again? At least they weren't at full strength. We would have been to the ceiling by now if they were.

"Come on, don't be like that! Once I'm a court poet,

I'll have a lot of influence. You're sneaking food out of a party. Clearly you're not doing so well. I can help you once I've beat out Inkling and become Sir Quill's apprentice."

The waltz ended. I pulled away, but Plume tightened his grip as the next dance started. We were several inches off the floor now, but the crowd danced around us as if nothing were wrong. I had to get away without drawing anyone's attention.

"I'll rise to the top once I get an audience. Name your price."

"I really don't know anyone who can help you."

I was sweating now. Would the baskets under my skirts hold up to this much motion? How would I explain it if the fabric fell out? What if someone noticed we were floating?

I took the napkin of tarts and pushed it into Plume's chest. He gasped as filling oozed out. His grip loosened enough that I could shake myself free.

Plume fell to the floor as soon as my hand left his. It wasn't very far, but he slipped on the tarts and landed on his backside. I moved the bracelets to one arm, recovered my balance, and ran.

Couples swirled around me and bumped into my solid skirts. Plume elbowed his way through the crowd, trying to follow me. I swayed slightly, feeling dizzy.

"Care to dance?"

I looked up and took the hand Shadow offered me. We attracted much less attention as a couple and worked our way to the edge of the dance floor.

"I see you know the new style of waltz," I said.

"Oh, these steps are old by now I'm sure."

We danced through the crowd and reached the door without trouble. I looked at the food table one last time, but Plume stood at the corner guarding it. My stomach growled.

Shadow staggered a little as we left the museum. Elsie and Edsel stood outside talking to a silver haired noblewoman in a dark green gown without a hood. Edsel nodded as we passed, and Elsie pointed me out to the woman. She watched me with a critical eye. I curtsied and hurried away. Plume came out of the museum just as we ducked behind the trees at the top of the hill. I watched him greet the noblewoman and speak to Elsie and Edsel. Shadow stared into the darkness.

"What took you so long?" Estrella demanded.

She had already changed into her peasant clothes.

"Shadow and I stopped to dance."

"You went into the ballroom? With all those chandeliers? Shadow, are you alright?"

"I'm fine."

He slumped against a bush and rubbed the sides of his head. Estrella watched him with concern.

"It was nothing," I said. "We just had a bit of trouble with poets."

Estrella turned to me, eyes narrowed and arms crossed.

"Then you'd better let me handle the pirates."

17

As Princess, I had been on numerous ships. Mostly for dinner parties, never for travel beyond the harbor. I had danced on vessels of gleaming wood with the decks covered in furniture and food. I had inspected naval vessels before breaking a bottle of champagne over their bows to name them. The Navy ships all looked the same. The nobles' ships were lavishly decorated to suit their owners' tastes. They had all been majestic.

The wreck of a ship currently beneath my feet seemed ready to sink at any moment. The whole vessel creaked and groaned as if protesting the rapid pace as we sailed along the coast. I jumped each time I stepped on a loose board.

And each time I passed a pirate. The ragged crew scurried around the deck and climbed the rigging. They looked to be in as much disrepair as their ship.

The moon and stars reflected in the ripples of the sea, the only sources of light. Shadow and Estrella stood beside me, unconcerned. We had stopped in the salt tunnels to change and pack the stolen goods into baskets before traveling to the coast to meet the pirates. Elsie and Edsel were still at the party when we left.

A thick black substance oozed from the deck. I

dodged a pirate with a scarred face and stepped in it. I grabbed Shadow's arm to keep from falling as I pulled my foot loose.

"Tar holds the boards together," Shadow said.

"Aye, nothing more waterproof than tar!" the scarred pirate said. He smiled at me, revealing a mouth full of black, crooked teeth.

"Don't get it on your clothes," Estrella said. "It will never come out. Not even with magic."

I stepped away from the pirate and into another patch of tar. Now both my shoes were stained.

"Elsie and Edsel won't be happy about this," I muttered.

"Yer shoes will be stronger than ever!"

A burly man with a graying beard stepped out of the cabin. He held a flickering lantern that emphasized the deep lines etching his face. The pirate greeted Shadow with a smack on the shoulder.

"Shadow, welcome! One outlaw to another, hey?" he roared.

Shadow winced and rubbed his forehead.

"Hello, Captain," Estrella said.

He examined Estrella and smiled.

"You look better than last time I saw you, Strella."

"So do you. No more fever?"

He laughed. The sound boomed throughout the ship and shook the boards. Shadow rubbed both his temples.

"Best healer this side of Castana!" Captain bellowed to no one in particular. Approving murmurs floated down from the rigging.

"We hear you're buying." Estrella said, ignoring his outburst.

Captain's eyes glinted.

"That depends on what yer selling."

"The usual."

"Strella, you've never been robbing the palace again?"

"Of course not, Captain. Do you have the gold on board?"

Captain led us into his cabin and set the lantern on a table. The flame flickered. Estrella shoved a pile of papers off a desk and spread a piece of fabric over it.

"Four baskets. All Lady Alma's original designs. Magic weaving. Guaranteed to have been worn by the Princess in the past year."

The pirate whistled.

"You've outdone yerselves. I suppose ye have the usual sketches?"

Estrella handed him a packet.

"Everything a tailor needs to recreate the looks from the fabrics. And there's more. A pair of ballet slippers made by Lady Alma herself and a ballet costume worn in the latest opera."

She handed a package to the pirate. A piece of red silk stuck out of the wrapping.

"Those are mine!" I protested.

Captain raised an eyebrow at me.

"Who be ye?"

"No one important," Estrella said. "She escaped from the palace wearing these, but has no further use for them."

She directed the last few words at me through gritted teeth.

"You've come from the palace?" Captain asked.

I nodded.

"I'll bet you have some stories. Is it true, the immortal kitten? I think they just replace it with a new one every year."

Estrella put her hands on her hips.

"I've already told you about Seda, Captain."

"And she eats roses for breakfast? The Princess, I

mean?"

"What?"

"I peek into the palace when we sail by. Spyglass makes it easy. You can see her at breakfast when the crowds switch. Roses on the table every time."

Pirates watched me eat breakfast?

"The roses aren't for eating."

"Why else do you put something on a table?"

I stared at him. He stared at me.

"We can swap stories later," Estrella said. "Do you want the goods?"

"We aren't exactly dress wearing folk around here."

The ship rumbled with laughter from the unseen crew.

"Don't try to be clever, Captain. You'll have them to Castana by the time the new Salara portraits arrive and name your price."

"And you'll name yours, no doubt," Captain said. "What if everyone already has those colors?"

"Please, you know Lady Alma. No one else in the world will have these colors."

Captain stared at the fabric on his bed.

"Five," he said.

"Seventy-five," Estrella said.

"Ten."

"Seventy-five."

"Strella, you know how hard it is to transport fabric? On a ship made of tar? With the Dragon on the prowl?"

"If you want to raid the palace, be my guest."

Captain's forehead wrinkled.

"Sixty-five."

"Seventy."

"Deal."

Captain put out his hand to shake Estrella's. A shrill whistle sounded from the crow's nest. Shadow covered his ears and sank into a chair. Estrella put her hand on his shoulder and glared at Captain.

"Royal Navy, Captain! Approaching fast!" a pirate called.

"By Salara! You three, stay here!"

Captain ran onto the deck. Estrella pried open a trap door in the floor and stuffed her baskets into it. I did the same with the fabric I carried. Shadow stayed in the chair.

Captain burst through the door and tossed a sack to Estrella. It jingled as she caught it.

"Sixty-five as promised."

"We agreed on seventy!"

"Joe has business on shore. You can ride with him. Where's the goods?"

I pointed to the trap door.

"Off you go then."

"Captain, we said seventy!"

"There's no time, Estrella," Shadow said.

"And he knows it! Is there even a Navy ship out there?"

"Yes," I said.

I stood on the deck, watching the pirates scurry. The Navy ship glowed in the darkness thanks to lantern shaped charms on its ropes. It looked small it was so far out to sea, but it grew larger each second.

"Come on," Shadow said.

"I look forward to our next conversation," Captain said to me as we boarded a life boat. "I'm still curious about them roses."

We climbed a rope ladder and boarded a rowboat. It rocked each time someone stepped into it. I gripped the sides, not eager for another swim in salt water. Joe rowed us towards the shore. Captain's ship eased towards the horizon, sails full of wind.

"Will they be alright?" I asked.

Joe nodded. "We avoid the Navy as a general rule, but

Captain knows what he's doing."

He stopped rowing and examined me.

"Joe," Estrella said, "Do you want to fight a Navy vessel from this rowboat?"

He shrugged and continued rowing.

"I didn't catch your name," he said.

"I'm Rook."

"Are all girls in the palace as pretty as you, Rook?"

"I beg your pardon?"

He chuckled.

"Have you ever considered going to sea? I'd be happy to have you on board any time."

"Joe!" Estrella said. "Less flirting, more rowing!"

"Nothing personal, Strella. Just because you turned me down doesn't mean every girl will."

"This has nothing to do with that! We are trying to avoid certain death at the hands of the Salarian Navy!"

"Oh, there's nothing to worry about. I could take them down with one hand tied behind my back. Pirates make good money, Rook. You can have roses for breakfast every morning if you want."

He winked at me.

"No thank you," I said. What was the proper way to turn down a pirate? It seemed like a good idea to be polite.

"Be quiet," Shadow said. "We're near land. There might be soldiers on the coast."

Joe grinned.

"I hope there are! I can take down a whole troop of soldiers with-"

"Hush!" Estrella hissed.

By the time we reached the shoreline, both ships were dots on the horizon. Joe jumped ashore, nearly capsizing us, and helped me out of the boat.

"Until we meet again, Rook. Unless you'd like to come

with me?"

I shook my head.

"Thanks for the ride."

We hiked through a field until we found a road.

"This bag feels light," Estrella said. "I'll bet there's only sixty coins here, at the most. That lousy pirate cheated us twice!"

"Please be quiet," Shadow said.

She bit her lip.

"I could try a spell," she whispered.

"It doesn't help."

Shadow quickened his steps and walked ahead of us. I tried to keep up, but Estrella pulled me back.

"So how did you meet the Captain?" I asked.

"Just Captain," Estrella said. "His name is Captain."

She stared ahead, watching Shadow.

"No really. How does one meet a pirate?"

"He worked with my father."

"Your father was a pirate?"

She scowled at me. Shadow turned a corner in the road and disappeared from view behind a group of trees. When we reached the corner, he was gone. I glanced around but couldn't find him.

"What's wrong with Shadow?" I asked.

"Nothing is wrong with him!"

Tears glistened in her eyes. She wiped them away.

"Nothing is wrong."

We walked the rest of the way in silence. The mountains were far away now. Captain and Joe had brought us nearly back to Castlemont. The sun rose. I didn't realize where we were going until we stopped at Elsie and Edsel's shop.

"Is it safe?" I asked.

"Do you see any soldiers?"

The streets were clear except for peasants bustling to

get ready for the morning. My palace shone in the distance like a gem in the morning sun.

Edsel and William rose to greet us when we entered the cobbler shop. The Salara sketches and shoes were gone, and the shop looked strangely empty without them.

"I have the coins," Estrella said. "Not as many as I should have. That blasted pirate cheated me."

"Where's Shadow?" William asked.

"Recovering. He had to rescue our newest bandit from an amorous poet in the tiara ballroom."

"It wasn't like that!" I said. "It only delayed us a few minutes!"

Estrella looked furious, but William chuckled.

"You should have seen the poet he rescued her from the night we met."

He stumbled towards me in his best imitation of a drunken poet.

"Roses are red, I'm a poet. So you should dance with me."

He grabbed my hand and spun me around. I giggled.

"This is serious, William," Estrella said.

"You shouldn't mock royal artists," Edsel said.

"I'm always serious about poetry, but we have bigger problems. The salt patch in Gerta's farm spread to Roslynn's. Half their fields are gone."

"But that is several miles!"

"And the town well has gone salty again."

"At least I know how to fix that. Come help me."

They left. I turned to Edsel.

"Where's Elsie?"

"Um, not here."

"Obviously. She would have noticed my ruined shoes right away."

"You ruined your shoes?"

His eyes darted down to my feet, then back to my

face.

"I'll make you another pair," he said. "Something to better suit you. I'll have enough money soon to make you something really grand."

"You must have sold a lot of things at the masquerade."

"We did, but that's not what I mean."

He stared at me with the intensity of a poet. I tried to ignore his gaze.

"Um, when will Elsie be back?"

"Rook, was there really someone in the palace with dishonorable intentions towards you?"

"What?"

"I've been wondering why you left the palace. Poets are sometimes overwhelmed by beauty, and you're beautiful. So maybe, if there was someone there being, um, rude to you, that's why you had to run away?"

His eyes did not leave my face. The poets weren't the only ones overwhelmed. I had seen looks like this before.

"Edsel, are you alright?"

"I was just- I'm trying to understand why you left. Then I'll know if you want to go back."

His eyes were wide, almost panicked.

"I've thought about going back. I've thought about it a lot."

At least, I had at first.

"If you had someone to protect you. If you felt safe. Would that make a difference?"

Sir Gilbert's face flashed through my mind. I shook it aside. He was halfway to the colonies by now.

"Maybe."

"You're not meant to be a bandit, Rook. I'm going to the palace today, and I want you to come with me."

"What?"

His face turned red.

"Oh, I know I'm making a mess of this. I love you, Sara."

"What?"

"I can't call you Rook anymore. It is just a reminder that I failed you. That you had to sell your hair because I wasn't there for you."

"Edsel, that's ridiculous."

I ran my fingers through my short hair.

"I'm asking you to marry me, Sara. You're the most beautiful woman I've ever seen. I can't imagine spending my life with anyone else. Elsie and I were offered a place in the palace. She's already there, but I had to see you again. I had to ask."

"I don't understand."

"It was because of you, really. A noblewoman at the party liked the hood on your dress so much that she hired us to design for her. You're good luck for us."

"What about the shop? What about the bandits?"

"Sara, marry me. Let me take you away from all this. Back to the palace where you belong."

I twisted my skirt in my hands, torn between laughing and throwing up. My face must have looked very strange.

"It is a good position, Sara. We'll have standing in society. You could be another lady's companion once your hair grows out. Or stay home and help us sew if you want."

"No, Edsel."

"You deserve better than this!"

He grabbed my hands and shook them.

"Please tell Elsie goodbye for me."

He blinked and released my hands. Then he took a few steps back.

"You don't know what you're involved in, Sara. These bandits are dangerous. Shadow served prison time for crimes against Princess Salara as a child. Estrella was dismissed from the palace in disgrace. They're not good people, and they'll take you down with them. I can bring you back where you belong."

I shook my head. Edsel's mouth tightened.

"I see. I wish you luck then. We're renting this shop to Madame Delilah, and I can't have bandits disturbing her. Tell Shadow you're no longer welcome here."

He crossed his arms.

"Edsel-"

"You should leave, Rook. I won't hesitate to turn any of you in if you interfere with us. Our loyalty is to Princess Salara, and it always has been."

I stared at him, trying to process this. Elsie and Edsel had been my first friends outside the palace. I was supposed to move in with them. And now Edsel was turning me out, and Elsie hadn't even bothered to say goodbye. I blinked back tears, feeling betrayed.

The door flew open. Edsel and I squinted in the bright light. William came in, carrying Estrella.

"She fainted trying to fix the well. Do you have any healing potions?"

"No," Edsel said.

William raised an eyebrow and looked at me.

"We should go, William," I said, putting my hand on his shoulder. "We're no longer welcome here."

"Don't be ridiculous! She's hurt!"

He stepped towards Edsel, ready for a fight. Estrella stirred slightly, and Edsel crossed his arms.

"If you do not leave, I will call the town guard." He turned to me. "Unless you've changed your mind."

"You're threatening me?"

I stared at him. He stared back, determined.

"Estrella just fainted trying to fix your well! You think they would arrest us?"

"If they knew the truth about you, yes."

"And what if they knew the truth about you?"

William and Edsel glared at each other. I pulled William towards the door. He flinched.

"Let's go, William."

"Oh, one more thing, William," Edsel said. "Elsie asked me to tell you that the flirtation between you two will not continue."

William snorted.

"To show you she is serious, she returns the hair ribbons you bought for her last fall."

Edsel pulled two tattered green ribbons from his pocket.

"Burn them," William said.

We left the shop.

18

"What happened?" I asked.

"Well, Madame Delilah was in town, and Elsie was admiring those ribbons-"

"Not that! What happened to Estrella?"

"Oh. Castanian style magic goes wrong sometimes."

"Lady Alma uses Castanian magic. She never faints."

"Neither has Estrella while she was making clothes. But the well had gone really salty, and that takes a lot of energy to fix."

"So she fixed it?"

He nodded.

"We'll go to Gerta's farm," he said. "Shadow will look for us there once he realizes we're not at Edsel's. That little traitor."

"He asked me to marry him."

"I'm surprised it took him this long."

He looked at me out of the corner of his eye.

"You weren't interested?"

I laughed.

"Just making sure. Love can be strange. Sometimes it takes you by surprise. In fact, there is something I've been meaning to say."

"Don't you dare, William!"

He winked at me.

"Well, I am apparently free now. Elsie's gone, and Roslynn is avoiding me like the plague. If you want to-"

"I knew you liked Roslynn!"

"What? Who told you that? Some people will say anything."

He propped Estrella against his shoulder and walked faster. I jogged to keep up with him.

"I hope those good for nothing cobblers are miserable as servants in the palace. If Estrella doesn't recover, I'm holding them personally responsible."

He clenched his fists.

"Does this happen to her often?"

"No, not often."

William shifted Estrella to his other shoulder.

"Ready for your turn to carry her?"

I stared at him. He winked, and I laughed.

"But seriously, she isn't light. Do you mind carrying the gold?"

"Of course not."

I regretted agreeing as I stuffed the bag of pirate gold into my apron. Gold was heavy.

We entered the forest. The salty stream rippled beside us. At least I had socks this time.

I stopped suddenly, staring. William stood beside me and stared as well.

It was as if autumn had come for half the forest. I stood in the summer side covered in green, leafy trees. But across a line, brittle leaves covered the ground. Bare branches stretched to the sky like skeletal hands.

I knelt and examined the ground.

"Salt," I told William.

He nodded.

I ran my finger across the blackened ground. A single green blade of grass on the edge turned brown and crumbled to dust. I gasped.

"It's spreading."

"Obviously."

"No, I mean it is moving right now. Watch."

William leaned over the best he could without disturbing Estrella.

"I don't see anything."

I traced the line between life and death in the ground. William shifted Estrella in his arms. I adjusted my apron, making the coins jingle.

"William, I saw it move."

"We need to go."

Estrella remained unconscious as we walked through the dead forest and blackened fields. Larger plants looked charred. Grass and flowers had disintegrated to dust that swirled in the wind like gray snow.

"Gerta may have to send the orphans to the docks to look for work," William said. "If this keeps up there won't be any food left to buy."

"Were you one of her orphans?"

William laughed.

"Hardly. My parents have a farm by the Weeping Mountains. Out in the middle of nowhere, but there's a mining station nearby that buys lots of food."

"Are they alright without you?"

"I have six older brothers. I'm not sure they know I'm gone."

"Why did you leave?"

"I wanted an adventure. Shadow showed up one night clearly in the middle of one. I packed a bag and followed him."

We reached the valley where the sleigh ride had been. I thought of myself in a carriage with Sir Gilbert and felt sick. It had been magical, but at what cost? Would this land ever grow food again? I turned to William, desperate for a distraction.

"How did you meet Estrella?"

"Oh, she knew Shadow from before."

"Before what?"

He shrugged.

From the top of the hill overlooking Gerta's farm, the ground was black as far as I could see. Thomas stood on a ladder, repairing the roof. He waved and called to us. I caught the word "angel." Gerta looked up from mending a shirt and smiled when we entered the house, but her face fell when William laid Estrella on her bed.

"William, not again! I don't have anything strong enough for this."

"Can you send someone to buy a crystal?"

William nodded to me, and I pulled the sack of gold out of my bag and put it on the table. A few orphans crowded around to examine it.

"Of course, but there isn't time. She needs something now."

I stared at Estrella. Her normally tan skin was pale. Except for a faint movement in her stomach when she breathed, she looked like a statue.

"What does she need?" I asked.

"A healing charm," Gerta said. "Something powerful. Her energy has been drained."

"I have this."

I pulled out the flat silver disk Lady Alma had given me. Gerta took it and placed it over Estrella's heart.

Nothing happened. Gerta shook her head.

"Not enough."

I reached out to retrieve the charm. As my fingers brushed the silver, a wave of dizziness swept over me. Something cold stabbed my heart. My vision faded, and I saw two children playing in a moonlit garden. The girl was tan with long blond hair. The boy's pale skin glowed in the moonlight, and his hair blended into the darkness.

I opened my eyes and pulled my hand back. Estrella opened her eyes and gasped. Our eyes locked for a moment. She took a few deep breaths, and I leaned against the wall until my head stopped spinning.

"What just happened?" William said.

"Rook saved me."

"You could have done that before I carried her across the country."

Estrella glared at William.

And at me.

"You said you couldn't do magic."

"I can't! I've studied techniques, but I've never been able to do a spell!"

Gerta picked up the charm and handed it to me. I slipped it into my apron.

"Questions later," she said. "You need to rest. Everyone, let's go to the barn and give Estrella some quiet."

She picked up the bag of gold coins on her way out. Estrella sank back into the pillows and closed her eyes. The orphans glanced at her with interest but followed Gerta.

"We need to get some of this money to Roslynn's farm," Gerta said. "They can help people without raising suspicion since their farm is larger. Thomas can deliver it."

"I'd rather stay here," Thomas called down from the roof.

"I'd better take it," William said. "The bag is heavy. I don't want Thomas to pull a muscle."

"I'm plenty strong enough!" Thomas said. He poked his head through the door and grinned at me. "I just want to make sure they have enough muscle around here. Some jobs take a man, you know?"

Gerta winked at me and handed the bag to William. He measured half the coins into his pack and handed her the rest.

"I carried that bag the whole way here," I said. "He didn't worry about me pulling a muscle."

"I had some weighty matters to attend to. Don't tell Estrella I said that. She'd kill me."

He left the barn. Gerta motioned to Thomas.

"Will doesn't know his friends are here," she said. "Can you tell him? Come back by nightfall if you can't find him."

"Tell him not to go back to Elsie and Edsel's," I added. "We're no longer welcome."

"Then they're crazy," Thomas said. "You know you're always welcome here. Can't you send Samuel, Gerta?"

"Samuel has other chores," Gerta said. "You can take the owl eyes charm. Will is probably in the tunnels."

"Really? I get to use the owl eyes?"

Thomas ran to the door then turned.

"You'd better not leave until I get back."

He winked at me and left. The rest of the orphans trailed after him. Gerta and I went back to the house.

Estrella sat at the desk writing a note. When she saw us come in, she folded it and snapped her fingers. A sealing charm glowed on the paper. Only the intended recipient would be able to open it.

"Estrella!" Gerta said. "You shouldn't be using magic right now."

"No, I shouldn't."

She glared at me.

"I don't know what I did."

"Well I do, and it doesn't happen by accident. Have you studied Castanian magic?"

"Of course not. Something just happened when I touched the healing charm."

Estrella raised an eyebrow.

I pulled the charm out and showed it to her.

"It looks like a typical healing charm," Gerta said.

"Something is wrong," Estrella said. "Who made this?"

"Is it defective? It was all we had. I brought it with me from the palace."

"Only a master of the Castanian style can make this sort of charm."

"Rook saved your life, Estrella," Gerta said.

"I know."

She handed the charm back to me.

"Don't use that again. Castanian magic can be very unpredictable. My mother once used it to heal my cat, and-"

She shook her head with a sad smile.

"I sent Thomas out to find Will," Gerta said. "And William took some coins to Roslynn's farm. All their crops have been ruined."

"How's your well?" Estrella asked.

"A bit salty, but don't you dare try to fix it!"

"I fainted before I could repair the village well. It will be salty again in no time, and this is the nearest place people can go. I want to at least look at it. I'll bring Rook."

"Estrella, you were unconscious for hours!"

"And now I'm fine. Rook can revive me again if I faint."

"You said the charm was dangerous," I said.

"I was joking. I'll be fine."

She didn't look like she was joking. Gerta shrugged.

"Don't let her do anything too reckless."

I ran out the door and followed Estrella to a well behind the barn. The ground crackled under our feet.

"The village well is more complicated than this one

because of the fountain," she said. "All the gold in the world won't do any good if they have no drinking water."

"How are you going to fix it?"

"I'm hoping you can help me. Apparently you have a natural knack for soul magic."

"For what?"

I tried not to look worried. Estrella tried not to look disgusted.

We both failed.

"Not every country is full of residual fairy magic waiting to be harvested and put into charms. Certainly not Castana. We use our life energy, our souls, to power spells."

"You're Salarian," I said. I couldn't think of anything else.

"My mother is Castanian."

Gerta's well was a hole in the ground surrounded by a rock wall. Estrella dipped her finger in the water, sucked it, and made a face. She rested her palms on the surface and inhaled. Her palms glowed white, and the rippling surface became still. The light pulsed, then turned red and disappeared. Estrella gasped.

"I'll definitely need help. Have you ever worked magic at all? Any kind?"

"No."

"Lovely. Got any fairy salt in your bag?"

"No."

"I was afraid of that. Listen carefully. When you're using soul magic, never push your life force into the spell directly. Do that, and you'll die."

"I don't know what you think I'm going to do, but I'm not going to do it."

"I need you to act as a secondary power source. I'll make a loop in your soul. All you have to do is stay still so it doesn't break."

I crossed my arms and glared at her.

She sighed and snapped her fingers. A handful of water rose from the well and formed a ring.

"You have energy in your body keeping you alive, but if you use that energy in your charms you'll be weakened and die. Instead, you focus it and move it like a water wheel. That movement powers your spell, and you get to keep your soul."

She picked a withered blade of grass and stuck it in the loop of water. The grass rippled in the current and became green again.

"The water powered the spell. But all the water is still in the loop."

She pulled the green blade out and handed it to me.

"So, my soul is made of water? Or is it the grass?"

Estrella threw her hands in the air. The circle of water fell back into the well.

"This is the basis of the Castanian style. You use your soul, the energy keeping you alive, to create magic indirectly. It is complex, but I'll be doing all the work. All you need to know is that I'll be moving your soul in a loop. If you interfere and push your energy directly into the spell, you'll die. Understand?"

"I don't like how often you keep saying I could die."

No wonder Lady Alma had refused to teach me Castanian magic.

"I've had years of training. I know how to control the loops and ration the magic. You'll be fine."

"But you fainted last time."

"I made a mistake. I tried to create a charm I didn't have enough energy to sustain. With both of us helping, that won't be a problem."

"You are not going to mess around with my soul!"

"I just need to move it around a bit!"

"You're insane!"

"Do you want people to die? Because that's what will happen if we can't fix this well. You think I want to pry around inside you? Normally I wouldn't even try. But we're already linked."

"We're already what?"

"When you healed me, you should have seen a flash of memory."

"I saw two children in a garden at night."

"That was me and Shadow. A memory from my childhood. You established a link between our souls. I'm just going to reopen it. This is a normal procedure in Castanian magic."

"I really don't want to do this."

"Rook, this is important."

She held out her hand.

I took it.

Her palm tingled with magic. The cold stabbed my heart again, and my insides churned. An internal whirlpool swirled from my head to my toes.

"You're just backup power," Estrella said. "Stay still."

The late afternoon sun faded into darkness. I saw a young girl being carried by a man in a naval uniform. Their hair gleamed the same golden hue. They smiled at each other, and a woman, unmistakably Castanian with her dark hair and tan skin, kissed the man and smoothed the girl's dress.

I snapped back to the present. The water in the well shot up like a geyser. Estrella and I jumped back. Most of the water fell back down into the well.

"What was that?" I asked.

Estrella's eyes were wide. She gasped for breath.

"Power surge. Apparently you have a very strong soul."

A green beam of light shot up from the well. Estrella traced lines on the water's surface, leaving glowing symbols.

"It is working," Estrella said. "Give me your hand again. I'll be more careful this time."

I thrust my hand into hers without giving myself a chance to think about it.

The green light faded. Estrella and a young man kissed under a tree in her garden. He had unnatural bright red hair. It flickered like flames and reflected red light onto her face. He pulled away from her, knelt, and held up a ring. Estrella clapped a hand over her mouth.

I came back. My cheeks burned as red as the man's hair.

"Almost done," Estrella said.

She snapped her fingers. The light became purple.

And then black. As black as the dresses Estrella and her mother wore. They each tossed a rose into the sea and walked away. Estrella wore the ring the man with red hair had given her. Her mother spoke, but I couldn't hear the words. Estrella shook her head. Her mother put a hand on her shoulder, but Estrella pushed it off, shouted, and ran away. Rage distorted both their faces.

I gasped and stared at the well. White light streamed from the water. Estrella snapped her fingers, and the light disappeared. I glanced at her hand, but she wore no ring now. My insides stopped churning.

"Don't touch it," she said as I reached for a drink. "It needs to sit undisturbed for a while."

"So do I."

She chuckled.

"We were at some of the same parties in the palace."

"How do you know that?"

She shrugged.

"Wait, did you see my memories? What did you see?"

Panic edged into my voice. How much had she seen? Enough to learn my true identity?

"Wow, you have that many embarrassing moments?"

"What did you see?"

"A few parties at the palace. I didn't notice much but Princess Salara. Always the center of attention. Even in someone else's memories."

My shoulders sagged with relief.

"I don't remember you from the palace," Estrella said.

"To be fair, I don't remember you either."

I really didn't. How long had she been my companion?

We both laughed. Estrella with amusement. Me with relief. We walked back to the house with the setting sun behind us.

"Do you want to know what I saw?" I asked.

"No, I don't. But thank you for helping. I couldn't have done that alone."

I opened the door. Gerta's sobs filled the air.

"Gerta, what happened?"

Estrella put her arms around Gerta's shoulders. Gerta shook her head.

"The Dragon stole another shipment of fairy salt. The warehouses are empty now, and the King reinstated the salt tax. Anyone who can't pay will be sent to the mines for a year."

Estrella pounded her fist on the table.

"Who told you that?" I asked.

"One of my girls just sent word from the city. And they've raised it! Two gold coins per person. I have twenty orphans living here. There's no way. I still need to buy food for the winter!"

She raised her head and met my eyes.

"How do I decide who has to go to the mines? And if I go, who will feed them?"

"No one is going anywhere," Estrella said.

"She's right," Shadow said.

We all jumped. As usual, I had not noticed him come

in.

"I thought the King was for us," Gerta said. "When he canceled the salt tax before, I thought-"

"Estrella, is Captain still in port?" Shadow asked.

"He usually stays about a week to buy supplies and things to sell. With the salt patches spreading, it might take him longer."

"We need to send him a message. If he can wait two days, we'll bring him our biggest haul yet. At least two hundred coins worth. Probably more. Tell him to have the gold ready."

"And we'll count it first even if we have to go through a naval blockade," Estrella muttered.

She pulled a quill and parchment from her apron pocket.

"You should sell him the gems from the museum," I said.

Shadow looked at me, confused.

"You were at the museum. We only stole fabric and a few books."

"The gems are heavily guarded," Estrella said. "Impossible to get to."

"I know I'm not supposed to know about them, but you can trust me. You stole a shipment of sapphires a few days ago. Surely the profits from that can pay for the salt tax."

Shadow stared at me and shook his head.

"I have no idea what you're talking about, Rook."

"But they went missing!" I said. "Everyone knows the Shadow stole them!"

"Hush," Estrella said.

She motioned to Gerta. I felt my eyes go wide. Had I given away the secret?

Gerta winked at me.

"I know all about it," she said. "But the children don't.

You'd better be more careful."

"She's not the only one," Estrella grumbled. "You didn't take long enough to recover, Will."

She put a lot of emphasis on the name.

"Are you feeling better?" I asked.

Shadow looked at me, but didn't answer.

"I mean, you seemed-"

"I just had some things to take care of elsewhere."

I searched his face. He seemed fine. Maybe I had just been on edge last night after my first heist.

And now for other reasons. He didn't know yet, I realized. I took a deep breath.

"Edsel and Elsie are gone. Some noblewoman offered them a position in Castlemont. Edsel said we're not welcome at the shop anymore, and they'll turn us in if they see us."

"He said what?" Estrella asked. She slammed her quill down on the paper and smudged the ink.

"Oh, I forgot you were unconscious then."

"You were unconscious?" Shadow asked. "Estrella, what happened while I was gone?"

"Rook and I fixed a well, Elsie and Edsel apparently turned traitor, and William went to Roslynn's farm."

"Well, at least one of those things isn't a surprise," Shadow said.

"And the salt poisoning spread to the forest," I said. "The trees are dying."

Estrella looked surprised, but kept her mouth shut.

"Maybe we can figure out what's going on when we're in the palace," Shadow said.

"When we're where?" I asked.

He grinned at me.

"A lot of people won't be able to afford the salt tax. We need gold coins and fast. As soon as William gets back, we're raiding the palace."

Estrella pulled a new piece of parchment from her apron, scribbled a few more lines, and sealed it. She handed the two letters to Gerta.

"Have one of your orphans take these to Joe at the docks. He'll know how to reach Captain."

19

Thomas returned just before dark. He frowned when he saw Shadow sitting at the table.

"When did you get back? I gave up a day with Rook to look for you."

He set a black charm ring on the table. Gerta wrapped it in a cloth and put it on a shelf.

"At least it wasn't a total loss. I heard all the latest gossip from the miners."

"Why would miners know gossip?" I asked.

"Thomas, you're not supposed to talk to anyone when you're in the tunnels," Gerta scolded.

"Oh, I know how to blend in. No one even knew I was there. They're mostly upset about the salt tax. Apparently anyone currently working in the mines won't have the option to pay it even if they have the money. They'll all be down there another year."

"The King must be desperate," Estrella said.

"Money troubles?" Gerta said from across the room.

"That opera can't have been cheap," Shadow said. "And since Divinia didn't show up, they didn't get to make any wishes."

"Not to mention the Dragon has made travel unsafe," Estrella said. "He's basically a one man blockade. It has been difficult to renew treaties because ambassadors can't get through."

"This doesn't sound like the King," I said.

Father never made quick decisions. It was one reason he spent so much time in council meetings. I wasn't sure what the salt tax was, but it seemed significant. He would not be hasty about it.

"Everyone shows their true colors eventually," Shadow said. "All nobles are the same."

"He's under pressure from Castana," Estrella said. "The Dragon hasn't attacked their ships, so they don't understand why the Salarian ships can't get through."

"The Dragon hasn't attacked any Castanian ships?" I asked.

Estrella shrugged.

"He must have a lot of fairy salt by now," Gerta said.

"And Salara portraits." Estrella smoothed her hair back from her face. "Several diplomatic ships have gone missing. Captain was worried the value of his stock would drop, but so far none of the Dragon's stolen goods have been sold."

"We have a problem!"

William burst through the door.

"Only one?" Shadow said.

I laughed, and Estrella glared at me.

"Was Roslynn at the farm?" I asked.

William shook his head. "The salt has spread all the way to the village! Their well is useless. Three more farms have been destroyed."

Gerta pulled Thomas aside.

"Go tell them we have fresh water," she said. "Anyone is welcome."

"Really? You're sending me away again?"

"You're my best rider. I'm sure Rook would love to see how fast you can get to the village and back."

"I am impressive," Thomas said.

He kissed my hand.

"Until we meet again, angel."

"So you were expecting this?" William said. "I ran all the way here to tell you. Roslynn's well is salty, but drinkable for now."

"If villagers are coming here, then we need to go," Estrella said.

Shadow nodded.

"I told Captain to meet us in the usual spot," Estrella said. "As long as Joe delivers our message, we're set."

William smiled.

"This is more like it. But we just had a raid."

"We're going to the palace," I said.

"They're having another gala already?"

Shadow shook his head.

"They've reinstated the salt tax. Two coins per person."

William clenched his fists.

"That's insane! Half the country will be in the mines! They won't have enough owl eyes for everyone!"

"What are owl eyes?" I asked.

Shadow stood.

"You keep the coins, Gerta. Get them to anyone who needs help."

"Thanks, Will."

Shadow, William, Estrella, and I walked through the moonlit night. The salt poisoned ground was blacker than the sky. When we entered the woods, our feet crushed dried leaves that had fallen from the dying trees. Moonlight illuminated our walk until we reached the line where the salt poisoning stopped. Then we walked in darkness as leaves rustled overhead and blocked the stars.

The path led to the Ghone. We walked downstream towards the sea. I expected to spend the night in a hole underground, but Shadow led us to a small cabin. He knocked. No one answered, and we went inside.

"This is used by boatmen traveling up and down the river," Estrella said.

I searched the bare cabin for beds but saw only a rough wooden table and chairs. I sat down and leaned against the table. Estrella snapped her fingers. A few stars flickered on the ceiling and disappeared. She sighed. Shadow pulled a candle from his pack and tapped it against the wall. A flame flickered as the wick ignited.

"We'll go tomorrow," Shadow said. "Tomorrow night."

"We've never performed a raid without an event as cover," Estrella said. "Where will we sneak in? What will we take?"

"Doesn't matter, as long as it belongs to Salara," William said.

I sat quiet, thinking. It was silly, robbing myself. But I knew exactly how to do it.

"I have a plan," I said.

They turned to me.

"Lady Alma has been stocking her studio thanks to your last few raids. It is full of fabric, jewels, and everything Salara. If we rob the studio directly, we can take as much as we can carry."

"That's ridiculous!" Estrella said. "She's sure to notice things are missing!"

I nodded.

"Lady Alma's studio is in the busiest part of the palace," Estrella said. "There's no way we can get loads of fabric out without people noticing. There are only four of us."

"So we're a skeleton crew," I said.

"What?"

"It's a nautical term. It means-"

"My father was a sailor. I know what it means."

She crossed her arms and glared at me.

"I know a secret passage," I said. "I know exactly how to get there. There will be plenty to choose from. There is at least a chest of rubies there. Possibly more gems. If we can find the opera costume, we'll have diamonds. She doesn't lock the drawers."

"Don't be absurd," Estrella said.

"Alright, Rook!" William said. He slapped me on the shoulder.

Shadow stared at me. I met his gaze.

"Are you sure the passage is a secret?" he asked.

"I used it to sneak onto the towers when I lived there. I never met anyone else in it."

"And how did you find it?" Estrella asked, arms crossed over her chest.

"It is behind a tapestry."

Mentioning Seda was just asking for trouble. He never left Salara's side.

What had Seda been doing while I was gone?

"This seems like our best bet, Shadow," William said.

Shadow nodded.

"Does anyone else have an idea?"

"We can go by sea and climb the walls," Estrella said. "We can raid the museum again and steal dresses off the mannequins. We can do anything else but this."

"Surely they'll have more guards at the museum after our last raid," I said. "There won't be any guards in Lady Alma's studio."

"We pretty much cleaned out the museum last time," Shadow said. "It would take too long to steal the displays. Someone would notice us before we got enough."

"Where can we enter the passage?" William asked.

"There are stairs that lead to the main garden. Once we get there, we're set."

"The main garden? We'll never manage to get across that undetected!"

"We'll have to take the prison route," Shadow said. "That gets us to the kitchens. We can easily get to the gardens from there."

Estrella's eyes softened.

"Shadow, we weren't going to take the prison route again. I know how difficult it is for you."

"You think everything is difficult," I said. "But I know this will work."

"I'm in," William said. "It doesn't sound any crazier than our last few raids."

"First we have to get into the city," Shadow said. "The gates are guarded. Can you get us in, Estrella?"

She laughed.

"I can get you anywhere."

"Except Lady Alma's studio," William said.

Estrella glared at him.

"I can get you anywhere worth going. We might get wet, but no one will see us."

"Are you sure?" I asked.

I had seen the sheer cliffs and jagged rocks circling Castlemont from the palace gardens. They did not look climbable.

Estrella shrugged.

"I can get us into the harbor, but there will be guards everywhere!"

"Then you'd better let me worry about the palace."

Her nostrils flared. I smiled at her. We were in my territory now.

We stayed up most of the night discussing details for our raid.

"What about clothes?" Estrella asked. "We'll stand out if we go dressed like this."

"We'll be in trouble if we're seen no matter what we're

wearing," William said.

Me especially. I had been lucky so far that no one had recognized me, but what if I ran into someone I knew in the palace? Even with my short hair and peasant clothes, they would surely know my face.

"With Elsie and Edsel gone, we can't get court clothes by tomorrow night," Shadow said. "If we find some in the palace we'll take them. Otherwise, just stay out of sight."

"The only time we'll be in a main room is when we're in Lady Alma's studio, and most courtiers aren't allowed there," I said.

The sun rose before we went to sleep. When I had first come from the palace, I thought that the mat on Elsie and Edsel's floor was barbaric. Now, with bits of splinters from the floor poking me, the memory of it seemed luxurious. Estrella shook me awake sometime around sunset. I plucked slivers of wood out of my dress until it was time to leave.

William pulled half a loaf of bread from his pack.

"Gerta insisted," he said. "Never risk your life on an empty stomach."

I chewed my portion as we followed the Ghone to the sea. The leaves were still green here, and the river bank rustled with grass. Stars reflected in the Ghone, and for once I understood why the poets compared it to my hair. Castlemont's lights shone through gaps in the trees.

"Point out the tower with the stairs once you recognize it," Shadow said. "I need to plan our route."

I nodded. Estrella rolled her eyes.

"How long has the salt tax been abolished?" I asked.

"King Nicholas removed it years ago, and he renovated the mines in the first year of his reign. Most of the people down there are working off debts or paying for small crimes."

"So you think the renovations were a good thing?"

"Yes. The King added charms to help with the digging so fewer workers could mine the same amount of salt."

"I thought you hated the royal family."

My family.

"Salara is detestable. In some ways, the Queen is worse. The King at least tries."

"Tries what?"

"To help people. To make things better."

That wasn't fair. As Princess, I had constantly worked to be better.

We reached a clearing. I had not realized how near we were to Castlemont. Torchlight flickered. I pointed to a tower.

"There. The second tallest one."

Shadow followed my gaze.

"It is near the prison," William said. "That works out well."

His face was grim. Estrella looked horrified. Shadow's face was unreadable.

"You're sure that's the one?" he asked.

I nodded.

Estrella put her hand on Shadow's shoulder.

"Let's raid the museum instead. We can break into someone's country estate. Anything else. You don't have to do this."

"If we wait, Captain will be gone."

Estrella tried to wrap her arms around Shadow, but he slid out of her embrace and quickened his step until he was ahead of us. I jogged to join him before Estrella could stop me.

We walked in silence. I could hear and smell the ocean now. I had missed the familiar rhythm of the waves.

"Will it be hard to break into the prison?"

"I know it better than any other part of the palace."

"Have you broken in before?"

"No, but I've broken out. We'll be fine."

He didn't look fine. I grabbed his hand. He flinched, but wrapped his fingers around mine after a moment. I realized what I had done and blushed, but he didn't let go.

"We'll make it out," I said.

His lips twitched into a small smile.

We stopped at the ocean shore. Estrella and William caught up with us.

"Pay attention, and you won't get too wet," Estrella said.

Shadow squeezed my hand and let go. Estrella walked along the coast and climbed under a dock. We followed her, climbing on boards slick with algae. Mist from the waves made everything damp, but the docks were high enough to keep us out of the water.

Estrella held a finger to her lips and grabbed a rope ladder hanging over the dock. As I climbed it, I realized it hung from a ship. We crossed the ship's deck. The sailor on guard duty raised his hand to challenge us.

"It's me," Estrella whispered.

"Oh, good to see you, Strella."

He sat and watched the moon while we crossed. Ships crowded together in rows, a few feet of seawater visible between each one. Estrella hopped from deck to deck, circling around the coast until we walked down a gangplank and entered the city. In the upper tiers, spacious gardens surrounded immaculate buildings. By the sea, buildings huddled in rows that stayed upright by leaning on each other like books on a shelf.

From the tower, the buildings in Lower Castlemont looked tiny. Up close, I was too busy wondering how they stayed together to think about how small they were. Newer patches, less faded than older ones, created a mottled effect.

"Welcome to the docks," Estrella said. "Home to sailors on both sides of the law."

Two men stumbled out of a building with a bottle painted over the door.

"Estrella! Long time no see!"

Estrella waved to them and smiled.

"I was never here, boys. Got that?"

"Hey, Joe, Estrella's not here!"

Joe stumbled out of the building. Bandages soaked with blood held his arm to his side. He grinned weakly at me.

"Nice to see you again, Rook."

"Joe, what have you done?" Estrella asked. "Did you get my message to Captain?"

Joe nodded.

"Thomas brought it to me. Captain sustained some damages after his run in with the Navy. He has to make some repairs before he can sail long distances."

He handed Estrella a note. She tucked it into her apron.

"What about your arm?" I asked.

"I was helping with repairs and got hit by part of the mast. I don't suppose you have time to heal it?"

He looked hopefully at Estrella.

"I'm sorry, Joe. All out of power."

Joe pulled a silver crystal out of his pocket. It swung on a chain, reflecting moonlight.

"You can keep it as payment when you finish."

Estrella stared at the crystal, then nodded and followed Joe to the leaning building.

"Estrella, we're kind of in the middle of something," William said.

Joe turned.

"I won't keep her long. I'd invite you in, Rook, but

this won't be pretty."

"Ignore them. They were never here," Estrella said. "And they definitely won't be meeting me back here when they finish their business in town."

She followed Joe.

"We'll be fine without her," Shadow said.

"Will we?" William asked. "Last time I checked, we were about to do something insane and needed all the help we could get."

"Rook knows the way."

"Can she carry the extra goods?" William said. "Gold is heavy."

"Rubies," I said. "We're stealing rubies. Diamonds if we can find them."

"Oh good. Those are much lighter."

20

We walked along the shoreline. The castle loomed overhead. The buildings got taller and straighter the further we went. Finally we reached the edge of the docks and stopped by a cliff. The castle's windows glowed hundreds of feet above us, but the prison tower's black stone absorbed the light.

"What now?" I whispered.

"Shhhh," Shadow and William said.

Shadow pulled a rock, and a piece of the cliff swung out like a door.

"That's it?"

"A secret entrance to the prison. Now be quiet!"

It seemed too easy. Shadow pulled the door shut. The world went black. I blinked and couldn't tell when my eyes were open or shut. Someone grabbed my hand. I flinched, but recognized Shadow when he entwined his fingers around mine.

"Where are you?" William asked.

"Quiet. I'll help," Shadow said.

After a moment of confused shuffling, William's hand found his way to mine.

Shadow led us through the darkness. I waited for my eyes to adjust, but they never did.

We walked for ages, always climbing upwards. I heard the gentle breathing of people asleep and the scuffle of our feet on the rock. Nothing else.

I held my breath as much as possible. The stench of filth and rot was overwhelming.

Shadow knew exactly where to go. Each footstep had purpose.

"Are there no guards?" I whispered.

"Of course there are guards," he whispered back.

I pushed closer to him.

After an eternity of darkness, Shadow let go of my hand and opened a door. I followed him through it and breathed the clean air. Moonlight from a window illuminated the room. I glanced around.

The kitchen was empty. The fires had gone out. Shadow shut the door, and it blended in perfectly with the plaster wall. No one would find it by accident. William dropped my hand and snatched a pastry from a shelf.

"They'll know we were here anyway," he said.

"But they don't have to know how we got in," Shadow said.

He passed the shelves of food without taking anything. I followed his lead, although my stomach grumbled.

We walked through the series of rooms in the kitchen. I recognized most of them from the night of the opera, although everything looked cold and gray without the light of the fires.

"Why is there a passage from the kitchen to the prison?" I asked.

"Prisoners need to eat," William said, his mouth full of food.

Shadow scoffed.

"They use prisoners to test food for poison before serving it."

"Poison?"

"Salaria hasn't always been peaceful. And cooks aren't always trustworthy."

I swallowed and followed him through another door.

"The ugly garden!" I said as we stepped into the fresh air.

I walked over to the plant where Shadow had hidden the night we met and stroked a leaf.

"What?" William asked.

"Well, these plants aren't exactly pretty," I said. "I think this is where they send gardeners who need more practice."

Shadow smirked. William shook his head.

"This is an herb garden," William said. "They grow plants to use in the kitchens. To flavor the food."

"Oh."

I looked up at the main garden to hide my embarrassment. It was dark and quiet. There would have been torches and music if anyone had been in it.

"How do we get up there?"

But Shadow was already up. He had scaled the wall.

"I'll help you up," William said.

"I think I can make it."

There were plenty of rocks to use as handholds. I climbed it without a problem.

Shadow grinned at me when I reached the top.

"We'll make a bandit of you yet."

I smiled back. We hid in a bush and waited for William to make the climb. I stared at my garden, taking in every detail. Plants grew in symmetrical pairs. Every bush trimmed, the grass a green, flourishing carpet. Flowers of every shape and color imaginable glowed in the moonlight.

It all looked a bit unnatural.

William swung over the wall, and Shadow turned to

me.

Right, I would have to lead now.

I made my way to the corner of the garden with the stairs, doing my best to use the plants for cover. Surely everyone was asleep by now. Surely no one was watching the garden.

But my heart beat hard by the time we stood at the bottom of the staircase. I nodded to Shadow, then began to climb. It was easier in the short peasant dress, but still terrifying. I clung to the stones, trying not to think about the sharp cliffs below.

No one spoke as we climbed. I gasped in relief when I climbed over the top of the tower. My chest with the books and opera glasses sat undisturbed. The trap door was shut. For a moment, I panicked. Would we be able to open it from the outside? Shadow pulled a knife out of his pack and worked the bolt loose.

We climbed down to the secret passage.

It was unsettling, being so close to my former life. I led them down the tunnel.

"There's the council chamber," I said.

"You didn't mention it was so close," Shadow said. "William, see if you can find any information about the salt tax. Rook and I will come back for you when we've got the goods."

"We could steal a treaty and ransom it."

"William!"

"Quiet, Rook. Do we get to Lady Alma's through here?"

I nodded and led the way. My breath caught as we passed the tapestry that led to my bedroom. Would Seda be in there? Surely they wouldn't lock him up all alone. I thought I heard a noise, but it was difficult to tell in the echoing tunnel.

I walked past. Shadow gaped when we crawled into

the studio.

Thankfully, Lady Alma had left the ceiling and walls as windows. Moonlight gleamed against the solid gold drawers and mirrors. I resisted the urge to stand on the pedestal in the middle of the room while fabric swirled around me.

"Everything is in the drawers," I said. "I'll get the rubies. You see what else you can find."

"They'll know we were here, so don't hold back," Shadow said. "We'll take as much as we can carry."

I opened the drawer where Lady Alma had stored the rubies and gasped. My Rosas Rojas!

I twirled it in my fingers, picturing Sir Gilbert's face as he gave it to me. His scent lingered in the petals, mixed with the floral aroma. For a brief moment, I felt homesick for my former life. Lady Alma's cheerful chatter. Seda's antics. The poets-

That brought me back to reality. I did not miss the poets. Although, it might be amusing to see what they would write if they could see me now.

"This is no time to stop and smell the roses," Shadow said.

I rolled my eyes and put the rose in my apron. I couldn't bear to think of it on Captain's ship, traveling to the black market in Castana. Besides, it came from there. It wouldn't interest them.

The rubies were still in the drawer. The room glowed red when I opened the chest. Shadow turned and smiled at me.

"Well done."

The rubies were heavy. I dumped them out of the chest into a basket and filled the rest of the space with silks so thin they were transparent. I could hardly lift the bag when I finished.

Shadow opened a wardrobe and pulled out something

round and shiny.

"What in the world is this, Rook?"

I blinked at the glare as it caught the moonlight and gasped.

"Those are the diamonds from the opera costume!"

"Yes, but what are they in? This silver thing?"

"Um, it's a hat."

He stared at me. I examined the contents of the wardrobe. The white triangular dress hung in the middle. It was as ugly as I remembered.

"This is the dress Princess Salara wore in the opera," I said. "I suppose we should take it?"

Shadow grinned.

"Captain won't have enough gold. We'll have to fold it."

I carefully folded the dress and wrapped it in a piece of green velvet. Shadow wrapped the hat full of diamonds so it wouldn't spill.

"Let's go get William's bags," Shadow said. "We can leave these in the passage while we fill the rest."

I nodded and followed him.

William waved at us when we brought the bags.

"I can't find anything about the salt tax," he said.

"Keep looking. Rook and I have just about cleaned out the studio."

I reached out a hand to stroke the tapestry by my room as we walked past. Someone snored on the other side. I jumped.

"What's that?" Shadow asked.

"Nothing."

I found a few more small chests of gems and some half-finished shoes. We filled our baskets in no time.

I paused again as we passed my room. I definitely heard something. Who was in there?

Shadow kept walking down the tunnel. I ran my hand

along the tapestry, listening to the rhythmic breathing of someone asleep. I pushed the tapestry forward. Just a little. Just enough so I could see inside.

Someone slept in my bed. Black hair spilled over the pillow, gleaming in the moonlight. A ghostly prism of colors shone on the walls.

I stared. The room was unchanged. I recognized the same tapestries, the same carpet.

The same blankets.

With seemingly the same person under them.

Something brushed against my foot. I jumped and bit back a scream. A blur of white fur pawed my skirt.

"Seda, no," I whispered.

Seda meowed. The sound echoed through the tunnel.

"Go back in."

He scratched at my leg and yowled. I picked him up and stroked him to keep him quiet. The figure in the bed moved. She turned. I could almost see her face now.

"What are you doing?"

I jumped as Shadow put his hand on my shoulder. I tucked Seda under one arm and put my finger to my lips.

Shadow pushed the tapestry back further and examined the room.

"Rook, what is this?"

I shrugged and turned to leave.

The girl in my bed sighed and turned further. Her hair fell over her face. Faint colors danced around the room. Shadow grabbed my arm.

"Is that-"

"Impossible," I tried to keep my tone light.

His entire body was tense. He reached a trembling hand into his pack and pulled out his dagger.

"Shadow, what are you doing?"

He blinked at the knife in his hand.

"I-"

Seda yowled. The girl opened her eyes.

We should leave. I knew we should leave. But I stayed, and Shadow did the same. I needed to see.

The girl sat up and turned towards me. Our eyes met.

We both stared.

"Who's there?"

Her voice sounded familiar and not at all enchanted.

Shadow pulled me back while the girl rubbed her eyes. Seda dug his claws into my shoulder, and I yelped. The girl leaned forward, and a moonbeam illuminated her face.

Impossible.

Her screams brought me out of the trance. I pushed Shadow through the tapestry.

In a flash of silver sparkles, Lady Alma appeared. She wore a night cap trimmed with Castanian stars and a pink silk nightgown to match. The blast of magic stunned me. I stared at the teardrop charm around her neck and fingered the similar one around my own.

Of course Lady Alma had a wig charm. She wore wigs every day.

"Princess Salara!" Lady Alma said.

Was she speaking to me or the imposter? I didn't stay to find out. I followed Shadow through the tunnels, and we ran to the council chamber.

"Still nothing about the salt tax," William said.

"Forget that! Hurry!" Shadow said.

We grabbed the baskets and sprinted to the end of the tunnel.

Shadow climbed the ladder first. William handed baskets up to him. As I tried to climb it, I realized I was still holding Seda. I tried to set him down, but he climbed onto my shoulder.

He dug his claws in as I climbed the staircase around the tower. Shadow climbed after me. William lowered the baskets to us with a rope before climbing down himself.

This was taking too long. Lady Alma would have sounded the alarm by now.

We each grabbed our baskets and ran across the garden. Instead of climbing down the herb garden wall, Shadow led us to the staircase.

"It will take too long to lower the baskets," he said.

"Why are we in a hurry now?" William whispered.

I shook my head and followed Shadow down the stairs and through the kitchens. We reached the room with the secret door, and Shadow pushed the wall. The door swung open. When Shadow shut it, the prison plunged into complete darkness.

"We should have brought a candle," I whispered.

"Darkness spell," Shadow whispered. "Lights don't work."

"Lights don't work," a voice echoed.

It was harder to follow Shadow while carrying the baskets, but he did not slow down. I sighed with relief when he opened the final door and we stood on the docks. I looked back at the palace, expecting to see it aglow with lights and crawling with guards. Most of the lights were out now. There was no sign of commotion.

We walked through the docks until we found the place where Estrella had abandoned us. We entered the leaning building. A group of sailors surrounded Estrella. She waved her hands up and down Joe's arm, filling the room with flashes of colorful light.

"We need to go," Shadow said.

Estrella ignored him. She moved her hand in small circles, and the light turned green. Joe flexed his fingers.

"What happened back there?"

William leaned towards me, waiting for an answer. I shrugged and dislodged Seda from my shoulder. He jumped onto William.

"What is this?"

"Nothing."

I took Seda from him and scratched behind his ears. The kitten purred.

William stared at me. Then at the papers he still held in his hand. He shoved them into a basket.

"We need to get out of here, Estrella," Shadow said.

"I'll sail you out of the city," Joe said. "Rook can see what she's missing by hanging out with bandits instead of pirates."

"Thanks, Joe," Estrella said. "And thanks for the crystal."

"Worth every ounce. Wasn't even that hard to steal."

Estrella turned to us, smiling. She noticed Seda and froze.

The kitten jumped out of my arms, ran across the room, and leapt at Estrella. She caught him and pulled him close.

"You brought Seda?" she asked.

"You did what?" Shadow said.

Seda stayed in Estrella's arms, playing with the silver crystal hanging around her neck. He turned to me, meowed, and clawed the crystal again. I watched them as we climbed into Joe's ship and sailed out to sea. Had Estrella set an enchantment on the crystal? Why was she charming my kitten?

"Where to?" Joe asked.

"Take us to Miner's Harbor," Estrella said. "But sail out a bit first."

She stood beside him, watching the waves hit the boat. Seda slept in her arms. William, Shadow, and I stood at the back watching the palace for some sign of alarm. It remained dark.

We sailed out to sea, then turned and sailed up the Ghone.

"So what exactly were you two doing?" William asked.

Shadow shook his head and nodded at Joe.

"Oh, don't worry about me," Joe said. "I know lots of Captain's secret plans. Never breathe a word of them. Even if Rook asked me about them, my lips are sealed."

"I could teach him a thing or two about being subtle," William whispered to me.

"Like you taught Thomas?"

We both laughed.

I held Seda while Estrella helped Joe adjust the sails. She reached for him when she finished, but I shook my head. What made her think she had the right to hold him? She glared at me but said nothing. The ship moved slowly up the Ghone as we sailed against the current and towards the mountains. Finally Joe dropped the anchor at a ramshackle dock surrounded by a cluster of equally rundown buildings. He lowered a ramp for us and held out his hand to help me ashore. Shadow jumped in front of him and took my arm. Joe frowned.

"So that's how it is, then?"

"We were never here, Joe," Estrella said.

"Only my arm remembers, and it don't know how to talk. Thanks, Strella."

"Anytime."

They smiled at each other, and Joe sailed away. Shadow released my arm.

Estrella turned on us.

"This is more than jewels and fabric!"

She gestured to the sleeping kitten in my arms.

"We had a bit of a run in with the Princess," Shadow said.

"You had what?"

"Just so you know, I wasn't there," William said. "I was in a completely different room."

"Do you have any idea how dangerous that is,

Shadow?"

I thought back to his hand clutching the knife and shuddered.

"It was my fault," I said. "I heard a noise and wandered off."

"We need to get to safety," Shadow said. "We can figure out what happened later."

"To the mines, then," Estrella said. "But this isn't over."

"At least I didn't abandon the mission before it started," I said.

"Don't you dare. Do you know what this is? What it can do? I can repair ten wells with this, at least. I might be able to extract the salt from the ground so they can grow crops next year."

She waved the crystal in my face. I pushed her hand away. The movement startled Seda. He jumped to the ground. Estrella caught him before he could run away and pulled him close.

"The tunnel entrance is this way," Shadow said.

"We're meeting Captain tomorrow night by the mountains," Estrella said. "As long as Joe remembers to tell him."

A boulder hid the entrance to the mines. Shadow and William pushed it away, and Estrella pushed it back with magic after we entered the tunnel. She snapped a dozen stars above us. The light glistened on Seda's fur.

He slept in her arms. I had not seen him in so long. It wasn't fair that she insisted on holding him. Worse, she did not offer to help carry the baskets. I stumbled through the corridor as the jewels grew heavier and heavier. The Rosas Rojas pressed through my apron and dug into my leg.

I replayed the events of the raid in my mind. Shadow thought he had seen the Princess. Lady Alma had called to her. But that was impossible, and for a moment in the moonlight, I had recognized the face.

Only it didn't make any sense.

Why would Elsie be sleeping in my bed?

21

We walked deeper into the tunnel and entered a cavern so tall Estrella's stars did not light the ceiling. Shadow snapped his fingers. Nothing happened.

"These mines have gone dark," Estrella said. "Miner's magic won't work here."

"Dark?" I asked.

"All the fairy salt has been mined."

She snapped her fingers and more stars appeared above us. They floated upwards, but still did not illuminate the ceiling. I could see the walls in the distance. It was larger than the largest ballroom in the palace.

Across the cavern, an underground lake reflected the stars so perfectly that I thought it was a mirror until a single drop of water fell. The splash echoed through the room, and the ripples disrupted the light in an ever growing circle until they reached the shore. Shadow led us through another tunnel. It sloped downwards. How far underground were we now?

We entered a small room with furnishings similar to the cabin on the Ghone. I glanced around for beds but saw none. I tapped my foot against the rock to see if it was as hard as I expected.

It was. I groaned.

Shadow put his baskets on the table and sat. We all did the same.

"Now," William said, "What in Salara's name did you do back there?"

"Not quite what we planned," Estrella agreed. "What were you doing near the Princess?"

But she smiled and scratched Seda behind the ears. He purred.

What was going on? Would she really enchant a kitten to make it like her?

"We ran into a bit of trouble," Shadow said. "But Rook and I took care of it. And we stole the gown Salara wore in the opera!"

Estrella raised an eyebrow.

"The one covered in diamonds?"

"It is one of a kind, thank goodness," I said. "Should be worth a fortune."

William whistled.

"And Captain will pay a lot for that cat. He's always asking about it."

"Seda isn't going anywhere," Estrella said.

She clutched the kitten as if he would disappear at any moment.

She didn't let him go as we settled into the cavern. The mines were surprisingly comfortable. Estrella's stars illuminated the room with twinkling light. A barrel and empty shelf stood in the corner. Several doors branched out from the main room. I saw furniture and shelves through the openings. Shadow and William chose an opening to the right as their room. Estrella and I claimed the one on the left.

"Beds!" I said.

I set my pack on a bed, grateful I wouldn't have to sleep on the rock floor.

"These were miners' rooms," Estrella said. "Once they

extract the fairy salt from a section of tunnels, they move on."

"So it is abandoned?"

She nodded. We met William and Shadow back in the main room.

"We'll need water," William said.

"You know where to find it," Estrella said.

She flicked her wrist and a few stars hovered above William's head. They followed him when he left.

"Did we get enough?"

I meant the question for Shadow, but he wasn't there. I glanced around the cavern. Sometimes he seemed to melt into the walls.

Estrella nodded and opened a basket to examine our haul. She pulled wrinkled papers from the top and frowned.

"William must have brought those accidentally," I said. "He was in the council chamber looking for information about the salt tax when we ran out."

Estrella frowned and smoothed out the papers.

"These are documents about the treaty with New Salaria. Not very useful."

She leaned Seda on her shoulder and skimmed the papers.

"Let me hold him while you do that."

She shook her head.

I patted my lap, trying to coax Seda away from her. He stretched, but didn't leave her shoulder.

"You can release the charm," I said. "We don't have to worry about him running away now."

"What charm?"

"Whatever charm you've enchanted Seda with. I don't know why you're so determined to make him like you, but it is unnecessary."

"I haven't enchanted him."

She set Seda down on the table. He looked at both of us, then ran into the bedroom and scratched on the bedpost.

"Why does he like you then?"

She shrugged. "He was my kitten first."

"What?"

"It was a long time ago, but I guess he never forgot. I found him on the streets, and my mother healed him."

I stared at her.

"He kept getting sick, so she created a soul loop for him. Like you and I did for the well. It should have used his life force to strengthen his healing abilities, but she made it a bit too strong."

"Just a bit?"

"By the time we realized what had happened, it was too late to fix it. The soul loop had been in place for months. Changing it would have killed him."

She turned her attention back to the papers.

"So your mother is the one that made him immortal?"

"I don't know if he's immortal. His aging has certainly slowed down or stopped. Loops are unpredictable."

Seda purred in the next room and jumped from bed to bed. Estrella smiled. She looked happier than I had ever seen her.

"Why did you give him away?"

She glared at me.

"I thought Princess Salara would like to play with him. I was stupid."

I tried to remember the first time I had seen Seda, but it had been so long ago. The usual sea of blond girls had surrounded me while I amused the kitten by reflecting light from my diamond bracelet for him to chase around the room.

"She cried when I took him home. It was strongly suggested that I might like to give Seda to her majesty as a birthday gift. I said I would like no such thing, but they took him anyway. The next day, I told Salara I hated her. I was banished from her presence."

This I did remember. A girl emerging from my sea of blond companions screaming insults. She managed to scratch my arm, to draw blood with her nails, before guards dragged her away. Lady Alma healed the wound with a wave of her hand. It left no scar, but I remembered the hatred in the girl's eyes.

"I'm sorry."

"It was boring. Incredibly boring, being a member of court banished from the palace. My father's position as Admiral kept me from serious punishment, but I couldn't attend any social function where Salara was present. Which was all of them. I spent a lot of time in our garden."

William returned and emptied two buckets into a barrel in the corner.

"Is that all?" Estrella asked.

"There are only two buckets. I'll get more."

"Let me," I said.

"They're heavy," William said.

"Heavier than diamonds? Or sixty gold coins?"

He laughed and shook his head.

Estrella snapped some stars to follow me and turned her attention to the papers William had stolen.

"These will lead you to the river," she said.

"We don't get water from the lake?"

"Too stagnant," William said. "Where's Shadow?"

Estrella shrugged. William pulled a paper from the back of the pile and read it.

"Look at this! The treaty with the colonies includes a proposed marriage between the delegate and Princess Salara."

I halted in the doorway.

"Sir Gilbert proposed marriage to the Princess?"

"Almost all treaties with Salaria include that," Estrella said. "It doesn't really mean anything. Kingdoms use it to show who their most eligible bachelor is in case the King is interested. Marrying Salara to a colonist would be a terrible political move."

"I suppose someone from Castana would be better?" William said.

"It would unite nations across the ocean. They could control trade routes."

"Always thinking like a pirate."

"I'm not a pirate!"

I left. Their voices faded as I followed the stars through unfamiliar tunnels. Thinking about Sir Gilbert made my heart beat faster.

He had proposed marriage?

Others had. I knew that. But I had never met most of them. And I had never felt-

What did I feel for Sir Gilbert?

The sound of rushing water echoed through the tunnels, and Estrella's stars multiplied to illuminate a long, narrow cavern. An underground river rushed through and poured into a black abyss edged with jagged rocks. Even with the stars, I could not see where it led.

I found the calmest part of the river and filled the two buckets. I set them on the shore and watched the water churn, reluctant to return.

A sound mixed with the rush of the river. A voice? I left the buckets and walked along the bank.

It came again. A scream, cut off suddenly.

I searched the water and saw a girl thrashing in the river. She clung to a rock in the center. The current pulled her towards the sharp rocks at the end of the room.

I waded in before I remembered I could barely swim. The girl's dress and long hair flowed behind her, caught in the current. Her hands slipped, and she drifted a few feet closer to the abyss. Her head hit a rock. She inhaled to scream and choked on water.

The river's bank was not deep. I waded towards the center and reached for her she floated past. My hands connected with something, and I pulled.

It was her hair, but she didn't scream. Her body floated limp in the current. Her head bobbed underwater.

I pulled her towards me with her hair until I found her shoulders and pushed her head above the water. Blood streamed past her closed eyes.

I dragged her to shore and laid her flat. I patted her face, not sure what to do. Her skin was hot.

"Please wake up," I whispered.

She coughed. Her eyes did not open, but she was breathing. Tears of relief streamed down my face.

"You're safe," I whispered. "Who are you?"

She raised her hand, felt the wound on her head, and winced.

"I have friends nearby," I said. "I can go get them. One is a healer."

"I can walk."

Her voice was little more than a whisper. She pushed herself to a sitting position. With her eyes still shut, she tried to stand.

"Let me help you."

I wrapped her arm around my shoulder. She leaned on me. I was practically carrying her.

She was much heavier than rubies or gold.

The stars led the way, hovering just in front of us. The girl moved slowly. Blood streamed from her cut, mixing with the water dripping from her hair. Her skin was red and swollen, and she kept her eyes shut.

We did not speak. I was too out of breath for conversation, and she was panting as well. The light grew brighter as we came near the cavern. A warm glow illuminated the tunnel up ahead. Shadow's voice mixed with William and Estrella's. So he was back.

The girl stopped walking. I waited for her to gather her strength.

"Turn off the lights," she said.

I turned to her. She covered her eyes with one hand.

"I can't."

"It is too bright."

She found the rock wall with her other hand and slumped to the floor.

"We're so close," I said. "You can make it."

"It's too bright."

She put both hands over her eyes.

"I'm going to run ahead," I said. "I'll bring back help. Will you be alright alone for a few moments?"

She rocked back and forth on the floor, grimacing.

I ran to find the others.

"What happened to you?" Estrella asked.

I had forgotten that I was soaking wet.

"I found something. Someone. I need help."

"You did what?" Estrella asked.

Shadow stood.

"Show us."

William reluctantly put down the food he had been eating, and they followed me. I had no trouble finding my way. I had left a wet trail on the floor. Estrella's stars followed us.

We heard the screaming before we saw the girl. She sat on the floor, curled into a ball with her face buried against her knees, wailing.

"Roslynn?"

William froze for a moment, then ran to her. He put a hand on her shoulder, but she did not stop screaming.

"What's wrong with her? What happened?"

He turned to me, and then to Estrella. Roslynn's screams dissolved into sobs.

"Light," she whimpered.

"Turn off the lights!" I told Estrella.

"What?"

"Just do it!"

Shadow nodded to Estrella. She snapped her fingers. The stars went out.

I stood in complete darkness. Roslynn's sobs grew softer. They stopped. Heavy breathing echoed in the dark.

"Roslynn?" William whispered.

"Are you alright?" Shadow asked.

"I searched everywhere," William said. "Where have you been?"

"Where are you injured?" Estrella said. "You're bleeding."

"She hit her head on a rock."

"I can heal you, but first I need to see what's wrong. If I turn on a light-"

"No!" Roslynn said.

"Don't," William said.

I stood where I was, trying to stay calm in the complete darkness. The floor seemed to shift, and I lost my sense of direction as the voices echoed around me.

"I can help."

Shadow's voice was a whisper. I heard him move towards Roslynn.

"I'm coming," William said.

"To do what?" Estrella said. "If I can't help you certainly can't.

"We'll be back soon," Shadow said. "You can turn the lights on after we've gone."

A pair of footsteps echoed through the cavern and disappeared. I heard a snap, and three stars appeared. I blinked in the sudden brightness, momentarily blinded. We walked back to our room.

"Where did you find her?" William asked.

"In the river, obviously," Estrella said. "Shadow found food if you want any, Rook."

I opened the boxes on the table, examining the contents. They all contained something shriveled that didn't look edible. I pulled a piece out and sniffed it. Dried meat, maybe?

"So that really is Roslynn?" I asked.

"What was she doing in the river?" William asked.

"What is she doing with Shadow?" I asked.

"Can you heal her?"

William turned to Estrella.

"Be quiet or you'll wake Seda," Estrella said. She gestured to the kitten asleep in a chair.

"I don't care about Seda," William said. "What's wrong with Roslynn?"

"She'll tell us when she returns. But surely you've guessed."

I had no idea, but William looked crushed.

"It fades, doesn't it?" he said. "It heals with time."

"Sometimes."

"Most of the time," he insisted.

I took a bite of a shriveled hunk of meat. It was tough. Impossibly tough. I gnawed at it, trying to break off a piece. My wet clothes dried to my skin. I slumped back in my chair and stared at Seda. He sharpened his claws on a basket, not caring that the humans around him had been thrown into chaos.

I was halfway through the piece of dried meat before Shadow and Roslynn returned. She wore a blindfold. The blood had been washed from her face. William gasped and ran to her. She flinched when he touched her shoulder.

"Sorry," she said. "Give me some warning next time."

"Are you alright?"

She nodded.

Estrella glanced to Shadow, who nodded as well.

"The cut on her head isn't serious," he said. "You should heal it. And the sunburn if you can."

Estrella waved her hands over Roslynn's head. A green light flashed, and she stepped back.

"What about her eyes?" William asked.

Estrella shook her head.

"Do you want some food?" I asked.

Roslynn nodded, and I handed her a piece of the meat.

"It is kind of hard to chew."

Roslynn smiled.

"Thank you. For everything."

"I'm Rook."

"I know. Shadow told me. Thank you, Rook."

"How did this happen?" Estrella asked. "Did they use a charm?"

Roslynn nodded.

"I already told Shadow. It didn't pierce my skin."

Estrella sighed.

"It shouldn't be permanent, then."

"So it will fade?" William asked.

His eyes glinted. With tears? I stared at him.

"Probably," Estrella said. "But the charm must have been strong."

Roslynn nodded and reached for William. She missed, and he grabbed her hand and pressed it to his lips. She smiled at him.

"The Dragon doesn't mess around."

22

"What?"

William jumped out of his seat. Roslynn flinched at the sudden movement.

"Sit down, William," Shadow said.

"What, did you already tell him about that?" William asked. "Where have you been?"

"Let her finish eating," Estrella said. "We'll hear the whole story in time."

"I'm done," Roslynn said. "I don't think my jaw can take any more of that."

She laughed. I was the only one who joined her.

"I'll find you some better food," William said. "I'll-"

Roslynn shook her head.

"I'm fine, William. Really, I am."

"You were supposed to help at the shop," he said. "Not go searching for pirates! You were supposed-"

"To stay on the farm while you flirted your way across the country?"

"That's not fair, Roslynn."

William looked hurt. Roslynn found his hand and squeezed it.

"I'm joking. Mostly. Don't think I don't know about Elsie. I helped in their shop, for goodness sake!"

Elsie. We all stiffened, but of course Roslynn couldn't see us. She continued.

"I didn't go looking for the Dragon. I couldn't have found him if I had. It was just good luck."

"Good luck?"

William looked ready to punch something. He let his breath out in a slow hiss. Roslynn patted his hand.

"A few days ago, I heard that a chest of sapphires was being transferred from the Salara Museum to the palace. It isn't far, so I thought security might be low. I went to check it out."

"You tried to steal gems? On your own?"

I leaned forward, impressed. Everyone else just looked shocked.

"Roslynn, how could you?" William said.

"Please, you've raided the palace how many times now? I found a Navy ship docked at the museum and sneaked aboard. Unfortunately, I couldn't find the gems. They set sail before I could escape."

"And the Dragon attacked them?"

"I'm not sure. I hid in a half empty salt crate and couldn't see much. We docked along the river for a while, and the sailors unloaded cargo. They carried my crate to shore. I tried to sneak out and hide in the woods, but someone hit me and knocked me out. I woke up in a cabin on a different ship. We were at sea."

William clenched his fists.

"How do you know it was a different ship?" Estrella asked. "You were inside a cabin."

"Navy ships have the same type of wood," Roslynn said. "That light gold sort of color. This ship was red."

Estrella gasped.

"Are you sure? Red?"

Roslynn nodded.

"How do you know the ship was the Dragon's?"

Shadow asked. "Did you see him?"

Everyone leaned forward.

"He told me he was the Dragon. He could have been lying, I suppose. I hadn't thought of that. I didn't see him. He kept me tied up in a chair and stayed behind me until he used the owl eyes."

"Were there any other prisoners?" Estrella asked.

Roslynn shook her head.

"How could you do this?" William asked. "What if he had killed you? Pirates are vicious! No offense, Estrella."

Estrella threw her hands in the air.

"For the last time, I'm not a pirate!"

"What did he ask you about?" Shadow asked.

"I admitted I had been trying to steal gems, and he asked me about Princess Salara."

"What does the Dragon want with Princess Salara?" I asked.

Roslynn shrugged.

"He wouldn't be the only pirate obsessed with her," Shadow pointed out. "If he got his hands on her, he would control Salaria."

"Is he sending in a marriage proposal and treaty?" William joked.

Shadow didn't laugh.

"The King is getting desperate," he said.

"You really think they'd give Salara to the Dragon?" I asked.

"They do need the trade routes open," Estrella said. "The peace treaty with Castana is in jeopardy if the fairy salt shipments don't make it."

"This is ridiculous," I said. "Absolutely ridiculous. They would never give her to a pirate."

But they would replace her. They would stop searching for her.

"How did you escape?" Estrella asked. "Why did he

curse you?"

"He was trying to get information out of me. He asked about the operas, life in Salaria, what the Princess liked. That sort of thing. If I didn't know something, he touched me with the owl eyes charm again. After a while, all I could see was white. Even with my eyes closed."

She shuddered and rubbed her temple. Shadow often used that same gesture as if trying to massage away a headache.

"I'll kill him," William said.

He didn't move. His expression didn't change. He meant it.

"I've never heard of using owl eyes for torture," Estrella said.

"He said he doesn't like blood staining his ship. Curses are clean."

William clenched his jaw and tapped his foot on the ground.

"How did you end up in the caves?" I asked.

"His crew threw me overboard. Expected me to drown, but I've lived by the Ghone all my life. I swam towards the shore and ended up in a mine tunnel. I was pretty weak by that time though. When I tried to get a drink from the river, I slipped and couldn't get out of the current."

She leaned her head against William's shoulder.

"You should rest," he said.

"She can take my bed," Shadow said. "I'll find another."

"I'm fine," Roslynn said.

"You just swam across the ocean. And you've been cursed. You're going to rest now," William said.

"It wasn't that far."

William picked her up and carried her out of the cavern.

Estrella sighed and picked up the papers from the King's council chamber.

"I'll look over the rest of these. If the Dragon made any demands, maybe Salaria and the colonies have a plan for dealing with them."

She took the papers back to our room. Shadow smiled at me.

"Who would have thought raiding the palace would be the least exciting part of our week?"

I laughed.

"We still need water," he said. "Let's go get some."

Instead of asking Estrella for stars, Shadow lit a candle. We walked to the river, picked up the buckets of water I had left, and strolled back to the cavern. We poured the water in the barrel and walked back.

Instead of going to the river, Shadow led me to the lake.

"Estrella said this water isn't good to drink," I said.

"But it is a nice place to sit."

We found a rock and sat side by side, watching the candle's reflection in the motionless water.

"Will Roslynn be alright?" I asked.

He nodded.

"Owl eyes is not life threatening."

"What is it, exactly?"

"Have you ever walked into a dark place? It takes your eyes a moment to adjust, but then you can see again?"

I laughed and looked at the mine around me.

"Now when have I been in a dark place?"

Shadow smiled.

"The same adjustment happens when you move from dark to light. The world seems too bright until your eyes adjust."

I nodded.

"When you are in a dark place, your pupil, the black

part of your eye, expands to let in more light."

He pushed his hair to the side and leaned towards me. His pupils filled most of his eyes. I gasped.

"The owl eyes charm expands the pupil larger than it normally would go. It allows people to see in the dark."

"What about in the light?"

"It is too bright. And painful."

"But Estrella said it isn't permanent."

Shadow shook his head.

"I hope Roslynn's isn't."

"But what about yours? How did this happen?"

Shadow examined me for a moment. He exhaled slowly.

"Before the salt tax was abolished, anyone who couldn't pay it would work in the mines instead. My family couldn't pay. My father would have been in the mines for a year, but it cut his sentence in half if I went with him. So I did. We were given owl eyes charms."

"And the curse went wrong?"

"I never touched one. My father was afraid it would cause permanent damage since I was so young. I followed him in that dark pit for six months. When we returned home, my father found work as a gardener. The family gave him an owl eyes charm so he could work at night."

"It was Estrella's garden."

Shadow looked surprised, but nodded.

"Her father was an Admiral, and her mother was a Castanian noblewoman. But Estrella and I became friends anyway. Her parents didn't mind."

"That's odd."

Shadow smiled.

"The neighbors minded. I had to hide anytime they came over. And their son came over a lot."

"So you used the owl eyes in the garden?"

Shadow held his hand up.

"I'm getting to that part. Estrella became one of Princess Salara's companions. She told me all about her. I wanted to see for myself, and Estrella decided that I should. She helped me sneak into a banquet. And I saw her. Princess Salara."

I held my breath.

"She was beautiful," Shadow said. "More beautiful than any poet had said. Every smile, every laugh, was perfect. I just stood there, watching her. No one noticed me. They were all focused on her as well. When the moon began to sink in the sky, I knew I had to go back. But I wanted to bring something back to my mother and sister. I needed to share this beauty, to prove it. So I grabbed the first thing I found with her face on it: a boiled egg.

"Someone saw me and shouted. Soldiers grabbed me. I looked for Estrella. She shouted for me, but her father held her back. Salara heard the commotion, and for a moment our eyes met. Then she laughed and turned away."

Our eyes met again. How many years later?

"I'm sorry."

"They took me to the prison tower. The guard smashed the egg over my head. I sat in the darkness while it rotted in my hair. The other prisoners said I would be executed. Then one night, I heard a familiar voice in the blackness. My father.

"I thought I had gone insane. But he was there, and he had a key. He took my hand, and we ran. It was easy, just like in the mines. At least, until the guards found us. They shot him. When he pressed his owl eyes charm into my hand, I saw the arrow had gone all the way through his chest. I grabbed it to help him and cut my hand.

"He told me to run. To follow the trail."

Shadow's voice broke. I waited.

"He had left pebbles from the garden to mark the way

out. I followed them and held the charm in my cut hand so I could open doors without leaving blood. By the time I got out, the charm had been absorbed into the cut. It was a part of me.

"I hid in the mines. I made it to William's farm a few days later, barely alive."

"Oh," I said. "But maybe Estrella, with her new crystal-"

"She's tried. So many times. When it absorbed into my bloodstream, the charm created a loop in my soul. That sort of magic is unpredictable. Hard to undo."

He held up his hand. Scars and calluses from the mines etched across his palms. One scar was lighter and smooth to touch. I traced my finger across it.

"How good is your vision?" I asked.

"Fine in the dark."

"So last night when we saw Princess Salara-"

"I saw her."

"And she looked the same? You didn't notice anything strange about her?"

"No, did you?"

I shook my head. I had seen Elsie dressed up as me in my bed, but surely that was crazy?

"I think I experienced owl eyes once," I told him. "I ran into a stagehand at the ballet, and all the lights seemed brighter."

Shadow nodded.

"Is that why they called you Shadow? Because you spent so much time in the dark?"

"My parents called me Shadow because I looked so much like my father. Because I followed him everywhere. It is the only name I've ever had."

We sat in silence a while longer, then Shadow stood and offered me his hand. He didn't let go until we reached the cavern. Estrella sat at the table reading through the papers. William and Roslynn were nowhere to be seen.

"Where will you sleep?" Estrella asked.

Shadow shrugged. He handed me a piece of dried meat. I chewed as much as I could and gave the rest to Seda. He jumped onto my lap and purred. I dangled my apron strings for him to play with and winced when he clawed my leg. He felt the lump of the Rosas Rojas and batted it.

"He likes you," Estrella said.

She smiled as if she had given me a compliment.

"Of course he does."

I carried Seda to the next room and lay on my bed. He sat on my feet, then decided he wasn't ready to sleep and ran back to Estrella.

The bed in the cavern was comfortable, but it took me a while to fall asleep.

In my dreams, Sir Gilbert smiled at me. A breeze ran through my hair, which was long again. Past my waist.

"Are you safe?" I asked. "Did you make it home?"

He laughed.

"I should ask you the same question. Where are you?"

"I'm serious. The seas are dangerous right now. The Dragon has been spotted in Salaria."

As if to prove my point, we suddenly stood on a ship. Dark waves pushed over the side. We each took a step back. He stayed on the deck. I stood on the shore now, watching him sail away. The wind howled.

I woke up to the sound of Seda yowling. Our cavern was dark, but a faint light drifted in from the main room. I stared at the ceiling, waiting for my eyes to adjust. Finally, I could see Seda as a white blur in the blackness.

He purred when I sat up.

"Estrella?"

She didn't answer.

I sat up in bed.

Seda had pulled all the covers off Estrella's bed. He jumped and twisted. I picked him up and realized he was tied to the bedpost. I undid the knots in the rope and carried him to the common room. He jumped out of my arms and onto the table. I handed him a small piece of dried meat and chewed on the rest.

A candle on the table illuminated the room with a cold light. Was it morning? I had no concept of time in the mines. Seda finished his meat and meowed for more.

William leaned in the doorway.

"Keep that cat quiet, or I'll throw it in the lake. Roslynn needs to rest."

"It isn't my fault. Estrella left him tied up."

"I don't care."

"Where's Estrella?" Shadow asked.

He sat next to me at the table.

"Wherever she is, she should have taken that yowling beast with her," William said.

"If she tied him up, she obviously didn't want him to follow her," Shadow said.

"She's probably fetching water," I said. "What time is it?"

Shadow and William shrugged.

"Um, isn't that a problem if we're supposed to meet Captain?"

"Estrella has been communicating with him. She won't let us miss the deadline," Shadow said. "We should ready the goods though."

"Have fun playing dress up," William said. "I'm going to check on Roslynn."

"Isn't she asleep?" I said.

"I don't want her to wake up blind and alone in a cave."

"Take a candle," Shadow said.

He pulled a candle from his bag and tapped it on the table. A blueish flame flickered to life. William took the candle and left.

"Miner's candles," Shadow said. "I found extras while I was looking for food."

He grabbed the papers from the top of the stack, and we walked to the cavern with the stolen goods. Seda followed us, running around our feet and chasing shadows on the wall.

"Going to do some reading?" I asked.

"I want to make a list of everything we have so the trade can go faster."

He turned the paper over and waved the blank side at me.

"Did Estrella find anything about the Dragon in the treaty?"

"She didn't mention anything. Most of it deals with trade and new laws."

He flipped the paper over and read aloud, "The Governor of Salaria will be replaced by the Duke appointed by the King at the end of year."

"If they're getting a Duke, they've become a province," I said. "That's interesting."

I should have known that already. As heir to the throne, I should have been informed.

"Yes, but that doesn't really affect us. They're not even changing rulers. The Governor is just changing his title to Duke. And past Governors will be awarded the title posthumously. What an honor."

"It isn't for them," I said, taking offense at his sarcastic tone. "It is for their families. Their children and grandchildren. That will raise their standing in court considerably."

"Yes the family of-"

"Yes?"

Shadow stared at the paper and frowned.

"What's wrong?"

"There's a list of the past Governors who will become Dukes, but it doesn't make sense."

I looked at the piece of paper.

The list of names seemed harmless. The past Governors differed in rank. Some had been knights or naval officers while others already held the rank of Duke or higher.

"Admiral Ethan," Shadow said. "He never governed the colonies."

"Have you been keeping watch on the rulers of New Salaria as well?"

I examined the notes on Admiral Ethan.

"He was appointed, but never actually held the office," I said. "Some council members wanted to exclude him from the elevation to Duke because of this."

"Admiral Ethan was Estrella's father," Shadow said.

I flipped to the next page and read the rest of the information about Admiral Ethan.

"Admiral Ethan was nicknamed the Red Star Admiral because his ship had a figurehead of a Castanian star and was made of red wood instead of the usual Navy gold."

I stopped. Shadow and I stared at each other.

"Red wood," he said.

"Surely not."

I turned back to the paper.

"Admiral Ethan disappeared one week before he was to become governor of the colonies. Witnesses said he had expressed concern about being tied to land when his true passion was sailing. Some speculated he had finally turned to piracy. He had long been affiliated with the pirate known only as Captain. His wife Lady Rosa denied all claims of piracy, but was herself rumored to be a Castanian spy."

"Impossible," Shadow said.

"Estrella's father is the Dragon."

"Impossible."

23

"Estrella is a duchess now," I said, skimming the rest of the report. "There wasn't enough evidence against her father to justify keeping him from receiving the title."

"We should look for her," Shadow said. "She's been gone a long time."

I nodded. We walked through the mines. I carried Seda so he would not slow us down. We passed the lake and the river. There was no sign of Estrella. The caves looked ominous in the cold, flickering candlelight.

"She might be scouting out our rendezvous point," Shadow said. "We've never met Captain this close to the mountains before."

"Let's check."

The further we walked without a sign of Estrella, the more worried I got.

"Surely he wouldn't work as a pirate all these years without contacting her?" I said. "At least he would have told Captain."

"They thought he was dead. Her mother went back to Castana."

"Maybe she kept it a secret. Why would she stay behind to become a bandit instead of going with her mother?"

Shadow shook his head.

"She didn't become a bandit. Not at first. She healed sailors at the docks."

And acted as an agent for the Dragon?

The path sloped uphill. We were getting nearer and nearer to the surface. Seda squirmed in my arms. I put him down, and he darted through the tunnel.

"Where are we meeting Captain?" I asked.

"You'll see it when we round this bend."

"What if it is daylight outside? Your eyes-"

"We won't need to go outside. Captain won't be there yet. We're just checking the location."

And looking for Estrella.

The tunnel turned to the right. We had to climb over a ledge to continue. The path ended at a narrow cliff at the top of an enormous cave. The front opened to the sea. Water and faint red light flooded through the opening. It was sunset, then. Or sunrise? Even that dim light was blinding after so much time underground. The cavern was big enough to fit a sea faring ship, and tall enough that the mast would not scrape the stalactites above it.

At least, the ship docked below seemed to have plenty of room.

"Captain's early," I said, still blinking in the bright light.

Shadow blew out the miner's candle and put it in his pack. I gasped as my eyes adjusted.

The ship's figurehead was a Castanian star. The red light wasn't tinting the ship. It was made of red wood.

"The Dragon?" I whispered.

Shadow and I remained silent for a moment, staring at the ship.

"Why is the Dragon here?" I whispered.

"Storage?"

A crew of men dressed as Navy sailors unloaded crates

from the ship and carried them into tunnels.

"We'll need a new rendezvous point with Captain," I said.

Seda yowled. The sound echoed through the cave. I caught him and pulled him close.

"We need to find Estrella," Shadow said.

"You don't think she's here?"

"If she thinks her father is on that ship, yes."

"So what? We sneak aboard? Ask one of the crew?"

A woman's scream rang out. Seda jumped out of my arms and climbed over the ledge. I watched as he jumped down the rocks and disappeared into the hoard of pirates.

"What's the plan?"

"Be very careful."

I rolled my eyes at him, and he winked. The gesture caught me off guard. I tripped on a rock and had to grab the wall for balance.

We were in plain sight. Any pirate who looked up would see us creeping along the ledge, working our way down to the cavern floor. But they were focused on loading and unloading cargo. We made it to the shore and crawled under the dock.

There was less to hold onto than there had been at Castlemont harbor, but we made it to the ship dry and undetected. I put my hand against the red wood, searching for something to climb.

There was nothing. The sides of the boat were smooth. Shadow moved farther across the docks, looking for a ladder.

Seda darted between the legs of a pirate. I froze. The pirate kicked at the kitten and kept working. Calling to him was not an option. How could I get his attention?

The sun rose above the horizon. It shone directly into the cave now. Seda darted along the floor, chasing light reflected off the pirates' swords.

I dug into my apron and pulled out the Rosas Rojas. It sparkled in the light, but it wasn't enough. I reached deeper and found the silver opera bracelets. The light gleamed off them. I put the rose away and moved myself under the dock to get the right angle. I pushed my arm through a space between the boards and found a sunbeam. Twisting the bracelet, I caught Seda's attention with the light and led him towards me. When he reached the edge, I grabbed him and pulled him under the dock.

He purred as if the whole thing had been his idea.

I slipped the bracelets onto my wrist so I could hold him better. Shadow climbed over to my side of the dock.

"There are no ropes," he said. "The only way on board is up the gangplank."

We would never make it up the gangplank. Pirates swarmed both the deck and the cave.

But maybe there was another way.

I looked at the bracelets. They had failed at the opera but worked at the Salara Museum. If they failed now it would mean disaster.

I handed Seda to Shadow and put a bracelet on each wrist.

"What are you doing?" he whispered.

I held a finger to my lips and stepped backwards off the dock.

My foot landed on something invisible and solid. I set the other foot down and let go of the wooden beam.

The platform remained solid. I stood in midair.

Shadow's eyes grew wide.

"Wait here," I said.

How long did I have before I fell into the sea? It was impossible to know. I walked around the ship until I was out of the pirate's view, ducking beneath port holes and openings for canons. At the front of the ship, I walked backwards up invisible stairs until I reached the deck.

Then I put the bracelets in my apron and found a rope behind a barrel.

I had not considered how difficult it would be for Shadow to climb the rope while holding Seda. He tucked the kitten under his arm long enough to climb aboard. I pulled Shadow up and grabbed Seda. He squirmed, and I scratched under his chin.

Shadow motioned to a structure across the deck: the captain's cabin. We worked our way towards it, ducking behind barrels and chests. The pirates were busy taking cargo from the hold and didn't see us.

I heard two voices inside, but couldn't make out words. The cabin had a window looking over the front of the ship. We climbed along the railing until we reached it and looked inside.

Estrella sat in a chair, her arms and legs tied down. The Dragon stooped with his back to us, rummaging through a chest. His bright red hair flickered like fire.

Not her father then. At least, he looked too young from the back.

Seda meowed when he saw Estrella. She looked at us and shook her head. The Dragon pulled something from the chest and stood. Shadow and I ducked.

"Just tell me where he is," the Dragon said. "You've chosen me over him before."

Estrella's reply was muffled. I only caught one word.

"Father."

The Dragon laughed.

I looked at Shadow. How were we going to get her out? He shook his head.

Something in the cabin clicked. Estrella's voice rose as she spoke. She sounded short of breath.

"Really, the owl eyes? Are you that desperate?"

"The sun is rising. Don't underestimate this curse."

Estrella gasped.

I raised my head and saw a thin trail of blood along her arm. The Dragon, his back turned to me, held a sword.

"Especially if it is permanent," he said. "You've never been able to heal this one, have you? Maybe it will be different if you're trying to heal yourself."

Shadow crawled towards the door. I followed him. The pirates remained focused on their tasks. We opened the door and rushed inside. Shadow turned the key and pulled it out of the door, locking us in.

And the pirate crew out.

"Stop," he said.

The Dragon didn't turn around, but he pulled the black charm back from the cut on Estrella's arm.

"Or what?"

It wasn't a threat. He just sounded curious.

"I'll burn your ship down."

Shadow pulled the candle from his pack and tapped it against the wall. It lit.

"Always so dramatic, Shadow."

The Dragon turned to us.

My arms went limp when I saw his face. Seda wriggled free, ran to the window, and climbed the curtains.

Sir Gilbert.

It was impossible. Shadow gestured to me, but I paid no attention. I stared at the pirate.

His hair was wrong, red and flickering like fire. But everything else was just as I remembered.

Sir Gilbert was the Dragon.

He ignored me, all his attention focused on Shadow.

"Nice of you to come, Shadow. Estrella was being stubborn as usual."

"What do you want?"

"You robbed the palace recently, yes?"

Shadow nodded. I snapped out of my stupor long

enough to realize I could do some good while they chatted. I edged around the room to Estrella and started working the knots loose.

"And you stopped by Salara's room?" the Dragon said.

"Get to the point."

"I would have asked Estrella and saved us all some trouble, but apparently she abandoned you again for that mission. Rumor has it the Princess is not well. She hides her face. She rarely leaves her room. Darker rumors say the Princess is not there at all."

I dropped the ropes and stared at Sir Gilbert. Estrella hissed at me, and I resumed my work.

"Of course she's there," Shadow said. "I saw her."

"No offense, but your eyes aren't-"

"Rook saw her, and her vision is perfect."

Sir Gilbert glanced my direction and shrugged.

"Another girlfriend, Shadow?"

Another?

"My turn for questions," Shadow said. "Why the piracy? Why steal the fairy salt?"

"Really, it should be clicking for you by now. I'm a hero for negotiating the colonial treaty. Salaria is in trouble unless the salt shipments make it to Castana. If the person who negotiated the treaty, delivered the salt, and stopped the Dragon also happened to be a favorite of Princess Salara, well, anything could happen."

"You want to be King," I said.

He shrugged.

"Everyone wants to be King. I want the Princess."

"I don't want either," Shadow said.

"Well, you always were stupid."

Sir Gilbert raised his sword. Shadow rummaged in his pack and found his knife.

I untied a last knot and freed Estrella's right hand. She fumbled with the ropes on her left hand while I untied her feet.

Across the room, Sir Gilbert lunged. Shadow deflected the sword with his knife and jumped backwards. Shadow was faster, but Sir Gilbert had a longer blade and more training. He sliced Shadow's shoulder, and blood seeped into his shirt. Shadow pushed him off balance and cut across his chest. Sir Gilbert laughed and pulled off his jacket. The blade had not pierced his skin. He tossed the jacket away and continued to fight in a loose shirt with a deep neckline.

I looked closer at his shirt and gasped. Around his neck hung a familiar teardrop shaped charm, although it was red and mine was blue. I gripped the chain around my neck.

Sir Gilbert swung for Shadow's head. Shadow dodged, but the blade cut his cheek.

"Stop!" I yelled.

They ignored me. Shadow dove under the sword and sliced Sir Gilbert's leg.

"This fight has been a long time coming," Estrella said. "You won't stop it that easily."

Well, there were other ways.

I took a deep breath and sang. The music echoed through the room.

"Stop that!" Sir Gilbert cried.

Their blows slowed. They blinked often, trying to stay focused on each other.

I filled my voice with enchantment, singing of peace and stillness.

"What are you doing?" Estrella hissed. "For someone who insists she doesn't know magic, you've got a lot of tricks up your sleeve."

Both men stared at me. They stood across the cabin from each other, dripping sweat and blood.

"This has gone on long enough, Sir Gilbert," I said.

"Hush, wench."

"We've met before, Sir Gilbert. Don't you recognize me?"

He stared at me. Something crossed his face. Recognition? Fear?

Shadow prepared to lunge at the pirate while he was distracted.

"Help Estrella," I said. "I'll handle this."

Shadow's gaze moved from me to Sir Gilbert and back again.

"Trust me," I whispered, as much to Sir Gilbert as to Shadow.

Shadow ran to Estrella and cut through the last of the ropes.

Sir Gilbert lowered his sword and took a step towards me. I walked to him, hands outstretched.

The Dragon. Sir Gilbert. Which one was real? I couldn't even answer that question about Rook and Salara. Maybe a combination of both. Our eyes met. I heard his sharp intake of breath. We stared at each other, our eyes darting around to note every detail before meeting in the middle.

With the snarl gone from his face, he looked handsome again. His cheeks were smooth, and his eyes dark as if he had not slept well for weeks.

"You," he whispered finally.

I offered him my hand. He took it and kissed it.

"I've been looking for you," I said.

He pulled me close. I reached around his neck, standing on my tiptoes to reach. His arms wrapped around my waist. I ran my fingers through his hair, down his neck, searching.

"You cut your hair," he said.

"It will grow back."

If this didn't work, I was really in trouble.

I found the chain and snapped it open. I pulled his hair charm off and threw it across the room. Estrella caught it and stuffed it in her bag. Sir Gilbert's grip on me tightened.

Hair exploded from his head, making up for years of growth in a few moments. The mass of beard shooting from his chin tangled around me.

The beard grew heavier and heavier until Sir Gilbert lost his grip on my waist. I fell and crawled through the mass of hair towards the door. The Dragon roared with rage. Shadow unlocked the door and grabbed my hand, pulling me forward. We stood for a moment, watching the cabin fill with hair. Shadow cut the hair tangled around my legs with his dagger, pulled me out the door and slammed it shut before the hair could follow.

The pirates, still dressed as naval officers, stopped their chores and stared at us. Their knives gleamed in the now-risen sun. Shadow brushed his hair over his eyes.

At some point, we had set sail. The open sea surrounded us, and the Weeping Mountains grew smaller and smaller on the horizon. Waves churned beneath us.

Sir Gilbert's muffled voice emerged from the cabin. The pirates scowled and moved towards us. They formed a line of knives and leers, trapping us against the ship's railing.

24

"Grab my hands," I said.

"What?" Shadow and Estrella said together.

"Just do it!"

I slipped a bracelet onto each wrist. Shadow understood and pushed Estrella's hand into mine. He grabbed my other hand and squeezed it.

"Step backwards."

"What are you doing?" Estrella asked.

The pirates lunged towards us. I took several steps backwards. Shadow and Estrella walked with me. We floated above the ocean.

A pirate threw his knife at us. It sliced Shadow's calf near his ankle.

"Faster," he hissed.

We turned and ran forward. Shadow leaned on me, limping more and more. His injury slowed us, but at least the Dragon's ship was sailing towards the open sea. The pirates scrambled to reverse course, but it would take time to turn the ship. Blood dripped from Shadow's wound and pooled on an invisible platform in the air.

We hobbled towards the shore.

Boom! Something flew past our heads. The splash drenched us.

"What was that?" I asked.

"Cannonball!" Estrella said.

Behind us, the ship turned.

We could not run. We couldn't even walk fast.

Shadow closed his eyes. The sun shone bright in the sky, making us easy targets.

"They're sailing against the tide, but they'll be faster than us," Shadow said. "If you let me drop into the ocean, you can-"

"Don't be ridiculous," Estrella said.

She snapped her fingers, and the sea below us churned. The crystal around her neck glowed silver. Waves capped with white foam assaulted the ship and circled around it. The ship turned as the whirlpool caught it. The water glowed green. Estrella waved her hands to finish the charm. The Dragon's ship spun in the sea while we walked through the air back to the caves.

"We need to talk about your voice," Estrella said. "Have you trained in magical music? That was a strong charm."

"You just created a whirlpool!"

"I never claimed to have no training."

She smiled at me. Shadow stayed silent. He kept his eyes closed until we arrived in the underground harbor. Estrella lit a single star, and we collapsed in the tunnel. I slipped off the bracelets and slid them into my bag.

"Can you heal my leg before we go on?" Shadow said. "They'll come after us as soon as the seas calm."

"That might take a while," Estrella said.

She examined the wound.

"It isn't bad. Just a deep cut."

She held her hand over Shadow's calf.

A red light flickered for a moment, then the cave went black.

"What was that?" I asked.

"Apparently it takes more magic to move the ocean than I thought. I'm out."

"But you said the crystal had enough power to-"

"It's empty. I am sorry, Shadow."

I heard a tapping sound, and a faint flame illuminated the cavern. Shadow's grimace flickered in the candle light.

"If you can bandage it, that will be enough."

Estrella nodded and pulled clean white bandages from her apron. She put a few drops of something on them and cleaned the wound. Then she stopped.

"Where's Seda?"

I stared at her, horrified.

"He must have been buried in the hair," I whispered.

"We have to go back," Estrella said. "We have to save him."

"We can't," Shadow said.

"Shadow, he's all I have left! My mother-"

"They'll be on the alert now, and we're in no shape to battle anyone."

"What kind of idiot brings a kitten to storm a pirate ship?"

"We didn't know we would be facing pirates when we left," I said.

"I tied him up for a reason," Estrella said.

A few tears ran down her face, but her expression was hard.

"Give me the bracelets," she said. "I have to go back for him."

"No," Shadow said. "You're weak."

"I am not weak!"

"I meant you're hurt. You need time to recover from your encounter with the Dragon."

"It's not bad."

"You were limping," I said.

"It will heal."

"But not fast," I said. "And you're out of power. I want to rescue Seda just as much as you do."

"Obviously not!"

Shadow put his hand on Estrella's shoulder.

"We can't go back," he said. "Not now."

She glared at both of us and stood. Shadow handed her the candle. Estrella walked away, leaving us in the dark.

"You don't think she'll try?"

"She knows it would be pointless."

"So now what?"

Shadow stood and took my hand. He pulled me to my feet and tucked my arm in his.

He leaned on me, limping. I kept my eyes closed, which seemed less disturbing than staring into eternal darkness.

"You're sure you can see?"

He laughed.

"It isn't funny. I can't see my own hand in front of my face. Is your leg alright?"

"It will probably leave another scar."

We made slow progress through the tunnels, but Shadow limped with certainty.

"What would you do if you were King?" I asked.

"What?"

"You told Sir Gilbert you don't want to be King. Why not? You're always helping people."

"There is much a King cannot do. Too many forces pushing against him."

"And you don't want the Princess?"

He laughed.

"Why would I want her? She has caused me nothing but pain."

He squeezed my hand. I did not feel reassured.

William and Roslynn greeted us when we reached the

cavern. Estrella lay on her bed in the next room.

"What happened?" William said. "Estrella wouldn't say a word to us."

"We met the Dragon," I said.

Roslynn shuddered.

"We need to move deeper into the mines," Shadow said. "He might come looking for us."

"They have the owl eyes. They can follow us," Roslynn said.

"Not if we're careful."

Shadow picked up one of the baskets of silk.

"What about the rendezvous with Captain?" I asked.

"No good," Estrella said from the other room. "Apparently that port is Dragon territory."

"So we'll change the location," Shadow said.

Estrella entered the room and crossed her arms.

"You'll have to deliver the message in person. Unless Rook knows how to work enchanted parchment."

Everyone looked at me. I shook my head.

"What about your super special crystal?" William said. "You know the one you abandoned us to earn?"

"Shut up, William."

"Just saying."

"There's a mine tunnel near the cove," Shadow said. "We'll contact Captain from there with a new location."

William combed his fingers through his hair.

"We'll have to split up."

Shadow nodded.

"Rook and I will send a message to Captain. You, Estrella, and Roslynn will move the treasure."

"That's not fair, Shadow," Estrella protested. "Captain is my contact. He'll be expecting to see me."

"You're injured."

"Why not just say I'm useless? I saved us back there!"

"I can't walk without leaning on someone. Two

injured people would make an easy target if the pirates are in the mines. And you still need to look through what we stole to make sure Captain gives us a fair price."

Estrella blinked tears from her eyes and muttered in Castanian.

We packed up camp. Shadow and I each carried a small bag of jewels to prove to Captain that we had the goods. William, Roslynn, and Estrella picked up the rest of the baskets.

Shadow took my hand and blew out the candles. Cloth rustled in the darkness as Roslynn removed her bandages.

"Be careful," Shadow said. "Roslynn should have no trouble finding her way without a candle."

I held his hand and followed him. The others' footprints echoed through the caverns, fading into silence.

My eyes never adjusted. I waved my hand in front of my face with my eyes open and shut. No difference. We walked on. Shadow stumbled on something, and I steadied him.

"So," I said after walking in silence for some time, "Sir Gilbert is the Dragon."

Shadow laughed, but didn't sound amused.

"He was our neighbor, growing up. Estrella and I used to call him Dragon, but I never thought. I should have realized who he was."

"Because of his red hair?"

"Yes. It wasn't always red. His mother hired Madame Delilah to dye his hair blond so he could be a companion to the Princess. The spell went wrong."

"And they couldn't fix it?"

"Estrella's mother tried. She said it was one of the worst loop spells she had ever seen and made him the wig charm instead. I expect he's been wearing it ever since."

"It seems silly, using a soul loop spell to change

someone's hair color."

I felt Shadow shrug.

I could not say when it became light enough to see the outline of my hand and crevices in the floor, but at some point I realized it had. The dim light outlined Shadow's face when he leaned against the wall to catch his breath.

"Will the others be alright?" I asked.

"I expect so. Roslynn can see better underground than I can right now."

"Are we going to the Dragon's cavern again?"

"To the side of it. I'm hoping we get Captain's attention before he sails into the cove."

Beams of sunlight filtered through the opening. Shadow sat, and I knelt beside him.

"Captain won't be here until dark."

He pulled dried meat out of his pack and handed me a piece. I chewed it.

"Are you worried?" I asked between bites.

"About what?"

"Everything. The salt tax. The Dragon."

The future.

He grinned at me. My heart beat faster.

"You beat him in a fair fight."

"I'm not sure I'd call that playing fair."

"Either way, you beat him, and he won't forget. He might come for you."

"For all of us."

"I'll do my best to protect you."

He spread his hand out, and I did the same. Palm to palm, I felt every scar. My hands were still smooth, but my nails were chipped and had dirt under them. I had a few scratches.

"You hate nobility," I said. "But you keep saving me. Why?"

"Does it matter?"

"Yes."

I examined his eyes. Light gray with a hint of blue circled around his shining, too large pupils. He gazed into mine. What did he see? I had seen hundreds of paintings of myself, and none of them looked like the girl I saw in mirrors.

"You're different," he said. "You think about things. You care."

"I'm not sure I am. I just wanted an adventure."

"You're not telling me you ran away to have fun?"

I laughed.

"It might seem ridiculous, but I've had more fun in a few days out here with you than I have in a lifetime in the palace."

"Just wait for winter then. Snow and cold, famine, winter parties to raid. The Fairy Snow Festival at the Salara Museum is not to be missed. They use diamonds to decorate everything. We got a few bags full last winter."

"You would let me stay that long?"

"Do you want to stay that long?"

I did. Sitting here with him, I wanted to stay forever.

Shadow leaned closer. Before I could think how to respond, he kissed me.

That brought me back to reality. I jumped back. His eyes grew even wider.

"Rook, I-"

"No, it isn't-"

"I just thought-"

"I know. But-"

What could I say? It couldn't be explained now. Maybe not ever.

We sat in silence while the golden light faded to red. I had so many things I wanted to tell him, but I couldn't.

Why would he want the Princess? She had caused him nothing but pain.

He didn't want me. And the worst part was, he thought he did. He thought he knew me.

"We should go now."

Shadow avoided my gaze, but offered me his hand. We rounded the corner and stepped onto a moonlit beach. Silver waves lapped the shore. Captain's ship sailed around a bend, coming toward us.

"How do we signal him?" I asked.

Shadow pulled three yellow flags with black stripes from his pack.

"Nautical flags. Used for signaling supply ships for the mines."

"What do they mean?"

He shrugged.

"I think it depends on what order you put them in."

"So how do we tell him to meet us somewhere else?"

"All we need to do is catch his attention. He can send someone in a life boat to talk with us."

"But how-"

"His spyglass is strong enough for him to watch Princess Salara eat breakfast while he's sailing the open seas. He'll see us."

I shuddered and helped Shadow set up the signal flags.

Another ship sailed around the corner. It cast a blood red reflection on the waves and flew a Salarian Navy flag.

"The Dragon," I whispered.

Captain's sails hung limp in the windless night. The Dragon's ship sailed across the sea, gaining on it. There was a flash of light, and the sound of canon fire echoed against the mountains and through the tunnels.

"He's been hit!"

Shadow pulled down the flags and stuffed them into his bag. We stood on the beach watching, helpless.

Sir Gilbert's ship drew alongside Captain's. At this distance, I couldn't tell who belonged to which crew. All I saw was motion. Men running on the decks of both ships. The glint of swords. Captain's ship tilted to one side and began to sink.

"Come on."

Shadow pulled on my arm, leading me back to the mine.

"What about Captain?"

I pulled out the bracelets. Shadow shook his head.

"We can't help him now."

A red glow illuminated the water as Captain's ship burned. The mast crashed into the ocean. Bits of the sail caught the wind and flew through the air like flaming birds.

"He'll be a hero," Shadow said. "Destroying a pirate ship this close to Salaria."

We descended the tunnel into darkness. Shadow's hand trembled as he led me through the mines. We walked in silence for a long time, crossing underneath the mountain.

I tried to keep track of the twisting pathways, but the only direction I could sense was the downward slope of the floor. How deep did the mines go? Shadow stopped and squeezed my hand.

Three taps echoed through the cavern. Estrella's face appeared above a flickering blue candle.

"What happened?"

"Why are you sitting in the dark?" I asked.

"Keeping watch. No one has come through. It looks like the Dragon has other things to do."

"Like torching Captain's ship."

I said it without thinking. Estrella clapped her hand over her mouth.

"Is Captain alright? Did they see you?"

"They set his ship on fire," Shadow said. "It sank. There was nothing we could do."

Tears glistened in Estrella's eyes. She led us deeper into the cave to a small room covered with badly done paintings. I stared at the faces for a moment, then realized what they were and turned away.

Salara portraits.

Was this where Mother sent the truly terrible artists? Deep into the mines?

Roslynn had removed her blindfold, although she kept her eyes closed in the candlelight.

"Captain is gone," Shadow said.

"The flags didn't work?" Roslynn asked.

"The Dragon attacked his ship," I said. "He's gone."

"Oh."

Roslynn wiped a tear from her closed eyes.

"So what do we do with this?" William gestured to the baskets of silk and jewels. In this setting, they seemed worthless.

"We can sell them locally," Roslynn said. "Salarian nobles won't dare to wear them in public, but they might still buy them."

"The opera dress is too distinctive," I said. "No one would risk having that in their home."

"It will take too long," Shadow said. "Half the country will be in the mines by then."

"Let's go after the Dragon," Estrella said. "We can expose him to the King and collect the reward."

"They won't believe us," I said. "To them, Sir Gilbert is a hero."

"And he's destroyed a pirate right off the coast," Shadow said. "His reputation will only grow."

"We should have ransomed the cat," William muttered.

Estrella glared at him.

"We could contact Lady Alma," I said. "She won't be happy to be missing all her supplies. We could ransom the silks and jewels back to her."

"Are you insane?" William asked.

"That's risky, but it might work," Estrella said. "With the Dragon raiding ships, she can't be certain when she'll get more supplies."

"Won't she just recycle some old outfits?" William asked.

Estrella raised an eyebrow. I shook my head.

"Never," Estrella said.

"She'd rather die," I said.

"We'll decide tomorrow," Shadow said. "Right now, everyone needs sleep."

Estrella volunteered to take the first watch.

Whatever beds the miners in this part of the cavern had used were long gone. I leaned against the smoothest rock wall I could find. Estrella blew out her candle, and I stared into the dark.

Would any of the nobility believe Sir Gilbert was the Dragon? I had seen it, and I hardly believed it. Maybe if we removed his wig and showed them his fiery red hair.

But what would that prove? Only that he was the recipient of an irresponsible spell.

I felt my way along the edge of the cavern and crawled. I had too many questions to sleep.

"Estrella?" I whispered.

"What?"

She tapped the candle so I could see well enough to crawl and sit beside her and then extinguished it. The darkness made me more aware of sounds. I listened to everyone breathing.

"Tell me about the Dragon. How-"

"I really don't want to talk about him right now."

"Please? Shadow mentioned you knew him as a child."

She sighed.

"He was my neighbor. And my friend. My fiancé for a

while."

I blinked.

"What?"

"We were young, but it was a good match. Especially for him. And I loved him. I stayed in Salaria with him when my mother left for Castana."

"Why didn't it work out?"

"Once his father was appointed Governor of New Salaria, he didn't need me anymore. What support could I offer? They left for the islands, and I was trapped in Salaria, penniless. Practically an orphan. Captain and Joe helped me find work as a healer on the docks. And when Shadow reappeared, well, I would have followed him anywhere."

She broke off with a sob.

"I'm sorry," I said. "It's just- I met Sir Gilbert at the palace before I left. I'm just trying to understand."

"He is the same as his father. Willing to do anything to get what he wants."

"His father has the islands. He's a Duke now."

"And Gilbert wants Salara. I used to tell him stories about her when I was her companion. He always loved the idea. An enchanted princess and a dragon, falling in love."

25

I dreamed of a dragon with green eyes and blond hair.

"Let me explain," he said. "Give me a chance to explain, Salara."

His voice was a growl. I understood his meaning in the way of dreams, not through individual words.

"You're a traitor," I said. "You're a monster."

"Because I killed a pirate? I'm a hero for that. He has terrorized the seas for years. Where are you? Let me help you."

He reached for me with his claws. As he got nearer, his claws turned back into hands. If I reached for him, if I touched him, he would find me. I pulled my hands back, and he dissolved into smoke.

I opened my eyes and saw nothing but darkness.

Did the sun rise that morning? It was impossible to tell in the mines. The entire right side of my body, where I had leaned against the rocks, felt bruised when I woke up. I felt around the cave until I found a mining candle and tapped it against the floor. Staring at the hideous Salara portraits in the flickering light did nothing to improve my mood.

Across the room, Estrella yawned.

"These candles give me a headache," she said.

"Morning already?" Roslynn said.

She didn't open her eyes.

"Breakfast anyone?"

William came in with a fistful of dried meat. Shadow followed him with two buckets of water.

"I'm not sure how much more of this my jaw can take," I said.

William laughed as I struggled to tear off a piece of the leathery substance.

"Be glad Shadow found that," Estrella said. "Without food, we wouldn't be able to stay hidden so long."

"We can't stay much longer," Shadow said. "How do we contact Lady Alma?"

Everyone turned to Estrella.

"I don't have any magic left," she said. "I can't even make stars right now!"

"What about soul magic?" I asked. "I could help. You could-"

"Soul magic has limits as well, and mine have been reached. If I try another spell I'll faint. And since you keep insisting you don't know magic, I can't count on you to revive me."

She crossed her arms and glared at me.

"Can we make a charm out of the salt in the mines?" Roslynn asked.

Shadow shook his head. "These have gone dark. There's no magic left."

"We could sneak into the palace again," I said. "We could leave a message for her."

"We were almost caught last time," Shadow said. "It would be very risky to break in again so soon."

"If we could make it in at all," William said.

"We could send a message to Edsel," I said.

"We can't trust him now," Estrella said. "He'll be looking to increase his position in the palace any way he can. He'd betray us in a heartbeat."

"Ok," Roslynn said. "What did you bring with you? What are our resources?"

Shadow pulled his dagger, several mining candles, and a Salara egg out of his pack.

"That's disgusting," Estrella said.

"I forgot it was there."

"I'm surprised it doesn't stink by now," I said.

William tossed the egg against the wall. A rotten smell filled the room.

"Great!" Estrella said. "Just great!"

She pulled a pen, parchment, and a few bottles of potions from a pocket in her skirt.

I put my silver bracelets and healing charm on the cave floor. My hand caught something else in my apron pocket, and I pulled out the Rosas Rojas. I put it to my nose to mask the smell of the egg. It smelled like a rose, then the smell shifted to perfumed wig powder. I jerked it back and stared at it.

The movement brought the flower into the candlelight. Glimmers of red and green reflected onto the cavern wall.

Everyone stared. Estrella's mouth hung open.

"Is that a Rosas Rojas?"

"Yes," I said slowly.

"A real one?"

"I think so."

She reached her hand out and stroked a petal.

"The souls of a hundred roses," she whispered. "My mother brought one of these when she left Castana."

"Great," William said. "We have roses, silk and jewels. Let's forget saving the kingdom and throw a garden party."

"As if anyone would invite you to a garden party," Estrella said. "The Rosas Rojas is a symbol of romance.

Castanian noblemen give them-"

"To the girl they like best," I finished.

"So how did you get it?" Roslynn asked.

"I took it from Lady Alma's studio."

That was the truth. At least, part of it.

"This is wonderful!" Estrella said. "A magical object that belonged to Lady Alma! I might be able to use it to reach her."

She reached for the rose. I pulled it away from her.

"I thought you couldn't work spells right now."

"That has a lot of power stored in it. I won't be working a spell. Just activating it."

I pinched the stem. The rose glowed.

"It does much more than that," Estrella said. "These aren't just given away because they're pretty. Mother used hers to communicate with friends back in Castana."

Reluctantly, I handed her the rose.

"I need quiet."

She held the flower to her nose.

"And fresh air."

She left the cavern. The rotten egg smell grew worse by the second.

"We should move the silks," Shadow said. "They'll be hard to sell if they absorb this smell."

We each grabbed a load. I couldn't carry the candle and the basket. I blew it out and walked with my shoulder against Shadow so I wouldn't get lost. We had to walk a long way down the tunnel to get away from the smell.

"If Estrella's plan works, we may need to get to Castlemont quickly," Shadow said. "William, you and Roslynn see if you can find a path to the Ghone."

"Sure thing."

They didn't light a candle. Roslynn took William's hand, and they disappeared into the darkness.

"Want to take a walk?" Shadow said

I nodded. I suppose he saw me in the dark. He took my hand and led me down the tunnels. After a while, he tapped his candle. The flame reflected off the floor but did not reach the ceiling.

"It's a shame I can't make stars," he said.

"I can't work magic at all."

It took me a moment to realize where we were. The lake reflected the cavernous ceiling, making it look like a pit in the ground. Our voices echoed in the open space.

We sat by the shore. I wanted to take my shoes off and dip my feet in, but decided not to disturb the dark water.

"Rook, about yesterday."

"We did everything we could, Shadow. There was no way for us to know the Dragon would attack Captain. We couldn't have saved him."

"I meant about what I, um, did."

Right. The kiss.

My cheeks flushed.

"I meant it," he said. "I like you. I know this is terrible timing. We might be swept away by pirates or soldiers or a famine. We might not make it out of this mountain alive. But I wanted you to know."

I should tell him the truth.

I couldn't tell him.

And really, did I have to? Why couldn't I be Rook forever? Elsie could be Princess Salara. She'd love that. It had worked so far.

Everyone would win.

My face flickered in Shadow's eyes. I leaned forward and kissed his cheek.

"I like you too."

He turned his head to look at me, and I kissed him on the lips. My heart pounded. What was I thinking? What would he-

Shadow wrapped an arm around me and pulled me closer.

"Shad- oh."

Estrella kicked a rock as she walked toward us. It fell into the lake, and the smooth surface erupted into ripples. The splash echoed in the cavern.

She stared at us. Her face hardened into a mask.

"Sorry," she said after a moment.

She didn't sound sorry. Her right hand clenched the Rosas Rojas with enough force to crush a normal rose.

"Did it work?" Shadow asked. "Can we use it?"

He leaned away from me but slipped his hand over mine.

"No. There's a trace of Lady Alma's magic here, but only a faint one. This never belonged to her."

"Then who?" Shadow asked.

"Salara."

His grip tightened on my hand.

"The Princess could use it. Or we could contact her through it. But it won't get us to Lady Alma."

I bit my lip.

"We'll think of something else," I said.

"We're running out of time," Estrella said. "Gerta's well might have failed by now, and I don't have any magic left. We don't have money for food or the salt tax."

She raised her hand to throw the Rosas Rojas into the lake.

"Don't!"

I stood and grabbed it from her.

"It's useless, Rook!"

I tucked it into my apron pocket.

"You never know when we'll need to throw a garden party."

Thankfully, the new cavern did not have Salara portraits. When we returned, I leaned against a basket of silks in a corner and stroked the Rosas Rojas. It smelled more like wig powder than rose now. What had Estrella done to it? Shadow and Estrella discussed possible strategies until William and Roslynn returned.

"We found a path to the Ghone," Roslynn said. "And the Dragon's store rooms."

She and William held up leather bags.

"Gold?" Estrella asked.

"Dried meat," William said. "But it is a few years fresher than what we have."

"And there are crates with the royal crest on them. We'd need a tool to open them. They were sealed."

"There's not much there," William said. "It looks like they cleared most of it out a while ago."

"Were you able to contact Lady Alma?" Roslynn asked.

"No luck," Estrella said.

"We can't just sit here," William said.

"We have contacts," Roslynn said. "You've sold directly to Salarian nobles before."

"Elsie and Edsel always set that up," Shadow said.

"What about you, Rook?" Roslynn said. "Surely you have friends you can contact."

"Maybe, but they're all in the palace."

"So we go back to Castlemont," Shadow said.

He said it slowly. Deliberately.

"You said that was a bad idea," I said. "That it was too dangerous."

"They'll be expecting us now," Estrella said. "At the least they'll have set up extra guards."

"We're out of options. We'll go further into the palace. Steal gold coins directly so we don't have to worry about selling anything."

"You want to rob the treasury? Without magic? Are you insane?"

"We don't have a choice," Shadow said. "This goes beyond saving people from the mines. You can survive the mines. But you can't survive without water. And if enough fields are ruined, there will be a famine. Merchants will import food, but it will be expensive. We need gold."

"I don't know a thing about the treasury," I said. "I can't help with this."

"Shadow, this is dangerous," Roslynn said. "You could be killed. It would be better to wait. We will find someone to buy all this."

"You're not responsible for the kingdom," Estrella said.

Shadow's eyes narrowed.

"After I escaped from prison, after my father died, there was no one to look after my sister. My mother was ill. They starved because no one was responsible. Don't tell me not to help people. Don't ever tell me to look away."

We sat in stunned silence. Shadow stared at each of us.

"I'll come with you," I said finally. "I'll do what I can."

Estrella shrugged, her eyes filled with tears she refused to cry.

"If that's how it has to be," she said. "Let's go tonight."

William shook his head.

"Roslynn is in no condition to raid the castle, and I'm not leaving her."

"We'll need your help, William," Shadow said.

"I won't throw away my life. Not when she needs me."

"We can contact nobles," Roslynn said. "Some of Gerta's orphans work for them. We'll find someone to buy this."

She gestured to the baskets.

Shadow nodded.

"Go then. Try to find exits close to nobles' houses. I'll scout the tunnels and find the quickest way back to the palace."

He left. I stood to go with him, but Estrella grabbed my arm.

"I didn't know," she said. "It was a long time ago, and I didn't know his family was in trouble. I would have helped them."

The tears in her eyes finally spilled over and ran down her cheeks. William and Roslynn slipped out of the room.

"He knows that," I said.

"Does he? Because we used to be close. We used to-"

She choked on a sob.

"He can't forgive himself. He won't forgive me. You think you know him. You think you know what you're doing. But you have no idea."

"And you do?"

She laughed through her tears but didn't smile.

"I'm going to get some water."

She took the candle with her when she left. I reached in my apron, but I had left my candle in the room with portraits. I crawled around the floor, searching for a light.

Nothing.

I fought back panic. I was trapped in the dark. How long would it take them to come back? If I tried to find them, there was no telling where I would end up. Roslynn had fallen in the river, and she had owl eyes. I found a basket and leaned against it.

I thought about Shadow. The kiss. It made me smile in spite of everything. He liked Rook, so I would be Rook forever.

It was that simple.

Elsie knew more about Salara than anyone. She had already impersonated me for days without a problem.

Father could arrange her marriage to a responsible younger son from a neighboring kingdom who would rule Salaria well. They didn't need me.

Shadow did.

26

I drifted to sleep thinking of the palace. Where was the treasury? Probably underground. There were rooms in the heart of the mountain. What hallways led to them?

In my dream, I stood in Lady Alma's studio.

"Princess Salara!" she said.

I stepped onto the pedestal and stretched out my arms. In the mirrors, I saw my hair was still short. Lady Alma waved her hands and blue fabric flew around me, replacing my peasant clothes.

"The salt curse has spread," she said in the same airy tone she always used for court gossip. "The year's crops have been destroyed. Everyone is eating their winter stores now. There won't be anything left when the frost hits. And Castana is threatening war unless they get their shipment of fairy salt. We'll have to send hundreds to the mines to get enough. The Dragon captured our last shipment yesterday. He sank it to the bottom of the ocean."

"Sir Gilbert is the Dragon," I said.

"Of course he is. I recognized the spells on his ship the moment he arrived. I tried to warn you about him, but you were quite smitten. Still, his Rosas Rojas came in handy. Clever girl, finding it where I left it for you."

Another voice, muffled behind a door, whispered, "Ask about their plans."

"In time," Lady Alma said. "All in good time."

"We're going to rob the treasury," I said. "Get enough gold to pay the salt taxes and buy food for the kingdom."

Lady Alma laughed.

"You overestimate the depths of the King's purse, and they've doubled the city guard since Castana threatened war."

"You're Castanian. Do something."

"You're the Princess. You do something."

"I'm trying! But everything is going wrong!"

The door opened, and Madame Delilah stepped through. Lady Alma frowned.

"We agreed you would stay behind the door."

"Well, you're making a terrible mess of this! She won't sleep forever, and you haven't told her what to do yet."

"Oh, that won't do any good. She never listens."

Lady Alma winked at me.

"This is serious!" I said. "Elsie is the Princess now. She can do something!"

"That charade can't continue much longer," Madame Delilah said. "At this point, a marriage treaty may be the only way to save Salaria. And to do that, they need you. More soldiers left this morning. They're searching the whole country. And someone started a rumor the Shadow has you in the mines."

I stared at my feet in the mirror. My peasant boots looked strange with the blue silk dress.

"Are you really in the mines?" Lady Alma said. "I can't think of a better place to keep your skin protected. You'll look perfect for the wedding."

"I'm not the Princess anymore! I'm not Salara!"

"You're fairy blessed, dear," Lady Alma said. "You can't easily escape that. Being a princess is tied to the deepest part of your soul."

"Watch what you say!" Madame Delilah said.

Lady Alma laughed.

"You're the one who wanted to tell her what to do."

Madame Delilah grabbed my shoulder and shook me.

"Wake up!" she said. "Wake up!"

Lady Alma's studio, the two women, and my blue gown faded. Madame Delilah's grip on my shoulder did not.

"Wake up," another voice said.

I opened my eyes and saw Shadow smiling at me.

"Ready to rob the King?" he said.

I gulped.

"Hey, we'll be alright," he said. "Didn't I promise I'd protect you?"

He took my hand.

My other hand slid into my apron and brushed against the Rosas Rojas.

Did it truly allow communication? Or had it just been a wishful dream?

Estrella ran into the room. Thomas followed a few steps behind her. He grinned at me.

"Hey, angel."

"Thomas? What are you doing down here?"

"Sorry to interrupt," Estrella said, "but we have to move!"

"Soldiers are everywhere," Thomas said. "They're questioning the miners, and someone has been stealing food from them. They're about to start searching."

He glared at Shadow.

"They're on their way," Estrella said. "They'll be here any minute."

"Why would they come here?" I asked.

"We'll outrun them," Shadow said. "No one knows the mines like a miner."

"The city guard has doubled," I said.

They didn't ask how I knew.

"Good thing you have two feet then," Shadow said. "There will be twice as much guard kicking to do."

He winked at me, but his face was tense.

"Hey," Thomas said. "Are you flirting with my girl?"

Shadow stared at him for a moment.

"It isn't safe here, Thomas. Go back to Gerta's."

"So you can make eyes at Rook? No, I'm staying."

"You know the miners, right, Thomas?" I said.

He nodded.

"Could you work with them to delay the soldiers? Direct them away from us?"

Thomas kissed my hand.

"Anything for you, angel."

He ran into the darkness. Right, he would have Gerta's owl eyes charm.

"That was a good idea," Shadow said. "But we still need to hurry."

I stared at his hand holding mine. He had promised to protect me. He was willing to die to protect me.

What was I willing to do for him?

I shook my hand out of his grasp and stepped back.

"We don't have to rob the palace," I said. "We don't have to risk anyone's life."

Estrella scoffed.

"We've thought through this pretty thoroughly, Rook."

"My name's not Rook."

Shadow laughed.

"Of course it isn't. Come on, we need to go."

"Salara."

It cost me everything to say that word. My name.

They stared at me, confused.

"Princess Salara," I said.

Estrella gasped.

"William joked about ransoming Seda, but if we kidnapped Princess Salara-"

"And ransom her! Rook, you're a genius! We've been to her room. We could get in again."

"There will be guards now," Estrella said. "Surely there will be guards."

"So we'll deal with them. There will be guards at the treasury as well."

Shadow squeezed my hand. Estrella smiled.

"We can plan on the way to the palace," Estrella said. "They'd do anything to get her back. I'll pick up some herbs in the harbor to knock her out. How much do you think she weighs, Shadow?"

He laughed.

It was too much. Hope had flickered back into his face. I closed my eyes so I wouldn't have to see his reaction.

"I'm Princess Salara!"

They stopped laughing. My heartbeat pulsed through my entire body. I opened my eyes. Their smiles had not faded, not entirely. More than anything they looked confused.

"You don't look anything like her," Shadow said.

"A decoy isn't a bad idea," Estrella said, "but they'd never buy it."

"I am Princess Salara," I said again.

"We saw her in her room," Shadow said. "She's in the palace."

"We saw Elsie wearing a wig made with my hair."

I shook my head, and my short hair rustled around my face. I willed my voice to be charming and sang Divinia's blessing.

Dark as a rook's wing, hair flows like the Ghone.
Night prism eyes reflect colors unknown.

Moonlight complexion, pearly reflection.
By every standard, you are perfection.

Radiant voice like the song of a star.
Reddest of roses, loveliest by far.

I name thee Salara, Salarian princess,
Born to be queen of them all.

Ideals align, beauty be thine.
Names, souls, and destinies all intertwine.

In my apron, the Rosas Rojas glowed. I pulled it out, and it lit the entire room. The light caused my hair's dark prism of colors to reflect on the wall. I felt a tingle against my chest as the wig charm pulsed with power. My hair grew a few inches, causing even more colors to dance.

Shadow let his breath out in a long hiss. His expression was hard.

"I'll go stop Roslynn and William," Estrella said. "They won't need to contact the nobles now."

"This is impossible," Shadow said. "I've seen the Princess. You look nothing like her."

But he believed me. I could tell. He slid sideways, blocking the cavern entrance.

Blocking me in.

He stood for a while, just watching me. Checking every detail as if he was seeing me for the first time.

Or would never see me again.

"Why?" he said finally.

"Shadow-"

"Why?"

"I've already told you. I wanted to get out. Wanted to see things. To see what it would be like to be just myself."

"So it was a game? Like your picnic on Gerta's farm? Pretending summer was winter just because you could?"

"Shadow, I'm still Rook."

His shoulders shook. I couldn't tell if he was laughing or crying.

Or both.

"You were never Rook. She doesn't exist."

"Shadow, I told you to protect you! To keep you from storming the castle."

"Can't you see you've made everything worse? They won't stop until they've caught us. Even if we return you! Crimes against the Princess."

He laughed.

"I think kidnapping certainly qualifies as a crime against the Princess."

"So bring me back. Ransom me. Once I'm in the palace again, I can help. I got the Rosas Rojas to work. I talked to Lady Alma. The salt patches have spread. There isn't any food left to buy. The Dragon sunk our last salt ship. She said they'll need hundreds to work in the mines, regardless of the tax. And Castana is threatening war. Lady Alma thinks a marriage treaty may be the only way to avoid it."

He made a sort of choking sound.

"It will make a good story in court, won't it? How you won the bandit's heart? Tricked him into falling in love with you and saved the kingdom? I'm sure your future husband will laugh harder than anyone."

"Shadow, that isn't fair."

I blinked tears out of my eyes and stared at him. If he

could only understand!

Shadow pulled his knife out of his pack. I stepped back and inhaled sharply.

"Don't worry, Princess. Your blood isn't worth spilling."

He pulled a piece of silk out of the basket and cut it into strips.

"Sit down."

I sat.

He tied my hands and feet together with the silk.

"Only the finest," he said. "You can tell the court we treated you well."

"Shadow, I know you're upset. And I am sorry. But I'm still the same person."

"We'll need quiet since your guards are coming."

He cut another piece of silk and tied it around my mouth, gagging me. Then he pulled a handful of diamonds out of the opera hat and sprinkled them around me.

"All the comforts of home."

I glared at him.

"I've thought about this moment a lot," he said. "Planned what I would say if I ever got to confront Salara. I'd tell you about my father. About prison and the mines. I never planned to tell you about my mother and sister. They're too good for you. But you already know it all, so my speeches seem a bit silly. The worst part is you're not even worth hating."

His voice cracked.

"I've spent so many years blaming you. Waiting to tell you how I feel about you."

I wanted to tell him how much stories of him had frightened me when I lived in the castle. He had been a terror that kept me up at night. But those had just been stories. Someone else's version of him.

Just like Princess Salara was someone else's version of me.

The cavern brightened as William, Roslynn, and Estrella entered with their candles.

"This is a mistake," William said. "This is ridiculous."

Roslynn opened her eyes a moment to look at me, then shut them again. Estrella watched Shadow.

"What now?" she said.

"According to Princess Salara, she used the Rosas Rojas to talk to Lady Alma. We have to assume the soldiers know where we are."

"How dare you?" Estrella said. "We trusted you! Even I trusted you!"

"We'll transport the Princess back to the palace," Shadow said. "Lady Alma will be expecting us. Hopefully we can negotiate with her. If we can get to the Ghone, we should be able to avoid the soldiers."

"We do have an advantage," Roslynn said. She tapped her eyes.

"That isn't funny," William said. "You're supposed to be hoping the curse fades."

"It will fade. It is fading. That doesn't mean I can't use it in the meantime."

"We should split up," Estrella said. "William and Roslynn can scout ahead. I'll escort the prisoner. Shadow can guard the back."

Shadow shook his head.

"I'm injured. I won't be any good in a fight. Besides, the sea is our only hope of getting into Castlemont fast enough. You run ahead and find a boat we can use. Try to make contact with Lady Alma. She should be expecting us."

"But you need help guarding her. You shouldn't have to deal with her any more. You shouldn't even have to look at her."

"We need to reach Lady Alma quickly. If the guards find us, everything is lost. I'll escort the Princess. You get a boat and make contact. We'll meet you by the mouth of the Ghone."

"Fine."

Estrella knelt beside me and loosened the silk around my feet so I could walk. She pulled me to my feet and tied a piece of rope around my waist. She handed the end to Shadow. Then she untied my apron and folded it.

"She might try to use the Rosas Rojas again," she said.

Shadow took the apron and slipped it into his bag.

"I won't run away," I said. "This was my idea."

At least, I tried to say it. The gag muffled my voice.

Estrella slapped my face. The sound echoed through the cavern.

"Not another word," she said. "We don't need any more of your help."

27

Estrella lit a candle and ran down the tunnel. Her rapid steps echoed through the mines long after the light faded.

"We'll get a head start," William said. "If there's anything in your way, we'll take care of it."

"Watch out for the soldiers. Whistle once if you run into trouble."

They blew out their candles. Shadow pulled the rope around my waist. I hobbled after him. We were going too slow! I struggled to walk with my feet tied.

Why couldn't they trust me?

Why couldn't he trust me?

Bits of silk stuck to my tongue. My mouth had gone dry.

Shadow's steps were uneven and slow. I could help him support his injured leg if he would lean on me.

But he wouldn't. I couldn't even suggest it with the gag in my mouth.

Tears streamed down my face. Why pretend I was alright? No one could see me in the darkness. And I had no friends left to care. The tears soaked into the silk gag until the salty taste reached my tongue. Still we walked, both of us shuffling.

If they trusted me, I could have contacted Lady Alma

with the Rosas Rojas and set up a meeting place. She knew I was in the mines, but had I mentioned I was with Shadow?

I ran out of tears long before our journey ended. The mountain must be far away by now since travel below ground was so much faster than it was above. I crashed into Shadow as he stopped suddenly. I heard footsteps coming towards us, but couldn't tell whose they were. Had the soldiers found us?

"The mouth of the Ghone is just ahead," Roslynn's voice floated from the darkness. "It looks clear. No sign of Estrella yet."

"It is daylight," William said. "Very sunny."

"We'll wait in the tunnels then," Shadow said. "Estrella will signal us when she's ready."

Behind us, somewhere far back in the mines, a sound echoed. It grew louder and louder. Footsteps. It sounded like an entire army.

And it very well might be.

"We'll distract them," William said.

"That's too dangerous," said Shadow.

"We'll lead them away from you," Roslynn said. "We can make noise in the other tunnels. At least slow them down until Estrella gets here. What matters is that we don't lose the Princess."

She and William walked away. Shadow pulled me forward. The tunnel grew gradually lighter. Even the dim light was blinding after so much time underground. It made my head ache. I had some idea what living with the owl eyes curse must be like.

I could see Shadow now. We walked side by side. He limped, and I shuffled as we fought to reach the Ghone. His eyes were red. Had he been crying in the dark? Or was it an effect of the owl eyes curse?

A flash of light caught me off guard and blinded me.

Sunlight shining off the Ghone. Shadow brushed his hair over his eyes.

"Sit," he said. "We'll wait here."

His voice sounded shaky.

Unstable.

It was difficult to sit with my hands tied together. I fell the last few feet. That would leave a bruise.

Shadow had difficulty sitting as well. He reclined against the wall with his injured leg stretched straight in front of him. Blood had soaked through the bandages.

Maybe Estrella could buy a crystal in town. Lady Alma would have a healing charm if either of them thought to bring it.

Reflections from the Ghone sparkled on the roof of the tunnel. Light caught my hair and refracted into the usual dark prism of colors.

The light became unbearably bright. I brought my hands up to my face, covering my eyes the best I could. I peeked at Shadow. He covered his face and turned away from the tunnel entrance. The light grew brighter and brighter. I glanced up. A single star floated on the ceiling, blinding us. Had Estrella sent it to let us know she was nearby?

"A bad day to have owl eyes."

A hand wrapped around my waist and picked me up. I screamed, but little sound escaped the gag. Shadow scrambled to his feet, but the person holding me kicked his injured leg. He gasped and collapsed on the ground. I heard the dull thud as my captor kicked him again. Felt the force of the blows through the arms that held me tight to someone's chest. I wriggled, trying to stop the attacker, and turned to see his face.

The Dragon.

He smiled at me.

"Should I kill him now?"

I shook my head.

He laughed.

"Whatever you think, you are too kindhearted to be a good bandit."

He kicked Shadow one more time and carried me out of the tunnel. We stepped into a rowboat with four pirates at the oars. They pushed off once we settled at the front and rowed towards the open sea.

Sir Gilbert tried to untie the silk gag, but the knot was too tight. He pulled a small knife from his belt and cut the cloth. I smacked my mouth, trying to spit out or swallow the bits of thread stuck to my tongue. Sir Gilbert handed me a canteen. I drank and spit out bits of thread. The water tasted slightly salty.

"Where are you taking me?"

"To my ship. Hold still, and I'll cut the rest."

He cut through the silk. I massaged my wrists and looked at the churning river. If I jumped in, could I make it to shore?

"This is the swiftest part of the Ghone," he said. "Even I can't swim in that."

"Take me back to Shadow."

He laughed.

"Don't be ridiculous. I've clearly just rescued you. You want to go back to the ruffian who tied you up? I should have stabbed him through the heart for hurting you."

"He didn't hurt me."

Sir Gilbert took my hand and traced the red lines the silk had left on my skin.

"Yes, he did."

He touched my cheek. I winced. Apparently the slap had left a bruise.

"Estrella did that," I said.

His smiled faded for a moment.

"I believe it. She punched me when I broke off our

engagement."

"Why did you leave? She loved you."

"Yes, but I was in love with someone else."

I didn't have to ask who. His every look and gesture gave it away.

"You don't know me."

"I know everything about you that can be known. And we started off very well. Don't tell me you didn't enjoy the picnic. Or dinner. Or walking through your gallery?"

"Yes, of course. But, you're a pirate."

He chuckled. The pirates at the oars joined him.

"And you're a bandit now! The life of a noble is often dull. We both understand that. We both found ways around it."

"You stole the fairy salt shipments to Castana and almost caused a war! You've murdered sailors! Sank whole ships! You sank Captain's ship!"

"And you've crept into people's homes while they slept and stolen their belongings. You kicked royal guards in the face and would have done worse if it had been in your power. You have blood on your hands too. Shadow's family is only the beginning of it. Do you know what has been done in your name?"

"I didn't order any of that."

"But you didn't ask about it either. Neither of us is innocent, Princess. Which works out well for both of us."

We were well out to sea now. I stared at the Ghone, fading from view. Waves pushed against the small rowboat. I didn't see the red ship anywhere.

"This boat is a bit small for the open sea, isn't it?"

"My ship is well hidden," he said.

"Did you really steal it from Estrella's father?"

He laughed.

"I'm flattered you think I had that much strength as a young boy, but I'm afraid my father took care of all that.

He let me borrow the ship when I wanted to go to sea. It wasn't doing him any good docked at the colonies."

"What happened to her father?"

He shrugged.

"Honestly, I have no idea. My father wanted to rule the colonies, and he did what he had to do. Neither of us is afraid to work hard for what we want."

"And you want to be King."

He raised an eyebrow.

"Is that really what you think?"

"Isn't that your master plan? Bring us to the brink of war with Castana, then sail in and save the day? You can marry me and have all the power you want. Once you fix the salt patches and stop the famine, you'll be a national hero."

"I didn't do any of this for a kingdom."

"Don't lie to me."

"I did it for you. I don't care about power. I don't care about a throne. In fact, I found my time in the Salarian court rather stifling. Say the word, and we'll sail away from here and never look back."

"But-"

"You like being a bandit? Being a pirate is better. The open sea. The freedom to sail wherever you want. You can explore new lands. We'll kidnap Lady Alma to design outfits for you if you want."

That made me laugh in spite of everything.

The rowboat hit something and stopped. I looked up. The Dragon's ship floated beside us. Bright red letters painted on the side declared its name: *Stella Rossa.* The Red Star. The water around the vessel showed no reflection of the red wood.

"Lower the carriage, men!" Sir Gilbert yelled. "We've come home."

28

The pirates lowered a golden platform from the deck of the ship. Sir Gilbert and I stepped onto it, and they hoisted us up. The mainland looked very far away. How far out had the ship been when Roslynn swam to shore? If I grabbed something buoyant and jumped overboard, could I make it?

Probably not, but this ship was clearly enchanted. Maybe I could use that magic to get back somehow. I just needed to know more about how it worked.

Sir Gilbert snapped his fingers, and the pirates vanished. I jumped and stared at him.

"What just happened? You never told me you knew magic."

"Would you like me to show you how the ship works? It really is a marvel."

"I am familiar with the concept of a ship. It floats on the water, the wind catches the sails, and-"

He laughed and waved to stop me.

"This entire ship is filled with magical charms. For instance, the crew."

He clapped his hands. I jumped and leaned towards him as skeletons appeared where the crew had been.

"A skeleton crew," I said.

"They are part of the ship. They sail it without asking questions, and they're excellent fighters. I usually keep them in naval uniform, but this is a great way to intimidate others."

"How does it work?"

"Not sure. I didn't set up the spell. The ship can also disguise itself. The most useful makes it look like a traditional Salarian Navy vessel. I can sail across the sea with a naval fleet and no one questions me."

"So right now, the ship is hidden somehow?"

He nodded.

"We're invisible unless you're within a few feet of the ship. Useful, although hard to keep up in crowded seas."

"Show me."

I grabbed his arm with excitement. He chuckled.

"The control room is in my cabin. And just so you know, I'm not wearing a hair charm. So don't get any ideas. It took my crew hours to cut me loose."

I laughed.

"I was mostly curious. Madame Delilah promised my hair would grow back to normal length in ten seconds. Obviously it didn't. Your charm seems to have worked better."

"It has grown since I last saw you."

I ran my hand through my hair. It fell past my chin now. Somehow, my singing had made it grow.

Sir Gilbert led me to the captain's cabin. The last time I had been here, he had tortured Estrella and tried to kill Shadow. Now he was the perfect gentleman.

"My best guess is this is some sort of fairy magic. I keep fairy salt on board just in case, but it doesn't seem to need it. This controls the disguises."

He pulled back a curtain and showed me a table covered with silver charms decorated with swirling symbols. They reminded me of the charms Lady Alma used to dress dancers in opera productions.

"So if we want to be a Navy ship?"

He pointed to a charm, and I touched it. The ship shook. Red wood transformed to the golden hue I recognized from dinner parties aboard naval vessels. Sir Gilbert's hair flickered to brown, then back to red. I blinked and pressed another charm. The ship shook and shifted back to the *Stella Rossa.* Sir Gilbert's hair flickered again.

I pressed the Navy charm. This time, I felt a slight coldness in my chest. The cabin faded to black, and I saw a man and woman dancing on the deck. I recognized them.

Estrella's parents.

I turned to Sir Gilbert. Had our souls just linked? Why would he have a memory of Estrella's parents? He noticed my gaze and grinned at me. Surely he would say something if he had seen one of my memories. I stuck my head out a window to look at the transformed *Stella Rossa* and smiled. The ship's reflection rippled in the waves now.

"Can we leave it as a Navy ship?" I asked. "It reminds me of home."

Sir Gilbert nodded.

"Anything to make you happy."

"I want to see the full effect."

I led him back to the deck. It looked just like a Navy ship. The skeletons had transformed into polished sailors in uniforms. We climbed to the top of the captain's cabin. From there, I saw the entire Salarian coast.

Not a trace of green remained. The salt had killed everything. It looked like a forest fire had burned the entire country.

"How did you create the fairy snow?" I asked.

"The skeletons used salt from the ships we raided.

Very symbolic."

He winked at me.

"I'm sure Mother loved it."

"Snow made of salt? It was all Sir Lefting could do to keep her from revising the opera on the spot."

"How did you spread it? It is covering the whole coast now."

I gestured to the shore. Sir Gilbert shrugged.

"We didn't do any of that. Something else must have triggered it."

"You killed an entire farm's crops to create that snow."

"And I'd do it again to make you happy."

I turned to face him.

"What if I don't want to be a pirate, Sir Gilbert? What if I want to be queen?"

"Since when do you want to be queen?"

A movement on the horizon caught my eye. I turned away, looking out to the open sea. Sir Gilbert followed my gaze.

I tried again.

"We've made a mess of things, you and me. Don't you think we should fix them?"

He examined me, bemused.

"There are crates of salt left, although it took a lot to coat the field. I can tell your father where to find them. We can deliver it to Castana personally if you want. You'll like it there. Lots of roses. The court magicians will figure out a way to remove the salt from the ground. They're far more qualified than we are."

"What about Salaria? I'm the heir to the throne."

"There are plenty of noblemen. They can have a tournament or some such thing. They'll find someone to rule. Oh, I forgot! I have a present for you!"

He ran below deck and returned with a small cage.

"Seda!"

I reached through the bars and scratched the kitten behind the ears. He purred.

"I had to lock him up. He kept climbing the mast, and I was afraid he would hurt himself."

"Thank you."

I unlatched the cage and cuddled Seda. I buried my head in his fur and stole another glance at the shore. Something on the ocean moved. Had Lady Alma sent a rescue party? I turned back to Sir Gilbert. The way his hair had flickered still puzzled me.

"Your hair is quite dashing," I said. "Is it a statement? To make you recognizable as the Dragon?"

He ran his hands through his strange, fiery hair and shook his head.

"When I was young, all I wanted was a chance to be near you. That hasn't changed, actually. I had dark hair, but they only allowed blond children to be companions. So my mother paid a wigmaker to dye my hair with magic. It went badly."

"But surely you could remove the spell."

"The idiot used a sort of Castanian magic. A soul loop, Estrella called it. Somehow, it draws energy from my soul and changes my appearance."

"And it can't be changed back?"

He shook his head.

"I'll wear a wig if it bothers you."

"It doesn't bother me."

His hair had changed back briefly even if he didn't know it. My mind raced. The *Stella Rossa* would need a lot of magical power to transform. Had it drawn power from his soul? Small charms did that, and Seda was proof that Estrella's mother knew how to work them. Would a small charm, like the one that changed Sir Gilbert's hair, fail if a larger charm needed power?

Not that any of this would help me. I couldn't work magic. But I could use the transformation charms. That was something.

Sir Gilbert misunderstood my silence.

"I don't mind wearing a wig if the red hair bothers you. I know you're used to blond."

"No, I wasn't thinking about that."

The ship had not only drawn magic from Sir Gilbert. It had drawn power from me. For a moment, it had felt just like when Estrella and I linked souls to fix the well. If I reactivated that link, maybe I could fight back somehow. Turn the skeletons against him?

But how?

The coast grew smaller every minute. We were sailing away. If I wanted to escape, I had to do it soon.

"They're looking for me, Gilbert. The soldiers know I was with Shadow. I can't just disappear."

"I told them you were with Shadow. They'll take care of the bandits, and I'll send your father a message to let him know you're safe. If we turn our love into a symbol, we'll have your mother's support. He won't dare go against her wishes."

"Perhaps, but what sort of symbol would it be? Beauty and the beast?"

He laughed.

"I wouldn't go that far."

"Salt and the fairy snow?"

"That sounds perfect."

"Great. You can be the salt. Sucking the life out of everyone to sustain your illusion."

He frowned and placed his hand over mine. His voice lowered to a growl.

"And what does the fairy snow do?"

"Removes the salt."

I threw Seda at him and jumped back. Seda clawed Sir

Gilbert's chest, alarmed by the sudden motion. I hated to leave him again, but what choice did I have? I reached into my apron to grab my bracelets.

My apron was gone.

How could I have forgotten?

I glanced around the deck for something to bring overboard with me. I found an empty crate and tossed it over the side. It spun through the air before finally hitting the waves. I looked down. It was a long way to the water, and the waves were bigger than the gentle rocking motion of the ship suggested. I hesitated, and the chance was gone.

Sir Gilbert grabbed my arm and pulled me back to the deck. His fingers dug into my skin. Lady Alma would have a lot of bruises to heal if I ever made it back to the palace.

"You've been in the mines too long," he said. "You're confused. Once you've had some rest, you'll feel better."

"I need to get back to the palace. I need to fix this!"

He dragged me across the ship.

"You'll like the room I prepared for you."

He opened a door. My jaw dropped. Salara portraits covered the walls. A wardrobe filled with replicas of my gowns sat in the right corner. A bookshelf filled with volumes of official Salara Poetry stood in the left.

"I haven't just been robbing salt shipments," he said. "It is amazing how many gifts your mother sends to other countries. They'll be disappointed to hear their ships have been attacked by the Dragon, but you'll have all the comforts of home here."

"This is-"

Words failed me. I stared with horror.

"And I have another gift for you."

He was calming down, fighting for control. It had been foolish of me to upset him. He pulled a small chest from a shelf and opened it.

Sapphires.

"It was you," I said. "You stole the sapphire shipment from the museum."

"And I am sorry it caused you distress. I had no idea they were intended for your gown. I sailed up the Ghone to search for a spot for the picnic and couldn't resist."

"And then you kidnapped Roslynn."

"You should lie down," he said, pulling me into the room. "You've been through a lot. I'll keep you company. We can read some poetry."

"I think the last thing we need right now is poetry."

Sir Gilbert and I ran out of the cabin and stared. Shadow hovered a few feet above the ship. He pulled a silver bracelet from his wrist and dropped to the deck. The impact made his leg buckle, but he recovered his balance and pulled his knife from his pack.

The Dragon growled.

Shadow looked terrible.

His eyes were still red, and he held a hand over his face to shield them from the bright sun. His clothes were torn and muddy. Dried blood crusted on his face, and bruises had already formed.

He slipped the bracelets into my apron and dropped it on the deck.

Skeletons appeared around him, swords drawn. Shadow held up his dagger, ready to defend himself.

Sir Gilbert laughed and snapped his fingers. The skeletons disappeared.

"I think I can handle this one on my own," he said.

I stepped forward. Sir Gilbert pulled my arm so hard I crashed into him. He held me close against his side.

"Shadow, are you insane?" I said. "He'll kill you."

"Maybe. But I love you. The real you. And I wanted you to know."

Sir Gilbert scoffed.

"She's a noble," he said. "She's one of them. And you tied her up and kidnapped her. Do you think she'll forgive you? Just like that?"

"Worth a try."

He took a step forward. His hurt leg trembled as he walked.

"Shadow, get out of here," I said. "Leave while you still can."

Shadow shook his head and kicked my apron across the polished deck, out of his reach.

"So," Sir Gilbert said. "We get to finish our fight. The Princess won't be able to save you this time. I'm all out of hair charms."

Shadow lunged forward. Sir Gilbert pushed me into the Salara room and dodged. Shadow lunged again, and Sir Gilbert stabbed him in the side. A red spot spread across his tunic.

"You should have at least waited until the sun set. Can you even see me?"

He stabbed Shadow's other side.

"I'll come with you. Gilbert," I said. "Let him go, and I'll come with you. We can read poetry together. We'll sail to Castana and visit rose gardens. It will be very symbolic."

Sir Gilbert laughed.

"We'll do all those things after I stab him through the heart. You can't get much more symbolic than that."

He was distracted. Shadow stabbed his shoulder. Sir Gilbert lunged for his head and missed.

I retrieved my apron from the deck and pulled out the Rosas Rojas. Did I have to be asleep to contact Lady Alma? I was on a magical ship. Surely she would have an idea.

Lady Alma, I thought. Please hear me, Lady Alma.

Nothing happened.

Even if I dared to sleep now, I wouldn't be able to. A blur of white caught my eye. Seda ran away from the fight and climbed the mast. He clung to the ropes with his claws, swinging above the ship.

I heard a groan, turned back to the fight, and screamed.

Sir Gilbert pulled his sword from Shadow's chest. Blood dripped from the blade onto the deck. The *Stella Rossa's* illusion flickered with each drop, switching from golden wood to red.

The frigid point of a soul link stabbed my heart as the ship changed appearances. My vision faded to black. Sir Gilbert's hair turned dark. He looked like an older version of himself. Shadow's turned blond as he transformed into Admiral Ethan. I watched, helpless, as Admiral Ethan crawled backwards, trying to escape the sword.

With a cold smile that looked just like his son, Sir Gilbert's father stabbed Estrella's.

I jumped back to the present and blinked back tears. Stay calm. I must not panic.

Shadow crumpled to the deck. His dagger slipped from his hands.

"Shadow!"

He didn't respond. Blood from his wound soaked his tunic.

"Shadow, answer me!"

Sir Gilbert wiped his blade on Shadow's cloak, slipped it back into his sheath, and walked towards me.

29

My hands trembled. My whole body shook. I shivered as an icy chill spread through my limbs.

My apron lay by my feet. I picked it up, slipped the silver bracelets over my wrists and stepped back.

I made it back a few more steps onto the unseen stairs before Sir Gilbert realized what was happening. He lunged towards me, but I ran backwards until I was out of his reach. Seda climbed down the rigging and pawed at a rope, asking me to play with him. Gilbert ran to the mast and climbed the rigging himself until he was eye level with me.

But I stepped away from the ropes. He could not reach me.

"You're a monster," I said.

My voice trembled.

"You're getting worked up over nothing. You want me to be a King? Fine, I'll be a King. I've just executed a criminal who was plaguing the land. You can't have it both ways, Princess."

"You're just a selfish, spoiled-"

He grabbed a loose rope and jumped. I stepped sideways to dodge him, and my foot went down instead of up. I had reached the top. Each step now would bring me lower.

"Obsessed, traitorous-"

Below, Shadow did not move.

The Dragon climbed higher, cutting ropes and swinging nearer. Seda scampered after him, clawing the dangling ropes.

The invisible platform buckled under my feet. Of all the times for the bracelets to fail! I grabbed the nearest rope, swung to the mast, and held tight. Below me, the *Stella Rossa* swayed in the waves. The motion felt gentle from the deck, but on the mast it seemed strong enough to shake me into the sea.

Sir Gilbert swung from rope to rope, getting closer and closer.

My heart pounded, but I still felt cold. Emotions churned through me in a-

Well, in a loop.

Moonlight complexion, pearly reflection
By every standard, you are perfection.

This was no time to think of poetry! I climbed up the mast to another rope and swung out of Sir Gilbert's reach.

How much magic would it take to change my appearance? To make me perfect by every standard? How did such a spell work?

Lady Alma's voice ran through my head.

"You're fairy blessed, dear. You can't easily escape that. Being a princess is tied to the deepest part of your soul."

Divinia's enchantment was a soul loop! Just like Seda's youth and Sir Gilbert's hair. That must be why I couldn't work magic! The soul loop absorbed power from my charms just like the ship.

Sir Gilbert swung towards me. I gripped a rope, jumped, and kicked him as we passed each other. He spun out of control. I stepped, landed on an invisible platform, and stood in midair, watching him.

Estrella had said my soul was strong, but what if it wasn't just my soul? If my soul was tied up in Divinia's spell, it would mean I had been absorbing magic to power it.

Magic I might be able to use.

I needed a way to focus my emotions. To control the loop.

I took a deep breath and sang my aria from the opera.

My enchanted voice connected to the spell Divinia had cast on me. I felt it now. Something foreign lodged in the deepest part of me. The song focused it.

"You won't distract me with that again," Sir Gilbert said.

He cut a rope loose and swung towards me. I stood my ground and focused all my energy on him. At the last moment, I jumped and swung towards him, still singing.

Power swelled up around me. Immense power. A silver mist swirled around me. My wig charm shattered into blue dust, and I felt a weight on my head as my hair grew. The *Stella Rossa* flickered through its disguises. My heart went cold. My foot hit Sir Gilbert's chest. Something in my ankle popped.

Sir Gilbert flew backwards and hit the mast. Silver light radiated from the point of impact, blinding me. I lost my grip on the rope and fell onto the invisible platform. Below, the *Stella Rossa* shuddered. The golden deck flickered, and the entire ship glowed red. It flashed so brightly I had to close my eyes.

When I opened them, the blaze had faded and Sir Gilbert was gone. I sat up and examined the ship. The mast was charred and black where he had hit it. The sail hung in tatters. Bits of rope, still burning at the ends, swung in the breeze.

What had I done?

There was no time to think about that now. I moved the opera bracelets to my right arm, climbed down the ship's rigging, and ran across the deck. I knelt over Shadow's body.

"Please," I whispered. "Please."

His eyes did not open. He did not move.

I leaned over him and felt a tiny puff of warm air. I held my hand above his mouth.

He was still breathing!

But blood gushed from the stab wound.

He was still alive.

He could be healed.

If only I knew how.

Gently, I put my hands on his chest. I focused on the movement in my soul and hummed a song.

Something deep inside me snapped. A cold, sharp pain pierced my heart. It traveled down my hand, and silver wisps of magic covered Shadow.

My vision blurred. I heard laughter. A boy with dark hair and peasant clothes stood in the courtyard at the palace. He was small and blended in with the crowd. No one noticed him as he walked towards the brightest lights. A smiling blond girl stood on a dais filled with people in brightly colored clothes. She knelt and offered him her hand. The boy took it, and she pulled him up. He wandered around with her, watching everything.

And then he saw her. She sat on a throne, elevated above everyone, the brightest light of all. Her pink dress and pale skin shimmered. Her hair was the night sky with strands of stars diffused in it.

He stood watching her. Hours passed. The crowd

swept the blond girl away. A painter pushed him aside to set up his easel. The boy watched the painting for a moment, then turned to go. As he left, he searched for evidence of this shining world. Something to bring back to the shadows.

He passed the food table and grabbed a painted egg.

My vision cleared with a jolt. I gasped for air as if surfacing from under water. Shadow's eyes opened and darted from my face to the strands of magic. He continued to bleed.

I focused on the loop again. It was less of a loop now and more of a stream, trickling towards Shadow's wounds. The bruises on my arm grew darker. My tears left traces of salt on his tunic.

It wasn't enough. I needed more power.

There had to be a weak point in the loop somewhere. I closed my eyes, searching.

My ankle twinged. I kicked my foot against the ground. The pain grew sharper.

Something still held the magic back. I focused on the magic and searched for the thing blocking it. There, on my wrist.

I pulled off the bracelets and threw them across the deck.

Pain roared through my ankle. Something deeper than bone shattered, and magic rushed towards Shadow in a current as swift as the Ghone.

His eyes opened wider. He stared at me. I glowed silver in his dark pupils. My hair floated around me in an unfelt breeze. Pain traveled up my leg into my chest. I couldn't breathe. I was submerged in magic.

Beneath my hands, the wound in Shadow's chest closed. His breath grew stronger.

Something else fractured inside me. I gasped. Shadow sank beneath me as I began to float above the deck.

I couldn't stop it. I didn't try.

The magic pulled me high above the *Stella Rossa.* The ship drifted towards Salaria. I felt the emptiness on the mainland, where life had drained from the earth itself. I felt that life inside me. Without realizing, I had absorbed it as I walked through fields and under mountains.

Now that my soul loop had broken, the magic flowed towards Salaria. As it returned, the grass on the edge of the shore turned green. I smiled. A breeze caught the ship's sails, and the *Stella Rossa* rushed towards the mainland. Green spread across the ground. Flowers bloomed, and trees grew new leaves.

There was no loop now. No distinction between my soul and the magic. Estrella had said that could kill me.

That didn't matter.

Fields of crops regrew in striped rows.

I felt the land.

A broken arm and bruised ribs.

I gasped as I recognized Estrella. She lay on the shore. A wave of silver light washed over her, and she sat up.

"Rook, what are you doing?"

She was too far away for me to hear her voice, but our souls were linked. I understood her thoughts.

"Help me."

I directed a stream of magic towards Estrella. She gasped and poured the power into the people, land, and homes we both sensed.

I found Roslynn. She and William stood outside the mines. Her eyes pulsed beneath her blindfold, desperate to absorb too much light. Estrella flicked her wrist, and the dim light Roslynn saw behind her blindfold faded to darkness. She pulled the blindfold off and smiled at William. He picked her up and spun her around.

Those I had healed became portals I could channel magic through. As if she understood my intent, Estrella used these people to push the magic further into Salaria. I gasped as something deep down tugged at my core, then resumed.

I found Gerta's farm and healed the soil. Bits of green rose from the ground. A silver rain began to fall. All of Salaria glowed. Crops regrew to twice their normal size. Charmed candles became beacons, shining to the sky. Under the magic, the land looked as if silver snow had fallen.

I had become connected to everything in Salaria. To the country herself. I felt every hurt. Every injustice my people had suffered.

And I knew exactly which I had caused.

I screamed and pushed more of my soul magic towards the country. I had to heal everything before my power faded. I could not stop it now. Bits of my soul chipped off and swept away towards Salaria. I looked at my arm. My skin was translucent, and whole patches were gone. I felt myself fading into the magic stream. Salaria's feelings became stronger than my own.

I found the wells that had gone salty and purified the water.

Estrella tried to stop me, but it was like reversing the current of the Ghone. Impossible.

The flow of power ripped me apart from the inside out. Silver mist swirled around me in a storm, getting thicker and thicker. The wind carried off bits of me as it blew past. I screamed, but no sound came out. My voice was already gone. My body rippled like water. I was losing my form, reduced to a reflection of myself. My hair swept around me like a dark cocoon.

In my last moments, I searched for Shadow. He was still weak, but he was breathing and the bleeding had stopped. He would live.

The stream of magic had slowed now. I aimed it at

him. His eyes shifted as I healed the owl eyes curse. My own vision darkened, and I faded into his memories.

A small boy knelt over a man, crying in the darkness. The man pressed something into his hand, and the boy could see. His father was dying.

"Run," he choked. "Hide in the mines."

The memory faded into red light. The sunset transformed the ocean into fire. I drifted higher and higher. I had no weight to hold me to the earth. The last of my magic trickled towards Salaria.

I felt cold.

Could you die without a soul? Or did you simply fade into nothing?

I inhaled one last time and closed my eyes.

Pain shot through my ankle. Something strong clasped it, holding tight. I floated higher and higher, and the weight grew and dragged me down. Caught between heaven and earth, my country and my body, I opened my mouth and screamed.

At first, there was no sound. Just a silent expression of agony.

Then, like the sun grows gradually stronger each morning, my voice returned. The sound took form. I grew more solid.

I looked down. Shadow held my ankle. Bits of magic flowed from him. His pupils grew larger and larger.

"Stop!" I said, kicking my leg to shake him loose. "I healed you! I made things right!"

More magic hit me as Estrella pushed energy land towards me. I sank lower as my body reformed.

But I still floated above the ship. I was not whole yet.

Wham!

Something strong and gold slammed into my chest. I crashed to the deck as I absorbed it. I felt enough pain to know I was solid again.

Shadow knelt over me. Behind him, two women appeared on the ship.

Lady Alma glowed with silver sparkles. She directed them at me, and the agony eased.

I had met the woman beside her only once, on the day I was born, but I recognized her instantly. I had seen her in paintings all my life

She stood tall with skin illuminated from within as if she were a lamp. Golden wings peeked out from under her long, flowing hair. She wore a green dress that rippled as if made of the ocean itself. Her hands glowed with golden magic

The Fairy Divinia.

I sat up to get a better look and fainted.

30

A scream rang through my head after I passed out. I think it was mine. It faded to music as magic knit me back together. The Fairy Divinia's power filled me with a golden light and warmth, but bits of my soul were still tied to Salaria. As they returned, grass shriveled and wounds opened. I sat up to stop it.

"Stay still."

The same force that had crashed into my chest pressed down on me. I stood in a completely silent white room. The walls glowed with golden light. Divinia stood next to me, sewing lace onto my gown.

"What is happening?"

"Lady Alma and I are patching your soul back together. There will be less damage if you hold still."

I stopped moving.

The golden light faded into silver, and a gentle tension pressed in my hand. The music faded into the sounds of the ocean.

I opened my eyes.

Moonlight and stars filled my gaze. I lay on the deck of the *Stella Rossa*. Shadow held my hand and smiled.

"She will live," the Fairy Divinia said.

"Don't sound so pleased about it," Lady Alma said.

"This whole mess is your fault."

I propped myself up on my elbows. Shadow helped me sit up.

"Don't be unreasonable, Alma. This is hardly a mess."

We turned.

The Fairy Divinia smiled at us.

"It's you," I said. "You-"

"I have come," she said. "And I'm glad to see there's no harm done."

"You have a strange definition of harm," Lady Alma replied.

"You saved me," I said, looking at Shadow.

"Are you alright?"

I looked into his eyes, and my heart sank. His pupils were just as wide as before.

"I healed you," I said. "And now it's gone."

"I'm still alive."

"I can fix owl eyes, no problem," the Fairy Divinia said. "Just let me-"

"No!"

Shadow, Lady Alma, and I spoke in unison.

"Divinia, be a dear and set a course for the palace," Lady Alma said. "And pick up Estrella when we sail past her."

"I don't know what you're upset about," Divinia said. "Everything turned out beautifully!"

"No thanks to you," I said. "You're my fairy godmother! You're supposed to give me help and guidance. Instead you gave me a soul loop as a baby and left!"

"You really think I didn't help?"

Divinia snapped her fingers. The glow of her skin faded, and she shrank. Her back hunched, and her face became a familiar mass of wrinkles.

"You're Madame Delilah?" I said.

She nodded.

"And you think that makes it better? You tricked me into cutting my hair! You-"

"Your hair took a lot of magic to sustain. It isn't easy, making hair shine like the Ghone. Or making a wig that keeps the enchantment going when separated from the source of power, but I managed. I also arranged for Elsie to impersonate you in the palace so you could keep gallivanting about the countryside."

She hobbled across the deck as she spoke, waving her hands. The *Stella Rossa* glowed golden and sailed towards Castlemont.

"I've been working with Lady Alma for years to help sustain the loop so it wouldn't drain you. Do you think all that salt crystal jewelry was really about symbolism? It was a power source, of my own design, to keep your loop spell running without taxing your soul."

"Quite a bit of my design went into that," Lady Alma said.

"You knew about this?" I asked Lady Alma. "You knew Madame Delilah was Divinia, and I had a soul loop? You helped her?"

She nodded.

"Don't be angry, dear. There wasn't a way to break the loop, so telling you wouldn't have done any good. Don't forget to pick up Estrella, Divinia."

Madame Delilah snapped her fingers and transformed back into a fairy.

"Why did you stay hidden?" Shadow asked.

"Oh, I wanted to give Salara a chance find her own way. Relying too much on fairy magic doesn't do anyone any good."

"My name is Rook," I said.

"Oh, you're not planning to keep that are you? I named you Salara. That's so much nicer."

"You just named her after the country because you couldn't think of anything else," Lady Alma said.

"Besides, she isn't Salara anymore," Shadow said. "The spell is broken. Salara is gone."

I gripped his hand.

"What do you mean?"

"I was going to mention that later," Lady Alma said. "The Princess has been through a lot today."

She glared at Shadow.

"What's wrong with me?"

I stared at my arms. They were dirty, but looked about the same. I felt my face.

"Nothing is wrong with you," Shadow said.

"What happened?"

I felt differences when I tried. My fingers were shorter. My teeth weren't as straight. I ran my hands through my hair, trying to stay calm. It had grown again. Past my shoulders. I pulled a strand of it forward, looking for differences. It was still black.

"Oh, Salara preserve us!" Lady Alma said.

She snapped her fingers, and a full length mirror appeared on the deck.

Shadow helped me stand. I walked towards it, one tiny step at a time.

The edges of my dress were charred from the explosion. My reflection swam and blurred. Standing too quickly had made me dizzy. I leaned on Shadow's shoulder and stared.

A strange combination of Father and Mother stared back at me. I touched the mirror, searching for a trick. The stranger behind the glass met my hand with her own pale skin. Pale, but not luminescent. The tangled black hair showed no trace of a dark rainbow when it caught the light.

I had Father's clear brown eyes. Mother's heart shaped

face and upturned nose.

"I don't understand," I said. My hand flew to my mouth.

Watching my face, paying such close attention, I realized even my voice was not my own.

"What happened to me?" I tried the strange voice again.

It was deeper than it had been. Less melodious.

I stared at the stranger in the mirror, trying not to be overwhelmed.

"You're beautiful," Shadow said. "You'll always be beautiful."

"It isn't that," I said. "I just- I don't look like myself. Who am I now? What-"

I tore myself away from the reflection and faced him. His face looked different as well. Had the spell affected him?

No, I realized. The shape had not changed. Only the expression.

He looked happy.

My new face crinkled into a smile. I didn't need a mirror to tell me I was beautiful. I didn't even need Shadow to tell me.

I felt it. Deep in the soul so recently knit back together.

Shadow leaned forward. My heart beat faster as he kissed me.

Divinia made a comment to Lady Alma. I ignored her.

A wind swept around us, and my no longer magical hair flew into Shadow's face. We both laughed.

"I guess you're both alright then? Everything worked out?"

Shadow kept his arm around me as we turned.

Estrella stood on the deck.

"Thank you," I said, feeling awkward.

She nodded.

"What happened to Gilbert?" she asked. "And Seda? Is he here?"

I turned to Lady Alma.

"Don't look at me. I was still in the palace at that point."

"I broke my soul loop, and there was an explosion. Sir Gilbert and Seda were both in the rigging."

I gestured to the burnt mast. The charred sail and ropes hung limp.

Estrella nodded.

"He's gone then."

Lady Alma started to say something, but Estrella shook her head.

"Leave it. Loops are unpredictable. Breaking one as strong as Rook's would create a massive surge of power."

She faced Divinia.

"That was a hugely irresponsible spell. Trying to meet everyone's idea of beauty? Do you know how much magical energy that took?"

"Do you?"

Estrella's eyes narrowed.

"I almost blew up a well doing a simple soul link, and I helped direct the power when the loop broke. I think I have a pretty good idea."

"How will we explain this?" I asked. "My parents-"

I glanced at the castle towering above us. The *Stella Rossa* sailed into the port. A few skeleton sailors, now disguised as Navy men, dropped the anchor and lowered the gangplank.

"It might be best to enter quietly," Lady Alma said. "Divinia, if you would be so kind."

"Oh, now you want my help?"

Divinia waved her hands, and a golden glow covered us.

"You are now veiled. Go where you wish. The spell will fade when you reach your destination."

"Aren't you coming with us?" Estrella asked.

"I think I've played my part here. And I must report the happy results of my blessing to the rest of the fairies."

Estrella stared at her, open mouthed. Divinia raised a hand.

"I know what is troubling you, but I cannot help now. I must return to Castana. You are welcome to visit any time."

She disappeared in a flash of golden light.

"I visited the Castanian fairies myself once," Lady Alma said. "I wouldn't trust them with anything too important."

She took Estrella's hand and led us towards the first gate.

"I was a good friend of your mother, you know. Actually, I am her stepsister. I suppose that makes you my niece."

"What?"

"We'll talk later."

Lady Alma opened the gates with a wave of her hands. The guards on duty didn't notice us pass. We climbed the ramps one by one, working our way up the mountain until we reached the castle.

We walked through the castle without speaking. A few servants bustled through the hallways, but no one questioned our ragged group. Guards stood just outside my room. Shadow tensed as we walked past them, relaxing only when Lady Alma shut the door. I smiled in the moonlight, letting the familiar place wash over me.

Someone screamed.

Elsie sat up in my bed, the wig made from my hair tangled over her face.

"Oh, I forgot about you," Lady Alma said. "Your

services will no longer be required."

Elsie stared at us.

"Shadow? Estrella? Lady Alma, these people are dangerous!"

Shadow pulled a miner's candle from his bag.

"Not necessary," Lady Alma said.

She snapped her fingers. The moonlight streaming through the windows intensified, filling the room with a silver glow.

Shadow brushed his hair over his eyes.

"What is going on?" Elsie said. "Who is she?"

She pointed to me. Did I really look that different?

"Rook," I said. "I'm Rook."

"What is the meaning of this noise?"

Mother rushed into the room and froze.

She stared at me. I stared back. With my new face, I looked more like her than I had thought possible.

"Who is this person?" she asked.

But I could tell she knew.

"Hello, Mother."

I sounded just like her.

She gasped and wrapped her arms around me.

"My poor baby," she said. "Alma, what happened?"

I patted her shoulder.

"The fairy's spell was broken," Lady Alma said.

"What do you mean broken?" Mother held me at arm's length and examined me. Her lips pursed together.

Father entered the room. He stared at me.

"Father?"

He ran to me and almost knocked me over he hugged me so hard.

"I feared you were lost," he said.

A few tears dropped onto my shoulder.

My eyes really did look just like his now.

"Lady Alma, I demand an explanation."

Mother sounded like she was about to cry. I couldn't see her from Father's embrace.

"As I said, your daughter's curse has been broken."

"What curse? The fairy blessing on Salara defined this country. Without it, we are nothing! Where is the Fairy Divinia? Why has she insulted us in this way? I declare war on the fairies until they-"

Sir Bristle ran into the room carrying an easel, canvas, and his painting bag.

"Your Majesty, I heard Princess Salara has returned. We should sketch the scene!"

He put a brush in Mother's hands. She dropped it and shook her head.

"I won't be painting tonight, Sir Bristle."

"What happened, Lady Alma?" Father asked. "Who are these people?"

He kept his arm around my shoulder and turned to face the crowd gathered in my bedroom.

"Your daughter broke the fairy spell and healed Salaria with its power. These people helped."

She gestured to Estrella and Shadow.

"This young lady is a powerful enchantress and the daughter of Admiral Ethan. Allow me to present the Duchess Estrella."

Estrella curtsied in the courtly fashion. Mother bristled.

"I remember you. You were banished from our presence years ago for attacking Princess Salara."

"And we welcome you back," Father said. "Thank you for your part in saving our land."

Estrella nodded.

I slipped away from Father's embrace and grabbed Shadow's hand. He gripped mine, and his hand trembled.

"This is Shadow," I said. "He has protected me since I ran away. He saved my life."

Shadow tensed, ready for a fight. Ready to run.

My parents gaped. Mother opened her mouth and shut it again several times, searching for words.

"Your crimes are well known, Shadow," Father said. "You have been convicted multiple times for crimes against Salara and Salaria."

Shadow nodded.

"And you have taken advantage of your people for personal gain. Sent them to the mines and let them starve so you could impress your friends with operas and paintings."

"How dare you?" Mother said. "My art is a national treasure! Kings and Queens travel across the sea to witness our opera productions."

Shadow gripped my hand tighter. Father met his eyes.

"Things have changed," he said finally. "And you provided protection to my daughter when she needed it most. I pardon your crimes."

"Pardon his crimes?" Mother screamed. "Nothing has changed. Lady Alma will restore Salara's beauty, and everything will be exactly the same! You cannot pardon him!"

"I cannot restore the spell," Lady Alma said. "And I would not even if I had the skill. It was a foolish enchantment. Do you know how much magic it takes to create universal beauty? The spell constantly shifted Salara's appearance, so she met each person's ideal. It stole power from her soul to please the eyes of strangers. Why do you think she has never been able to work magic?"

"Nonsense," Mother said. "What you describe is impossible!"

"Just look at the paintings," Lady Alma said. "You have many skilled painters in Salaria. Each painted Salara exactly as they saw her. Each saw her differently."

"Thank goodness!" Sir Bristle exclaimed.

We looked at him.

"I thought I was mad. I have trained countless talented painters, but none of them could ever paint the Princess. Even my own paintings never matched those of the Queen. Sir Quill has been tormenting me about this for years!"

I glanced at Shadow and smiled. He still looked tense.

"What about the peasants?" I asked. "Why did no one recognize me? I didn't have nearly the same effect on them as I did the courtiers. Although one proposed marriage."

"I suppose this means you turned him down," Elsie said. "Edsel must be so disappointed."

"Your soul alone wasn't strong enough to sustain the illusion," Lady Alma said. "Here in the palace I kept you surrounded by fairy salt to provide power. In the villages, the spell was weakened. It took magic from whatever it could find. The charms in the wells, the trees, even the land."

"The salt patches were my fault," I whispered. "I thought Sir Gilbert was making them."

"No one is responsible," Mother said. "You're all talking in the most ridiculous way. We'll simply write to the fairies in Castana and have them restore the spell. We have plenty of salt to provide any extra power needed. As long as Salara doesn't leave the castle, everything will be fine."

"I won't be enchanted again."

"Darling, you don't know what you're saying. Have you seen yourself yet? You look terrible."

"She is beautiful," Shadow said. "And she's exactly the person needed to rule Salaria."

"We can talk about all this later," Father said. "You need to rest."

He took Mother's arm and led her out of the room. Sir Bristle followed.

"I'll find rooms in the palace for you two," Lady Alma said.

Shadow squeezed my hand and followed her to the door.

"What about me?" Elsie said.

She removed the black wig. Her blond hair had been cut short to fit under it.

"Your services are no longer required," Lady Alma said. "Please show yourself to the door."

Elsie nodded and blinked back tears.

"I am sorry, Rook," she said. "I never meant- I mean, I've dreamed about the palace for so long. When they offered-"

She bowed her head.

"Find her a room, Lady Alma," I said. "You can't turn her out in the middle of the night."

Lady Alma raised an eyebrow at me and pushed everyone out the door.

I opened my wardrobe and pulled a nightgown out of it. The same one I had worn my last day in the castle. The hem was tattered from Seda's claws.

Poor Seda.

I blinked back tears and unbuttoned the top button on my dress.

Then I stopped and stared at the nightgown.

The curse had been broken. Did that mean-

I had seen Lady Alma perform the charm thousands of times. I had read about the proper technique.

I raised a shaking hand, closed my eyes, and snapped my fingers.

Fabric rustled against my skin as the nightgown replaced the peasant dress.

31

"Please, just a quick walk in the garden! The sunshine will do me good!"

Lady Alma stared at me, arms crossed.

I had been under her care for the past two days, and she had not allowed me to leave my room.

"Your soul was ripped from your body and scattered across the land. What part of 'you need rest' do you not understand?"

"Gardens are restful. Estrella can come with me to make sure I don't faint."

"I'm busy."

Estrella did not look up from her book.

"Roslynn then."

"Roslynn and William are at Gerta's farm for the morning," Lady Alma said.

"Just let Shadow take her," Estrella said. "A walk in the garden is hardly inappropriate."

"This is not a question of propriety. If the soul link between them is reconnected, it could hurt Rook."

I turned to Lady Alma.

"Please, you haven't let him into my room since we returned. I am recovered. I feel fine."

It was true. Other than feeling like a dancer

permanently in costume, I had suffered no ill effects.

It wasn't that my new body was ugly. It just didn't quite feel like me. I avoided mirrors and wore the simple, comfortable clothes Lady Alma made for me.

"The rest of the palace is still recovering from the shock. Your mother has insisted I keep you from Shadow."

My hands went cold.

"What has she done to him?"

"Nothing! Don't look like that, dear. This is exactly why you shouldn't go out."

"Where is he?"

"He's fine," Estrella said, still not looking up from her book.

"You can't keep me locked up here forever!"

"Then maybe you would like to take a walk with me?"

I turned and faced Father. My face flushed. Of course he would walk in when I was throwing a tantrum.

I nodded.

"She must not overexert herself," Lady Alma said.

Father bowed.

"I value the care you have given my daughter, Lady Alma. Thank you."

He offered me his arm. We walked slowly down the hallway. He stopped often to let me catch my breath. I was more tired than I had realized. Courtiers bowed as we passed. When we reached the garden, we sat at a bench overlooking the harbor. The *Stella Rossa* floated near the dock. The charred mast and sail set it apart from the other vessels. Beyond, Salaria stretched to the Weeping Mountains, green and alive.

"You did well," Father said.

I looked at him.

"You prevented famine and war at great personal risk."

"I wasn't- That wasn't my goal. I ran away to find freedom. And adventure."

He chuckled.

"Nothing is wrong with freedom and adventure. But we have a responsibility to the people of this kingdom."

I nodded.

"And we chose that responsibility. Both of us did. I chose Salaria when I married your mother. I hope I have not disappointed our people."

He looked at me.

"For the most part, the people of Salaria are happy," I said. "Will you cancel the salt tax, Father? Reinstating it has placed a heavy burden on our people."

He raised an eyebrow.

"I never reinstated the salt tax."

"But, we heard that you had."

He shook his head.

"Sir Gilbert started many nasty rumors with the help of his friends. Perhaps that was one of them."

"Oh. So you won't be sending people to the mines?"

"We will still need miners. But I will not be hasty in sending anyone."

I nodded. He cleared his throat.

"When it became clear that you would be our heir, I assumed you would do as your mother did and marry someone responsible to look after the kingdom. Ingrid began considering marriage proposals immediately. But things are different now. Many of those contracts will be void since you are no longer blessed."

A dull pain, as if my soul were being ripped apart again in slow motion, welled up in my chest.

"I don't- That is- I don't need someone to help me run the kingdom. I don't want-"

He raised his hand to stop my stammering.

"You have proved that you are responsible and

resourceful. But take it from someone who knows. Running a kingdom on your own is difficult. You may-"

"I don't want any of them! I don't want to marry any of them!"

"Please, let me finish. Running a kingdom on your own is difficult. You may, at some point, want a partner to help you."

"Please tell me you haven't signed a marriage contract. I'll do anything!"

He put a hand on my shoulder.

"Apparently I'm doing this badly. I am trying to give you good news, Rook."

I blinked at him.

"That is the name you've chosen for yourself, isn't it? I must confess, I wasn't happy when that blasted fairy named you Salara. Naming you after the country. Ridiculous. I wanted to name you Mary. Your mother fancied Ermentrude."

I smiled.

"You are young yet. But if you decide, when you are older, that you want to have a partner in running the kingdom, I will support your choice. Especially if I have already seen evidence that you work well with the young man in question."

He smiled and turned around. I followed his gaze.

A hooded figure emerged from the trees. He wore dark courtier clothes and gloves.

"Shadow!"

I tried to stand, but Father held me back.

"I promised Lady Alma I wouldn't let you overexert yourself. Stay seated."

He left, bowing to Shadow as he passed.

"May I join you?"

Shadow sat on the bench beside me. We stared at the ocean together.

I felt self-conscious, then self-conscious for feeling self-conscious. Without the spell, I didn't know if others found me beautiful. It was strange, vulnerable.

"I have missed you," I said.

Shadow nodded.

"I tried to see you, but Lady Alma said you needed rest."

"She was worried about our soul link draining me again. She wanted to give it time to fade."

"I hope our souls will always be linked."

He took my hand. I leaned against him.

"How do you like living in the palace?"

He laughed.

"Your mother hasn't been happy about having commoners as guests, but it has given an air of excitement to the court. She's already planning an opera about our story, so she's been asking me lots of questions."

"Someone else will have to play me. I'm not sure I could sing at all now."

He put his arm around my shoulder. We sat in silence for a bit.

"Is it too bright for you out here?" I said. "The sun-"

"Lady Alma made this hood for me to block the light. The fabric is enchanted."

"Oh, good."

Another silence.

"I have to be a princess now, Shadow."

"Salaria needs a good ruler. And you will be."

"I hope so."

I gathered my courage and faced him.

"Shadow, I'll be queen someday. And I can't think of anyone who would be a better King than you."

He blinked.

"I know this is sudden, but I mean it. I know you

don't want to be King. I know you hate nobles. But I want you with me, Shadow. I can't leave, and I want you to stay with me."

Tears streamed down my face.

Shadow kissed my forehead. Then my nose.

Then my lips.

"As long as we don't have court poets," he said.

Someone cleared their throat. Lady Alma stood in front of us, arms crossed.

"So this is the King's idea of a peaceful walk with his daughter?"

Then she winked at us.

"It appears the soul link will not cause further damage. Someone has requested an audience with you, Rook. You may come as well, Shadow."

"I thought I was too ill to do anything," I said as we followed Lady Alma to the dining room.

"Oh, this isn't much. Just light brunch and a guest."

Shadow pushed back his hood when we entered the palace. A few courtiers stared as we walked.

"They're waiting for you in the breakfast room," Lady Alma said.

We met Estrella in the hall.

"Do you know what's going on?" she asked. "Lady Alma sent me here, and I don't have time for this. I'm studying."

"Studying for what?"

She shrugged and pushed the doors open.

A bedraggled figure stood at the table, hunched over a vase of flowers.

"So there really are roses," he muttered. "I hope there be other food. Not sure how them will taste."

"Captain!" Estrella ran across the room and embraced him.

"Strella! You've never been living in the palace again?

You look well."

"You look terrible. What happened? They told me the Dragon destroyed your ship!"

She glared at us.

"Please, have a seat," I said.

Servants brought food on silver trays. After clearing two plates, Captain spoke.

"Aye, me ship is no more. The Dragon shot three cannonballs through her and set her on fire."

Captain wrung his hands.

"The force of the blast threw me overboard. It threw me, see? I didn't jump. Didn't abandon ship."

"Of course," Shadow said.

He surveyed the array of silverware, overwhelmed. I pointed to the correct fork.

"Just when I was sure I'd sink, a board drifts by. Lots of driftwood from the canon blast. But this board, it had a lump of tar on it. Enough for me to stick together some wood and make a raft. Nothing better than tar. So I floats back, until I sees that coward's red ship in the harbor. I sneaks aboard, no one there. But funny thing, I found a cage. Not for a parrot. Wrong shape. So I know there's something aboard. And then I found this."

He pulled a cage out from under the table.

"Seda!"

Estrella opened the cage and hugged the kitten.

"He was hiding in the hold, chasing mice."

"Thank you, Captain," I said.

He examined me.

"Lady Alma tells me you're the Princess. You looked a might different when I seen you before. But then, they always said the paintings were no good. And through a telescope, well, who can say?"

"The fairy blessing was broken," I said. "And the Dragon is gone."

"Well, goodbye to one and good riddance to the other."

"What will you do now, Captain?" Estrella asked.

"Hard to say. A Captain without his ship ain't worth much."

"You're welcome to stay here," I said.

What would Mother think of a pirate living in the castle? I smirked at the thought.

"Well that would be-"

"Don't stay here," Estrella said. "Come with me. I'm leaving tomorrow."

We all stared at her.

"I'm sailing the *Stella Rossa* and personally escorting the fairy salt shipment to Castana. Pirates won't dare attack us if you're on board, Captain."

She winked at him.

"Well, I suppose you could use some protecting, Strella. I'm not sure about taking to the water so soon though."

"Please, Captain, you couldn't stay away. Saltwater runs in our veins."

"I knew it!"

William and Roslynn ran into the room. Roslynn's blue eyes sparkled with excitement. Her dark brown hair was pulled back with a red ribbon.

"I always said she was a pirate," he said. "Now that she's got a ship, she's gathering her crew to set sail!"

"Oh, shut up."

He and Roslynn joined us at the table.

I watched the white kitten in Estrella's arms. A lump formed in my throat.

"You should take Seda," I said. "He likes the ship. And he was your pet first."

Estrella smiled.

"Thank you, Rook."

The door swung open. Sir Quill and Sir Inkling entered.

"Princess Salara!" Sir Quill said. "At last you are recovered! The palace has been devastated without you. We had nothing to write about."

Sir Inkling leaned over and examined my face.

"The change is not so great," he said. "She can still serve as inspiration once Lady Alma has restored her."

He reached to touch my hair. I slapped his hand away.

"Don't touch me."

Sir Quill shook his head sympathetically.

"I understand you may feel self-conscious about your new appearance, Princess. But you are our nation's greatest treasure. Our art must resume as soon as possible."

"Get out."

Sir Quill took a step towards me. Shadow stood. Both poets froze.

"Who do you think you are?" Sir Inkling said. "We are the official poets of the Royal Court."

"This is the Shadow," I said.

The poets turned to each other.

"His skin is not so luminescent," Sir Quill said, "But we could possibly compare it to pearls."

"The way his hair swoops over his face," Sir Inkling said, "There must be a metaphor there somewhere."

They surrounded him, pulling out their quills and parchment. Shadow stared at them in horror. I grinned.

"Get out," I said. "I'll deal with you later. Especially you, Sir Inkling. Sir Quill, if you remain Minister of Poetry, I insist you choose a new apprentice."

"A poem about Salaria's greatest villain," Sir Quill muttered, almost in a trance.

"In the same room as Princess Salara," Sir Inkling whispered.

"I must begin the opera immediately."

"Please escort the poets from the room," I told the guards.

"You are interrupting art!" Sir Quill protested as the guards pulled him out of the room.

I smiled at Shadow as he sat back down.

"So," I said, "The poets have a new muse."

He grimaced.

"Can we banish them from the palace?"

32

When we finished eating, Captain insisted on seeing the ship. We followed Estrella to the docks.

"Not to dampen your spirits, Strella," Captain said, "But your sail is a bit scorched. Won't make it far, that ship."

"Stand back, Captain."

Captain stood on the edge of the dock. We gathered around him. A small crowd of sailors, curious about the bedraggled vessel, joined us. I waved at Joe, and he smiled back.

Estrella stepped onto the deck and waved her hands. A soft red glow, like fire, surrounded her. The black patches on the mast faded. The sail and ropes reformed. When the glow disappeared, the *Stella Rossa* looked as good as new.

"I don't suppose you'd work that charm on my boat?" Joe said. "My sails could use patching."

He jumped aboard and leaned on the newly repaired mast.

"Certainly not," Estrella said. "Unless you have another crystal to power it."

We joined them on the ship.

"Will ye sail with us, lad?" Captain asked. "We'll be

needing a crew."

"We won't," Estrella said. "I've got a crew."

Joe raised an eyebrow.

"I can't come anyway. In case you've forgotten, I've got my own ship now."

"That harbor tub?" Captain said. "That ain't a ship. It'll sink in the first stiff wind on the open seas."

"I'm not sailing the open seas. I've given up piracy. Going to be a fisherman."

Estrella crossed her arms.

"You? A fisherman?"

Joe nodded.

"I've even hired a lad to help me. Time to earn an honest living."

"What are you really up to, Joe?"

"Well, since you're determined to sail off, I suppose you'll never know."

He ran and jumped off the side of the ship towards the harbor. I gasped and ran to the side. There was no splash. When I reached the edge, I saw him standing on the deck of his small boat. Thomas held the wheel.

"You've hired Thomas?" I asked.

Thomas looked up just as Shadow put his arm around me.

"Shadow, are you cheating on Rook? If you've hurt her, so help me-"

"I am Rook!" I yelled.

The boat sailed away, and the wind muffled his response. But he waved, and I waved back.

"Princess!"

I turned and frowned. Lady Alma stalked towards me, her four chins jiggling.

"I said you could take a walk with your father and have brunch. What are you doing in the harbor?"

I protested as she dragged me back to my room, but I

fell asleep almost immediately.

The next morning, Lady Alma woke me.

"Your father wants you to make an appearance today," she said. "Typical man, to give so little notice."

"But I- Is that necessary? No one will want to see me now."

"Nonsense. Be at the studio in one hour. I'm having breakfast sent to your room."

She snapped me into a dressing gown.

Shadow brought the breakfast on a tray.

"No roses?" I joked. "We have a reputation to uphold."

He smiled.

"I'm supposed to be serving you breakfast in bed, but do you feel up for a climb?"

"Always."

We walked through the secret passage. When we reached the end, I used a charm to lift the tray up to the tower and only dropped one apple.

"This one's yours," Shadow said as he picked it up.

I leaned my head on his shoulder as we looked over Salaria. A crowd of people had already gathered in the courtyard. Even more had lined up at the tiers below, waiting for the guards to let them up to the castle.

We sat again the wall and used my crate as a table. Shadow opened it when we were done eating and pulled the books out.

"Your private library?"

"I'll be able to work magic now that the loop is broken. We could come up here to practice. There are plenty of fairy salt charms around. No soul looping required."

He grinned.

"I can take the stairs from the garden and meet you here."

"Princess Salara!"

The voice echoed through the secret tunnel.

"I suppose I should go now."

He nodded.

"You don't want to keep that crowd waiting."

Even more people stood in the courtyard now. I couldn't help feeling nervous.

We took the secret passage to Lady Alma's studio.

"Absolutely not," Lady Alma said when Shadow entered. "You have to wait to see the Princess just like everyone else."

She shooed him out the door.

"Hello, Rook."

Elsie curtsied. She wore a simpler version of Lady Alma's purple gown and an amethyst headband. It helped her short hair look less bare.

"What are you doing here?"

"Elsie is my new apprentice."

"But she-"

"Loves fashion and is dedicated to Salaria and you," Lady Alma said. "You're the one who asked me to find her a room. Anything else?"

I shook my head.

They had rearranged the studio. Only Elsie assisted Lady Alma. The mirrors had been turned into windows with views from the sea to the Weeping Mountains.

"Something simple," Alma said. Elsie nodded and pulled out fabrics.

Lady Alma selected a light pink silk and draped it around me. With a snap of her fingers, it became a flowing gown that rippled like the Ghone at sunrise.

Elsie brushed out my hair.

"Would I pass the rook test now?"

"Who wants to have hair like a bird?"

She left my hair loose. Lady Alma added a few white

flowers and dusted my face with some sort of powder. She stepped back, thought for a moment, and added a thin gold chain and bracelet to my ensemble.

With a knock, Edsel bowed and entered the room. He handed a pair of silver shoes to Lady Alma. She examined them and nodded her approval.

"Princess," he said. His face turned pink.

I glanced at Lady Alma.

"Someone has to make the shoes," she said, shrugging.

I snapped the shoes onto my feet before Lady Alma could. She jumped when they disappeared out of her hands.

"Beautiful," Elsie said.

"I doubt that."

"When have I ever let you down?" Lady Alma said.

I could think of a few outfits that had not brought out my best. The salt-shaker opera costume, for one. Lady Alma snapped her fingers, and a single mirror descended from the ceiling. I stared at myself.

I was beautiful, in a way. The pink silk did not make my skin look like a pearl or star, but I had a healthy glow. My hair flowed past my shoulders in soft waves. My eyes were kind like my father's. When I smiled, the bright enthusiasm of my mother caught up in her latest art project beamed back at me.

The combination was all my own. It would be easy to capture in a painting, but impossible to duplicate with a spell.

We walked to the courtyard together. Lady Alma at my side. Elsie and Edsel behind me.

"Go on," Lady Alma whispered.

I stepped through the doorway. I heard the cheers before I saw the crowd.

Shadow, William, Roslynn, and my parents waited for me on the balcony. Sir Bristle stood in a corner, sketching the scene. Lacquer assisted him, his frizzy red hair blowing in the breeze. Hundreds of people waited below, clapping and shouting. Gerta and her orphans stood at the front of the crowd. They all waved. Thomas tossed a red rose towards me. I snapped my fingers and created a gust of wind to blow the bloom up to the balcony. His jaw dropped.

People in the back climbed the walls of the courtyard to see over the crowd. I spotted Plume the poet climbing sideways along the wall, clinging to the stones until he reached a spot with a foothold. He pulled a feather from his inkwell hat and wrote.

Beyond the crowd, the harbor, and the Ghone, a fleet of Navy ships led by the *Stella Rossa* sailed out to sea. I imagined Estrella and Seda standing in the rigging, the wind tangling their hair. I waved, sure that Captain was watching me through his telescope.

Shadow took my hand and pulled me to the front of the balcony. Everyone cheered louder. I turned to him.

"You're smirking, Shadow."

"What do you mean?"

"You have a weird look on your face. What are you thinking about?"

"You're beautiful."

"And?"

He hesitated. I leaned closer.

"Well, now that your hair is long again, I couldn't help thinking it really does look like the Ghone."

I elbowed him and waved at the crowd. Their cheers drowned out our laughter.

About the Author

A.G. Marshall loves fairy tales and has been writing books since she could hold a pencil. She perfected storytelling by entertaining her cousins at sleepovers and writing college papers about music (which is more similar to magic than you might think).

She fills each book she writes with magic, adventure, humor, romance, and other things she loves. Her stories are designed to sweep you away to magical places and make you laugh on the journey.

Visit her website for free bonus scenes, blogs, music, artwork, and a list of her other novels.

www.angelagmarshall.com

Acknowledgements

I started writing this book over ten years ago. (At this point, Salara is one of my oldest friends.) While the story, my life, and our world have changed, the support I receive from my family and friends remains constant. Over the years, I have shared *Rook and Shadow* with friends in high school, college, and around the world. The people who have influenced it are too numerous to count, but I want to thank a few special people who had a large impact.

My parents have always supported me and surrounded me with stories. Abby and Allen listen to my crazy schemes and join in. My extended family supports all my projects, and their love means the world to me. Both my teachers and students have pushed me to be my best.

A huge thank you to my most recent round of beta readers (Some of whom have followed this story for years. Sorry to keep you waiting.): Kristin, Mommy, Abby, Aunt Cindy, Alex, and Whitney. Their helpful feedback, questions, and chats made this book better and better.

Many thanks to Whitney for being my cover model. Aunt Cindy read draft after draft and always found just what the story needed. Alex took the book and a purple pen and helped me search for typos like a pro. Mary agreed to write a review with such enthusiasm, that it made me determined to actually finish it this time around.

Calthyechild's wonderful brushes and map making tutorial made the map of Salaria possible. Check her out on DeviantArt at http://bit.ly/1y8tV6K

Made in the USA
Lexington, KY
08 November 2017